To Mr S
The last time I saw yc
were very young. It wo
minutes ago if I recall.
Here's to growing up – never c
or should that be the other
way arand?

THE MACHINE

Book One

The Blood and Destiny Series

E.C. Jarvis

By the way this book sucks until
about chapter 9 – then on it's rather
entertaining.
All the Best

ISBN 978-1523642007

Second Edition January 2016

www.ecjarvis.com

For Dave and Bonnie.

Thanks also to those who helped with their invaluable opinions along the road:

Dan C. Boutwell
Addison Smith
L. Byus (Cicero Grade Editing)
Rich
Ian Jordan
Bear
Anton Almgren
Kat Hutson

This is a work of adult Steampunk Fantasy.
Possible triggers are present within the book including
but not limited to sex, murder, torture, and violence.

Chapter One

A flush raced across Larissa's face as an entirely improper thought entered her mind. She stifled a grin and turned away from the ledger of credit accounts, placing her hand on her necklace to fiddle with the stone.

Beyond the window and the ferocious blizzard, she could still see the outline of the Hub rising over all of Sallarium City, two of the great towers obstinate in their visibility. The city administration building had stood in place for hundreds of years; it would take far more than snow to blot it out of view. Imagining the freezing air outside didn't help to lower the temperature in her cheeks. A wry grin spread across her lips once more as her mind conjured more inappropriate imagery.

She forcibly shook her head and stretched her back for a moment, smoothing her hands down the lines of her purple corset, wriggling to adjust the garment's position on her hips. The tightness of the corset hadn't been too bad at the beginning of the day, but as the afternoon drew on her ribs started to ache. No doubt Mother would have told her she needed more meat on her bones. But Mother was dead and gone, and friends were few and far between. Except for her elderly boss, Mr. Greyfort, and she could hardly discuss the discomfort of such impractical attire with him.

Heat returned to Larissa's face yet again; the issue of her corset could be resolved if a certain person were to come in and rip the thing open. She imagined Greyfort's stunned expression at seeing her spread across the cashier's desk with reckless abandon.

Larissa sighed and looked back to the ledger, scrunching her nose up at the odd column marked *SC*. Greyfort still hadn't explained those income entries to her, yet. They'd had no patrons today. It was a wonder they bothered opening the shop at all in this weather. So the shop was empty, save for the racks of clothing that stretched up to the rafters. Some were filled with suits for gentlemen, brushed leather jackets, waistcoats, cloaks, and hats. Interspersed racks were filled with ladies' shirts, skirts, hand-crafted corsets, and every type of footwear for which the finest denizens of the city could think to ask.

The fireplace in the corner cracked and whistled as the coals warmed the shop. The consoling heat lulled her imagination to far-off places and secret desires. She pondered romantic gestures by a good-looking gentleman.

"Well, come on..."

Mr. Greyfort had appeared from the back room, shaking his head in disapproval. Larissa hastily scribbled out the last nonsensical ledger entry and looked up at him, blinking.

"What's his name?" Greyfort continued.

"I...who?" Larissa dropped the quill back into the inkpot.

"The boy who's on your mind."

"Boy?" She picked at her necklace again, fiddling with the stone.

"Good gracious, girl! You've been smiling like a Cheshire Cat all day, counting down the minutes, and I'm sure your cheeks are actually glowing. It can only mean one thing. So, what's his name?"

Larissa's mouth dropped open at the realization that her fantasies were so easy to read.

"Mr Greyfort, I-I don't know what you're talking about." She turned back to her paperwork, dropping the stone of her necklace beneath the top of her corset, and retrieved the quill.

"Fine, don't tell me about it. Though mark my words—" Mr. Greyfort was cut off as the trill sound of the shop bell rang out for the first time all day.

A tall figure entered, dressed in a dark red robe, the hood obscuring his face. The customer immediately turned to push the door closed and gave the briefest nod to the window. Sparks burst from the fireplace and the heat inside the shop intensified in an instant. Larissa watched with interest as the man pulled his hood down, revealing his short, spiky blond hair. Greyfort wrung his hands together as he approached the man.

"Good afternoon, sir. Welcome to Greyfort's Clothing Emporium. Please let me know if I can be of any assistance."

The customer waved Greyfort aside and took slow, measured steps between the racks of clothes, idly thumbing the material as he passed.

Larissa felt a lump catch in her throat; through the window and a flurry of snow, on the opposite side of the street, she spotted a figure looking at the shop. The olive-skinned man wore a thin, white doctor's overcoat, and despite the cold and snow the sleeves of the coat were rolled up to his elbows.

"Perhaps a wealthy patron who lets his man do his shopping for him?" Greyfort whispered as he appeared at her shoulder; he too had spotted the mysterious figure outside.

"Perhaps," she said.

Larissa turned her attention back to the man in the robe as he met her eyes with his pale green stare. A shiver coursed through her when she managed to place his attire. He was a Priest; a Cleric, someone who should be tucked inside a Dolanite Citadel praying to the Gods, not out shopping for clothing.

She felt a pressure forming across her throat, as though a set of fingertips were digging into her skin. Her eyes widened as she grasped at her neck, relieved to find nothing there but the necklace.

Without warning, the man pulled his hood back over his head and marched to the door. Once he had left, the fire died down again, though a strange tingling sensation ran over Larissa's skin.

"What an odd pair," Greyfort muttered. "I suppose we won't require a new account to be opened today." He tapped his finger on the ledger in front of Larissa, a clear indication that she should get back to work.

Long minutes passed and the ledger became filled with neat black ink. Larissa found herself so wrapped up in her musings about the mysterious visitor that she didn't notice the cool air rushing in again and the shop bell ringing a second time.

"Ah, Professor!" Greyfort exclaimed, his tone jumping a full octave.

Larissa froze, the quill hovering over the parchment as drops of ink fell from the nib, bleeding across the page. The door slammed behind the Professor, shutting out the biting cold.

"Greyfort," the Professor acknowledged in his aristocratic dialect, pushing flecks of snow off the shoulders of his black cloak. "I was passing this way and thought I would stop to inquire after my waistcoat."

Larissa watched through the corner of her eye as he removed his top hat, revealing white-blond hair that trickled down just past his shoulders.

"Oh," Greyfort said, absentmindedly wringing his hands. "No, it hasn't arrived. The roads have been closed due to snow and the trains have stopped, causing delays to our shipments. I do apologize."

"Ah, yes, it's having an effect everywhere." The Professor paced the shop. As he reached the cash point, he glanced at Larissa, and she suddenly felt compelled to look up at him. Their eyes locked. "Good day to you, Miss Markus," he added. Then he nodded briefly, placing his top hat on the counter and hanging his walking cane on the edge.

"Perhaps, Professor, you'd enjoy a new cloak?" Greyfort sauntered over, turning his salesman's voice on for the richest man in the city.

"No, thank you. I'm not in need of a cloak." The Professor didn't drop his gaze from Larissa's eyes as he spoke, eyes which flashed with fire as a wicked grin crossed his mouth.

"I do believe you are unlikely to receive many more patrons today, Greyfort. You may be snowed in within the hour. You wouldn't let Miss Markus get trapped here with you for the weekend, would you?"

"Uhh..." Greyfort mumbled something under his breath.

The Professor turned to face him. "I shall pay you her wage for the hour if *that* is your chief concern."

Larissa watched on wordlessly, fiddling with her necklace again as the Professor handed Greyfort a palm full of gold. She was sure it came to a far larger sum than was necessary. Greyfort's eyes widened at the offering and he accepted it with a nod.

"Miss Markus." The Professor turned once again, stretching his hand out to her. "I'm heading to the Hub. I shall escort you there if you wish. I'm sure the cabs are still running to take you home."

Larissa flashed a brief look to Greyfort, who nodded to her, before wrapping her own cloak around her shoulders and taking the

Professor's hand. In one wordless motion he scooped up his hat and cane and led her out into the snowstorm.

Outside, the street was coated in thick snow. The dull light in the gas streetlamps fought against the rapidly darkening streets, and only a handful of people struggled against the flurry. The Professor wrapped his arm around Larissa's shoulders as they trudged towards the center of the city.

The Hub was an enormous, domed administrative building that housed numerous government offices and a few private businesses, though only those wealthy enough to afford the rent. The tall central dome stuck out toward the sky, built on the orders of Emperor Fastidus hundreds of years ago during the *Golden Age* of the Empire. Four great, external towers connected to the dome through a maze of covered moving walkways. The vast number of rooms and offices were joined by these impermanent passages, which could be reconnected when required through a series of mechanical switches and levers controlled from the top floor. That was the Professor's realm. Through fortunate birth, respectable schooling, and feats of political posturing, he had managed to work his way quite literally to the top.

They reached the imposing brass doorway, which swung open as they rushed through past a team of men who swept away the flurries of snow. The inside was as hot as a steam room, thanks to a series of vents that allowed the heat from the massive furnace below to penetrate above.

Within the large foyer, scores of people rushed to and fro beneath giant paintings depicting the last line of Emperors before the fall of the dynasty. Larissa stared up at them, their foreboding presence an odd extravagance for an administration building in one of Daltonia's largest cities.

The country had been a Republic for almost eighty years. Larissa wondered why there wasn't a picture of the first President, Henry Hague Senior, or their current President, Hague Junior, and made a note to ask the Professor about it as soon as she managed to find her voice.

The Professor pushed the snow off his shoulders again. Larissa turned to speak; instead she was knocked to the side by a tall oaf who appeared, huffing and puffing.

"Professor! Thank the Gods you're here."

"Mr. Mendle," the Professor barked as he brandished his cane in the man's face. "How dare you act so rudely to my companion!"

The taller man spun around and glared at Larissa for a moment. He wore an open white shirt, displaying the dark brown hairs on his chest, and a pair of black suspenders that held up his trousers. She noticed a brass pin on his collar that read "Cid Mendle – R&D". His hair was a ruffled mess of dark, reddish-brown curls with silver streaks, pushed back from his face by the thick goggles wrapped around his skull. Despite the heat, he wore thick leather gloves.

"My apologies, Miss," Cid sputtered at Larissa. "Professor, it's extremely urgent, sir, since the trains have stopped, you know, and the airships are grounded, you realize, and the machine—"

"I understand." The Professor turned to Larissa, his cool blue eyes catching hers as the corner of his mouth softened into a half-smile. "I'm afraid, my dear, that I will have to take my leave of you." He stepped in closer and she felt her heart racing. "I do hope you have a safe journey home. Good evening."

With that he brushed past her, heading with Cid towards a travelling walkway that led to the upper floors. It wasn't until she had watched him turn out of sight that she realized she hadn't spoken a single word to him.

I suppose I'll be taking my corset off myself tonight.

Chapter Two

Larissa hated using the cab system; a collection of burrows that sprawled throughout the city underground. It was serviced with filthy carts connected and moved by pulleys, and usually riddled with unsavoury characters who took interest in pretty young women. Especially those who were dressed in revealing attire. Despite her misgivings, the journey was mercifully uneventful. She pushed through the door into her tiny apartment and set to lighting the fire.

So cold.

She collapsed into her high-backed chair and absentmindedly picked at the faded fabric; Imago, her cat, jumped onto the arm and looked at her with disdain. She petted him, then removed her boots. Her feet throbbed from standing in those high-heeled contraptions all day. After kicking them to one side, she grasped at the lace of her corset and flung it away. Too cold to take off her cloak, she settled back into the chair, curling her legs under the black ruffles of her short skirt before Imago landed in her lap. The fire gently cracked and hissed to life, and Imago began to purr.

Larissa frowned at the framed cameo of her parents on the wall above fireplace, still feeling uncomfortable about having used her father's infamy to secure the job at Greyfort's. Would she ever stop feeling as though something didn't quite fit? Even if that was possible, she still had no clue where to begin trying to correct it.

Perhaps if she had even a small inkling of where her father had gone, she might make some attempt to find him. Yet Father was lost to the world and his exploits consigned to history; her only link to the man she couldn't even remember was the stone on the chain around her neck. Such a pitiful memento. Her eyes fluttered and her head fell back against the chair.

Just for a minute...

Larissa was unsure whether the knocking or Imago's claws in her leg woke her. The fire was nothing more than smouldering embers. She jumped out of the chair, unceremoniously depositing the cat on the floor, and opened the door.

"Miss Markus," the Professor greeted her. She felt her face begin to burn as she realized her feet were bare and her chest was covered by only a silk blouse beneath her cloak. She blinked at him, searching for something to say. Was he really at her door? She had been thinking of him all week, plagued by images that might make a harlot blush. She squeezed her thighs together and tried to suppress the inappropriate things that came to mind.

Imago jumped onto the chair and turned his head away, pretending not to watch.

The Professor glanced down the hallway nervously. "May I come in?"

"Yes...yes, of course," she breathed.

"I apologize for leaving you so abruptly earlier. You should know I am not in the habit of breaking dinner-date engagements." He paused to remove his cloak and hat, neatly placing them on the chair beside the cat. Larissa heard her heartbeat pounding in her ears. "Then again, I'm not in the habit of making dinner engagements."

"It's not a problem," Larissa said, looking at her feet and clutching her cloak around her body.

"I could still take you out."

She froze and somehow managed to suppress a frown. *Out* was not what she had expected. She looked around at her apartment, wondering if a man of his stature felt uncomfortable in such a humble setting.

I'm not ashamed—at the very least it has a bed.

Perhaps her quiet voice and all-too-shy reaction to him had made him second-guess his approach; perhaps he thought she wasn't ready. She was ready, *more* than ready. Gods, if only she could muster the courage to say so!

He gently brushed his knuckles across her cheek, and her body responded with a shiver, bolstering her nerve.

"Or we could stay here," Larissa said. Her pulse raced and she allowed her cloak to slip down her shoulders, the thin straps of her silk shirt falling with it.

The Professor stepped forward, clasping her shoulders and preventing the shirt from falling completely. He ran the tips of his fingers along her necklace, tracing his nails across the skin behind the silvery-white stone at the end of the chain. His fingers continued down the front of her chest and she held her breath. He brought his mouth close to her lips.

"Miss Markus, I cannot recall a time when I have been so easily seduced." His blue eyes studied her, and she pushed up on her toes, parting her lips, expecting him to bend down and follow her lead. Instead, he reached down and collected her cloak from where it had pooled around her feet and brought it back up to cover her shoulders.

"However, I'm afraid I do need to stay close to The Hub this evening. It is a critical time. Perhaps you'd like a personal control-room tour?"

What?

"Oh. Um, yes, that would be delightful." In spite of the sudden change in his demeanour and her utter embarrassment, the prospect of being allowed into a place that was usually so secretive thrilled her.

"Good, then let's leave immediately." He turned his attention to Imago, roughly rubbing the cat's head and giving Larissa time to redress herself.

She finished strapping up her boots, half-eyeing a more practical pair sitting beside the door but dismissing them in favour of the sexy-yet-painful pair. The Professor stepped forward, wrapped her arm through his own, and led her out, marching down the hallway to the cabs.

Awkward silence hung over their journey back to the Hub. She played back the moment she opened her door to him over and over, wondering if she had done something wrong. She wasn't a complete stranger to romantic encounters, but something about the Professor turned her into some sort of novice school-girl angling for her first kiss.

Even though he had rejected her, she was still a quivering bag of hormones; she lusted for him, and she was as sure as she could be that he felt the same way toward her. Yet here they sat, travelling through the night. He was domineering, arrogant, and utterly charming, and she had fallen for him in spite of herself.

Only a few weeks earlier, he had bumped into her in the street. She had toppled off the path, twisting her ankle yet landing neatly in his arms. It had seemed a little like a ridiculous fairy-tale at first, but when he invited her to dinner at *The Praze* as recompense, she almost choked on her tongue. It had seemed a whirlwind romance ever since.

The Hub was quiet now. The crystal light shades in the foyer had dimmed, the steam from the furnace rising in eerie trails through gentle streams of gaslight. The travelling walkway to the upper floors had ceased working for the night, so they had to climb the stairs. Sounds echoed through the emptiness; a door slamming in the distance, quiet whispers seeping through the air vents. The Professor gripped her arm that remained looped through his, slowing his pace to give her a chance to negotiate the steps in her high-heeled boots.

Why didn't I put comfortable shoes on instead?

An ornate door guarded the control room on the top floor; the Professor pulled a brass key from his waistcoat pocket and unlocked the door, which slowly swung inwards. He gently clasped her hand and she felt a fluttering in her stomach at the touch. Perhaps it was a promise of more to come later. She felt a smile tugging on her lips and tried to suppress it, lest she get carried away and start stripping clothes off again.

A humming came from up ahead and as they drew close, the corridor opened out into a colossal room. They came to a balcony and Larissa looked down on the area below. All around, the space was filled with an array of machines. Men in blue overalls busied themselves by monitoring a system of brass poles linked to intricate connecting cogs that clicked around in automation.

In the center of the room stood an enormous machine built of brass and silver, the like of which Larissa had never seen. She spotted Cid bent over an open hatch as he mumbled incoherent expletives to himself. Cid turned slightly and gave them a disapproving glare.

"This is my machine." The Professor's voice was laced with pride. "It is nearly complete."

"What does it do?"

""It's a small-scale fission reactor, used to generate power through a sustained chain reaction. The heat generated from the reaction with the core element is passed through a fluid, which releases steam. The steam powers a set of turbines, which pass a charge to a generator." He paused.

Larissa tried to maintain a captivated expression, but he may as well have been speaking Eptoran. The Professor's expression softened as he realized she had no idea what he was talking about, and she bit her tongue. She didn't want him to think of her as an idiot.

"This will give us incredible power, make our furnaces obsolete, and block out the winter. With this, we'll be masters of our enemies. His face darkened with another pause. "I need only one more element to make it work." He let go of her hand. She shifted uneasily on her feet and gazed at him.

What?

"I am a man of honor, Larissa. If I give my word, I do not go back on it. And I am going to give you my word, now." He closed the space between them as he reached out to lift her chin with the slightest touch of his finger.

"I will be everything you desire, everything you need. You will never want for anything again. If you ask for my love, you will have it. If you wish to be married, I will be yours. If you want me gone and to leave you free, you need only say the word. I will give you everything and anything within my power to give, you must understand this. I ask for only one thing from you."

Her heart thumped so hard against her ribs she almost couldn't hear him speak. Eventually, she mustered enough courage to speak.

"What is it you want?"

"This." He reached up and touched the silvery-white stone hanging from her neck.

"My necklace?"

"It's *Anthonium*, a precious and incredibly rare element. There are deposits of it hidden somewhere. However, I cannot gain funding to search for it until I have proven that this machine works. And to do that I need only a small piece. The only small piece I have managed to find, I tracked down to its last owner."

"My mother," she whispered.

"And that is how I found you."

A lump began to form in her throat. "So that's all you wanted from me? You sought me out for *this*?" She gripped her necklace.

"At first. However, now I want the *Anthonium...and* you. I am a greedy man, after all." He reached up and pushed a curly lock of hair behind her ear. Her mind fell silent as she scanned the room again. The workers and Cid all looked up at them.

Greed.

A small voice at the back of her mind seemed to shout a warning; she had been vaguely aware of its presence for days now, along with an uncomfortable fluttering in the pit of her stomach. Mother would have called it a premonition, as she had a tendency to *feel* signs in everything, but Larissa had stopped paying attention to Mother's whimsical notions a long time ago.

Her arms moved as though propelled by an absent force. She unclipped the necklace and dropped it into his expectant hands. The Professor immediately bent down to kiss her with such passion that she stumbled backwards. He caught her, swinging his arm around her waist. He didn't stop kissing even as he held the necklace over the balcony and let it slip through his fingers down to Cid.

Their passionate embrace continued as the machine hummed to life, filling the air with static. The Professor tightened his hold on her waist and she slipped into heedless bliss as a warming glow wrapped around them.

Chapter Three

"**B**y the Gods!" Cid yelled. "It's working, Professor. It's bloody working."

The Professor looked over the balcony, his eyes alight with joy. Larissa grabbed his neck and pulled him back to resume the kiss when an odd noise emanated from the door behind them. It started with a keen scratching at the bottom, as though a cat were trying to get in, followed by a series of distinct thumps at each corner. The Professor tightened his grip on Larissa's hand, turning his back on the door as he swung his arm around her body.

The air inside the control room seemed to disappear, followed by the entire doorway compressing inwards with an almighty blast, sending shards of wood and chunks of plaster flying in all directions. The boom was deafening. In the aftershock, the Professor was slammed against Larissa and they both crashed over the balcony.

A shot was fired, causing a dull clunking noise, followed by a hiss. One final, massive explosion rocked the entire Hub to the core.

Darkness descended, enveloping everything. For a moment, she could feel only a bolt of pain through her body to the tips of her extremities. The numbing silence was replaced by a dull, uneven humming, and muffled voices came from somewhere nearby.

Larissa regained consciousness; the Professor lay on top of her, his full weight restricting her ability to breathe. At first, his crushing body was all she could focus on, until somewhere within the humming and voices she heard a feint whisper against her ear.

"Play dead."

She felt the weight on her chest shift with speed, and willed her eyes to remain closed. Directly above, the sound of a fist connecting with flesh and bone cut through the air, followed by a pained cry.

"Good evening, Professor." A deep and oddly accented voice hovered above Larissa. "Perhaps you'll accept my invitation now that I have your attention."

"Doctor, what should I do about this girl?" a second man asked, and Larissa felt a swift kick against her ribs. She sucked in a sharp breath but instantly held it, forcing her body to lie still.

"She's of no use. She hasn't got what we need. If she's not dead already, she will be soon. Burn it, burn them all." Scuffling noises amid mumbled protests slowly faded into silence. Time fragmented. Larissa's head thumped with pain. In the few minutes that passed, she could barely tell up from down, seconds from hours.

Panic caught in her chest when she saw the roaring flames surrounding the Machine and burning the body of a fallen worker nearby. It was all she could do to wiggle her fingers and roll slightly to one side. In the corner of her eye she noticed a glimmer. Lying neatly beneath the debris was the stone from her necklace, the *Anthonium*. She reached for it, the flames licking at her skin. The world around her lightened as though she were rising towards the sky, and then darkness descended once more.

. . .

She heard someone choking as consciousness returned, the coughing mixed with disgusting spitting noises.

"You dead, girl?" an unfamiliar voice called, setting off another round of his harsh coughing. She tried to open her eyes but her body seemed uncooperative. A sharp thump assaulted her ribs and inwardly she cried out, but still her body would not respond.

"Girl!"

A second jolt to the ribs was enough to bring her around. She felt gentle flecks of snow landing on her cheeks, running down to pool at the base of her neck as they melted. Another thump to her ribs alerted her to the searing pain throughout her body, her aching back and head, the bleeding cut on her arm, and the layer of bubbling burns on her exposed skin.

Carefully, she sat up; the world wobbled into focus, and she saw Cid beside her in the snow, his gangly legs splayed wide, hands on knees, staring intently at her. The ringing in her ears was replaced by the clanging bells of fire trucks, followed by shouts from people nearby. She gasped as she saw the Hub.

Fire engulfed the entire Hub, its structure collapsing in on itself. Metal beams twisted and contorted like live animals submitting to the flames; each of the four pillars buckled and swayed. A plume of thick smoke stretched up to the sky, mixing with the dark snow cloud above, the falling snow peppered with ash. The air wasn't frigid enough to dampen the ferocious heat from the fire. The building that had stood for hundreds of years, filled with artifacts and history, was fading to a shell of dust.

"Well, that's fucked," Cid stated.

"What happened?" Tears pricked the corner of her eyes.

"Doctor Orother," Cid muttered.

Larissa sat up fully, her eyes darting everywhere as she tried to piece together everything that had just transpired. Cid raised his knees and rested his blackened forearms against them.

"The Professor thought he might be after him, although I don't think he expected anything like this."

"Where is the Professor?"

She looked over to Cid, who only gave her a plaintive look. She felt her chest give way to fitful sobs.

"Is he dead?"

"No. Worse."

"What can be worse than dead?"

"Taken." Cid sniffed indignantly and then released another round of harsh coughing as he rose to his feet, offering his gloved hand down to her. "Come on. I'll see you home."

They journeyed to her apartment on foot through a fresh layer of snow. The storm had reduced to a gentle, somber drift. Larissa ached and sobbed quietly to herself, wanting nothing more than to curl into bed. Cid walked alongside her, ignoring her for the most part but occasionally tipping down to catch her when her legs buckled.

The sound of frenzied citizens, enforcers, and firemen faded into the distance as they reached her building, her landing, her door. She reached into her pocket to find the key then paused, looking down at her hand. Inside her clenched fist she saw the stone, the *Anthonium*. She had been clutching it so tightly that her fingernails left bloody marks on her palm.

Cid loomed over her shoulder, his gaze fixed on the doorknob, chin sticking outwards in confusion. Larissa's fingers tightened around her stone.

The lock on the door was broken.

The apartment was trashed, the bookshelf thrown to the floor, the desk battered and emptied. The fabric of her chair had been cut, its innards strewn across the floor. Her bedroom door lay on its side, ripped from the wall, and her clothes and belongings had been tossed around and ripped to pieces. Larissa stood, her arms dangling by her sides and feeling as though they had weights tied to them. Silent tears rolled down her cheeks and her body shuddered with each breath. The sight was too much to handle. Her eyes widened with fearful shock.

Imago

"Imago."

She had meant to call out to him, but instead her voice was a quiet whisper. Stepping carefully into the apartment, her feet crunching on the debris, she called out again.

"Imago...please."

The curtain twitched slightly and the meekest mewing came out from behind it. Imago coiled his head around the fabric to look at Larissa. Immediately, he jumped in one great leap towards her. She sank down to her knees and cradled him in her arms while the cat rubbed his forehead passionately across her face and hands.

"Doctor Orother is very thorough. He must have come here looking for the *Anthonium*. You can't stay here," Cid stated from the doorway, his voice still husky from the smoke. "If Orother knew you were involved, he'll have tipped off the city enforcers and they'll come looking for you. They'll have questions. Too many bloody questions, and you won't be able to answer them. We both know where that will land you."

"Why? I haven't done anything wrong." Larissa clutched Imago to her chest and the cat mewed again.

"Won't matter to them. They'll want to pin this on someone. You'll be an easy target."

"I don't even understand what happened. What am I supposed to do? I don't have any money, I can't just disappear, and the Professor... Maybe if I explain to the enforcers, they'll go after Orother."

"Are you bloody daft?" Cid stepped inside and knelt in front of her as she sat huddled with Imago. She looked up at him, her face full of pleading innocence, and for the briefest of moments Cid's expression seemed to soften. "The enforcers won't believe a word of it, and even if they do, they don't have the resources or the intelligence to go after Doctor Orother. They'll blame you because they can, because it's easy, because you are nothing to them."

"I don't have anywhere to go." She watched as Cid ran his gloved hand through the mess of tangled brown curls of hair, muttering incoherent words to himself.

"Fine, come with me. Only for a day or two, mind," he half shouted at her, leaping up with a stride to the doorway. "And don't even think about bringing that bloody fleabag with you." He waved his arm frantically at her. "Well, are you coming, or not?"

She looked down at Imago, who had wrapped his paw across her arm in silent ownership. She set the cat down and stood up, quickly gathering a few items into a bag, before heading towards the doorway where Cid waited impatiently. Imago watched on, his tail flicking side to side. Cid walked down the hall and Larissa took one final look around her apartment. She tapped her fingers on her shoulder and Imago pounced up, wrapping his tail around her neck as she followed Cid out into the cold night.

21

Chapter Four

L arissa followed behind Cid in silence through the city. They passed through the residential district, past the Dolanite Citadel where the priests could still be seen at candlelight prayers through the stained-glass windows. A pair of stone orbs flanked the building's entrance, looking almost as though they glowed green in the dim night light.

Their journey continued on for several blocks before Cid turned and noticed Imago on her shoulders. The man stopped dead in his tracks. "For fuck's sake, didn't I say you couldn't bring that thing?" he snorted at her.

Larissa blinked at him, motionless for a moment. For the first time since the explosion, she felt anger boiling in her veins instead of despair.

"I have just lost everything." She spat the words out in a staccato, almost yelling at him. "When I left work a few hours ago I was a normal, respectable citizen. And now? I'm a wreck. Thank the Gods my mother isn't alive to see this, and all because of this stupid little stone." She threw the Anthonium at Cid. It bounced off his chest and disappeared into a pile of snow between his feet.

"I've been exploded, burnt, my apartment's been trashed, and now I'm a marked woman, all because a man I cared for tricked me. And that same man has been taken by some maniac." She threw her arms in the air and Imago jumped down from her shoulders.

"I can't even begin to process all this absurdity. I'm grateful that you pulled me out of the fire, and I appreciate that you're taking me...I don't even know where we're going. If you think that means

I'm going to leave behind my cat," she pointed down at Imago, "the only friend I have left in this world, just because you told me to, you are mistaken."

Cid puffed out his chest, taking a deep breath as he bent down to pick up the Anthonium.

"How the hell did you get this?" he asked, turning it over in his hand.

"What?" All her fight drained away at his change of topic. "Oh. It must have broken free from the machine with the explosion," she said, shrugging.

"This must have been what Orother wanted from you. Hmmm." Cid walked away, quietly mumbling to himself.

She watched him turn down a darkened alley as she tried to take in her surroundings, and she followed. He led her to the city outskirts in the Storage and Manufacturing Quarter. The Hub was now hidden from view by lines of tall buildings, warehouses, and storerooms, although the black smoke cloud could still be seen spreading across the sky. The streets were wider here, catering to larger steam-powered vehicles. A nearby signpost pointed to Sallarium City Limit Station.

"You coming, girl?" Cid yelled from up ahead. Larissa managed a weak smile to herself as she followed.

Around the corner Cid stood in the darkened doorway of a colossal wooden structure, a warehouse of sorts. She felt a sudden twinge of discomfort at the prospect of entering such an odd place with an equally odd man. Cid had saved her life and been kind enough so far. If she wanted to make sense of everything that had happened, Cid seemed to be her best bet. Imago padded his way through the snow beside her until they turned into the warehouse.

Cid struck a match and lit a gas lamp. Immediately, the flame spread throughout a system of linked lamps to light the entire building. Larissa's mouth dropped open when she saw what was hidden inside.

Spanning the entire warehouse length was the finest airship she had ever seen. The keel was built of dark-stained oak with cedar planking; the hull was curved with small portholes dotted across the length, their frames emblazoned with ornate carvings. Two large rotors protruded from either end of the ship, and the only missing part was the large balloon that sat in the center. It lay folded neatly along the warehouse floor instead.

Imago found a wayward piece of string to claim and Cid immediately busied himself with rummaging through a large cabinet propped against a wall. Larissa ran her fingers along the ship's wooden panels, studying them in detail. As she reached the end, her breath stopped short. Upon a brass plaque, in fine gold lettering, she read the ship's name—Larissa.

"The Professor asked me to do that last week," Cid yelled to her, nodding at the nameplate. With a shrug he resumed his rummaging.

"We only met two weeks ago?" Larissa mused openly. She couldn't stop the stupid grin that spread across her face at the memory and the thought that the Professor was so enamoured with her as to name such a beautiful ship after her. Then the smile faded and an ache caught in her chest at the realization that he was gone.

"Won't Doctor Orother come looking here?" she called back to Cid, who had disappeared. He reappeared up on deck and threw a rope ladder over the side, beckoning her to climb up.

"Orother has the man he came for. Besides, the Professor kept this beauty quiet."

He spoke as she climbed. Cid shoved a tattered box in her arms which was filled with vials and bandages. He ripped the goggles off his head, revealing a permanent indent in his skin. Then the gloves came off; the skin on his hands were pearly white, contrasted by his darkly tanned arms, now black with burned soot and covered with pockets of bloody blisters from the fire.

Cid picked up a bottle of yellow liquid and poured it over his arms, hissing through his teeth at the sting, then deftly bandaged each arm. Finally, he poured some more liquid into one hand, rubbed his palms together, and roughly rubbed it into his face with a growl of pain. Larissa noticed he had tucked a pair of pistols into hooks on his suspenders; her heart sank when she considered how suddenly dangerous her world had become.

"I'll sleep up here in case anyone comes in. You can sleep in the Captain's cabin up front. If you hear anyone come in, there's a trap door beneath the ottoman in the corner. Get down there and sneak out back as quick as you can." He waved her off towards the cabin door.

"And take that bloody cat with you." Imago arrived beside her feet as though he had understood, and Larissa entered the cabin.

Inside, a single candle lit the room from the huge desk at one end. The dark wood panels on the walls were decorated with more ornate carvings and the cabin smelled faintly of wood polish. Through the small stained-glass porthole windows, Larissa could see the lamps outside in the warehouse dimming as Cid extinguished the flames. She set the medical box down on the desk and sunk into the ornate leather chair. It was hard to know where to start; every inch of her body ached in one way or another.

She began by removing her boots, which were mostly destroyed, anyway. She hadn't noticed the fact that her left boot had lost the heel completely. The corset had turned out similarly, hanging off her body as a torn rag, the inner boning twisted beyond use. Her skirt was singed and part of the fabric still stuck to her skin. The tights beneath had filled with unsightly holes, the exposed skin patchy with mottled soot and blood. The only thing that wasn't completely useless was her cloak, which had somehow survived the ordeal virtually unscathed.

She set about oiling herself with the yellow liquid as Cid had done, combating strained screams through gritted teeth as it touched open wounds. Imago curled up atop the desk, watching her from the corner of his eye. After battling with bandages for some time, she scanned the cabin for a bed.

It had grown dark, the single candle giving a small field of vision. Eventually she noticed the hammock hanging at an angle in a corner. After two unladylike attempts to drag herself into the hammock, she succeeded on the third try, almost falling straight out again when Imago leapt in with her. Within moments, exhaustion took hold and she slipped into a disturbed slumber.

Chapter Five

Voices echoed in the darkness. The words seemed to linger in the air unnaturally, fading into nonsensical mixtures of syllables. Occasionally, a light shone and evaporated at irregular intervals. It was difficult to focus, impossible to comprehend the passage of time. It was as though a cloudy haze wrapped around his mind. Eventually, the Professor managed to maintain consciousness. He opened his eyes to virtual darkness. A single flickering green candle flame wavered on a nearby table, illuminating the wall and not much else.

He tried to move, instantly regretting the attempt. A rush of pain swept across his body as though he were being stabbed by a thousand tiny needles. His wrists were bound and tied with rope hooked to the ceiling, his body elongated so he was forced to stand on tiptoe. He had been stripped at the torso, cold air prickling his chest and feathering it with goose bumps. He strained against the bindings, testing them for weakness; it appeared to be a futile task.

A lurching feeling took over in the pit of his stomach and his head seemed to loll from side to side. Somewhere within the room the sound of a ticking clock came into focus. He tried to count the seconds and the minutes. By the time he counted twelve minutes his mind started to fog again and he lost count.

"Professor."

The voice caught the Professor's attention and he forced his eyes to open once more. He saw the familiar shape of a man dressed in a long, white, unbuttoned overcoat with the sleeves rolled up to his elbows, leaning in the doorway ahead.

"Doctor Orother."

The Professor's voice was dry with an unfamiliar sound. The Doctor stepped inside, followed closely by an extremely tall and muscular male and one short, slender female. Through the doorway, a third figure dressed in a dark red robe loomed in the shadows.

The Doctor lit a lamp, which shone with a bright green flame; the Professor flinched as the light scorched his eyes. How long had he been in there?

"I am going to make this simple for you. I want the design for your machine. When I have built a working copy for myself, I will kill you mercifully. Until that time, if you do not cooperate, I will make you suffer." The Doctor brought his nose up to the Professor's.

"I see."

It was all he could think to say in response. A drop of sweat formed in the wrinkle of his forehead, dripping down his nose until it paused at the tip. The Doctor moved in closer still until his own nose almost brushed against the drop of sweat. His wild eyes darted left and right as his focus shifted between the Professor's eyes. The corners of Orother's lips curled into a sickening grin. His chin-full of long brown stubble did nothing to hide the sneer of delight, making him look quite at home in the role of tormentor.

"Hans," Doctor Orother shouted to the tall man at the back of the room. Hans stepped forward; he was so tall his head almost brushed the ceiling and his shirt barely contained the thick muscles of his arms and shoulders. A dark, bushy moustache sat above his top lip, but the top of his head was bald and his grizzly face pulled down into a permanent scowl. Hans squeezed his knuckles and they crunched and cracked. The Doctor stepped backwards, regaining his composure.

"This is Hans. He used to be a military recruit trainer. Unfortunately, he wasn't much good. Used to beat the poor creatures to death before they had a chance to learn, and so he needed a change of career." As Orother chuckled, the Professor felt his stomach churn.

"And this is the lovely Amaria, my engineer." The woman stepped into view beside the Doctor; she was small and homely, with mousey hair and thin-rimmed spectacles perched on her nose. She took small steps within the tightness of the pinstripe skirt that hugged her thin thighs; the skirt didn't quite manage to hide the top of her stockings. Her feet clacked along the wooden floor as the points of her high heels tapped with her steps. Orother latched an arm around her shoulder.

"She will be here to notate your designs. Now, let us see how *amenable* you are going to be."

Hans pulled a large whip from his belt and moved to stand behind the Professor. The Professor clenched his fists to prepare for the pain. The drip of sweat finally fell from his nose as the torture began.

. . .

Daylight seeped through the cracks in the warehouse walls and in turn spilled through the ship windows, illuminating the Captain's cabin. Larissa awoke with a woozy head and it took a few moments before she remembered where she was. The memory of the night's events came flooding back like a recollection of some nightmare. She rolled over and jumped down from the hammock, managing to avoid breaking any bones. She stretched up, elongating her spine, which gave a satisfying crack. The poorly twisted bandages unwrapped from around her arms and fell to the floor. Out of nowhere, Imago pounced upon one end, scuttling away with it under the desk. Larissa smiled, though the smile turned to a frown as she noticed something odd.

I feel...fine?

She stroked the skin on her arms; it was cold to the touch and felt unusual, as though it didn't belong to her. The burns and blisters were gone, healed over in one night. She approached the medical box on the desk and picked up the yellow oil, wondering what exactly the liquid was. Imago moved underfoot, still chasing the bandage. He knocked into the desk, causing a pile of papers to flutter to the ground.

"Imago," she scolded him as she bent down to tidy the papers, "this isn't our home. We can't go around messing up..." The document in her hand caught her eye.

Summary Report – Target: Markus, Larissa

"I would normally find the act of snooping abhorrent," she said to Imago, who sat upon the bandage and regarded her coolly.

"However, in this case I think I have a right."

She opened the file to find it empty save for a scrap of paper inked with poor handwriting, which read:

Theft of items – price to be agreed based on size and value.

Interrogation – 50 gold.

Assassination – 150 gold.

General threats, beatings, and mutilations ranging from 20 – 100 gold.

You know where to contact me should you require further services.

- S

A streak, both hot and cold, ran down her spine and settled in her unpleasantly tingling toes. Her mouth fell open and she shook her head in disbelief. She read the words on the paper over and over, as if she hadn't read them correctly the first time. Somewhere in the back of her psyche she heard her mother tutting in disapproval, the all-too-knowing sound that said, *What did you expect from throwing yourself at a complete stranger?* Larissa shook her head, refusing to believe the worst without further evidence.

The sound of boots clunking on the deck above made her jump. She stuffed the note in her bra.

"You awake down there?" Cid yelled as he thumped on the deck, making the ceiling bounce.

"Yes. I'll be up in a minute," she yelled back.

She quickly shuffled through the remaining papers; there was nothing of note save an invoice for materials made out to "Professor Maximilian Watts".

"Maximilian." She tested the word out loud, wondering why she hadn't thought to ask him what his first name was.

Because you're a stupid, naive child.

After setting the remaining papers back in place, she made her way to the deck. Cid was perched on a handrail, legs dangling; he tinkered, jamming a spanner into a metallic box. She regarded him for a moment, his bandages still in place and his face still covered in unsightly, blistered burns. She smoothed her fingers across her face; the skin was cool just like the freshly healed skin on her arms.

"What now?" she asked, drumming her fingers on her thigh when he did not answer immediately.

"Breakfast," Cid said. He sniffed, cocking his head down and to the side without looking at her, indicating to someplace over the rail. She glanced over the side and saw a gas cooking ring burning, utensils and a few odd ingredients scattered haphazardly across a table.

31

"You're a girl," Cid stated inanely, bashing at the box in his hand with the tool.

"You have powerful observation skills, Mr. Mendle."

"I can't cook. You'll have to do it," he barked.

"As much as I look forward to serving you your breakfast, I was actually asking what your longer-term plans are."

Cid shrugged his shoulders and looked up at her, his face setting into a frown, and the wrinkles in his forehead deepened. She presumed his expression was a reaction to the speed at which she had healed.

"I'm an engineer, not a boss. I build, not plan."

"What about the Professor?"

"He's a clever man. He'll figure something out."

"What? And you think we should just sit here, wait, and hope he turns up?"

"You got a better idea?"

"We should..." She flailed her arms in the air in exasperation. She had hoped Cid would have some idea of what to do, but his lack of action was as frustrating as her own lack of a plan.

"We can't just... There must be someone who knows where this Doctor is."

She glanced at the box in his hand as he placed the *Anthonium* inside it. He swung down from the handrail and handed her the box.

"It's a lock-box. You choose the code and no one else can open it unless you tell them."

"Why can't I just wear it as a necklace again?"

"Gods!" he spluttered with a shocked laugh. "It's An-thon-ee-um. It's bloody poisonous. I'm surprised you haven't grown an ear on your forehead or something after you've been wearing it so long."

She regarded the box then looked at Cid, who scratched his chin and gave her an odd appraisal.

Yes, he's definitely wondering why you healed so quickly.

Her mind seemed to rush with a thousand questions—about the *Anthonium*, the note in her bra, the machine, the Doctor, and the Professor. Unfortunately, Cid was not the greatest conversationalist, and she realized she would have to pry information from him piece by piece. Above all else, she needed to do something, and she needed to convince him to help her.

She began by turning the dials on the box over. There were eight separate sections, each with twelve different symbols and numbers from which to choose.

This will have to be easy enough to remember or I'll forget.

"You said Doctor Oro..."

"Orother."

"You said he knew I had the *Anthonium* and he trashed my apartment to look for it."

Maybe my birthdate?

"I guessed that. Doesn't mean I'm right. Don't choose anything obvious like your birthday."

Damn.

"So he either found out that I had the *Anthonium* because the Professor had shown an interest in me, or he found out I had it the same way the Professor traced it to me."

That one looks like a cat. I'll start with that.

She pushed the first symbol down, locking it into place.

"Well?" she looked up at Cid.

"You didn't ask a question."

"Oh. Right. Well, do you know how the Professor traced the *Anthonium* to me?"

Three. I've been on three dates with the Professor—if I count the time he was kidnapped and I almost died.

She locked the second dial in place.

"I don't think he would want me to tell you that." Cid spoke slowly, seeming to choose his words carefully for a change.

"I'm sure that would have been the case yesterday. Given everything that's happened, I'm sure he would allow it."

A top-hat, perfect.

The third dial clicked into place.

"What exactly is it that you're planning on doing, Miss Markus?"

She looked up at him; his eyes narrowed. She wasn't sure if she was more worried about the fact that he'd used her actual name for the first time or that he could read her so easily. She tried her best to appear unperturbed by his question and turned her focus back to the box.

A dirigible, hmmm.

The fourth dial locked.

"Well, I don't intend to sit here and do nothing for goodness knows how long."

"I only said you could stay a couple of days."

"You haven't told me how he traced the *Anthonium*." She bit her tongue as she tried to stifle a sigh. This was not going very well. In her frustration, the fifth and sixth dials clicked into place on the number two and a picture that looked a bit like a snake.

Damn, how am I going to remember those?

"He didn't share the details with me." Cid scratched his nose. "I do know he had a lot of communication with one person in particular."

"Oh?"

An M...for Machine? Good as any, I suppose.

"I think the name was Serenia. A mercenary. Ruthless-looking woman. Always made me nervous when she showed up."

Larissa's eyes widened at the name. Serenia—could that be the *S* on the note in her bra? The list certainly seemed like the sort of services a mercenary might offer. Not that Larissa knew anything about those sorts of people.

"And how would one go about contacting this mercenary?" She couldn't believe the words coming out of her mouth. Yesterday morning she was a respectable citizen, a sales clerk with a good position and a hopeful future. She had only heard of mercenaries in hushed stories that almost always ended up with someone dead or brutally maimed, and now she was actually considering contacting one. A fish out of water, indeed.

Fish. That's me.

The final symbol locked.

"I know what you're thinking. Do you have any idea what you're getting yourself into?" Cid tucked his shirt into the top of his trousers and adjusted his braces.

"I have some clue."

Liar.

"I had a feeling you'd be a bad idea the moment he said he was going to take you to dinner instead of just buying that stone off you."

"Who says I would have sold it to him?"

"He's a shrewd businessman with vast wealth and charm. If he wanted to, he would have gotten you to name a price, and he would have paid. That simple."

"How do I contact the mercenary?" She shifted her tone, hoping a more authoritative voice would make better progress.

"No idea. They did often meet in one particular place."

"And where was that?"

"At Misty Bar in Sherwater."

Larissa smiled. It felt like a small drop in a very large ocean, but at least it was more information than she had at the beginning. The box in her hand automatically clicked and whirred into life, the dials scooting round and jumbling themselves up.

"I hope you don't forget it." He prodded the box with his grubby index finger, the nail chewed down to a stub.

"I won't."

Chapter Six

It had taken Larissa the entire morning to prepare. She had cooked Cid his breakfast as requested in the hope that it might appease him, although he hadn't appreciated it when she asked him why a single man of his age couldn't cook for himself.

"I worked as an engineer at the Hub since I left school," he had explained, obviously irritated. "They always brought food to the workers, and I was always working."

"Where did you sleep?" she asked.

"Nowhere."

It seemed her cooking had been as hopeless as his conversation skills.

She had managed to find a boiler suit and boots that would work as better protection against the freezing air than her tattered clothing. It was at least two sizes too big in the most unflattering shade of grey, but in their current situation, a shopping trip for a new outfit was out of the question.

She emerged from the cabin onto the deck. Cid fiddled with the controls, a box full of tools scattered around his feet. Out of habit she reached up to her neck, expecting to find the necklace. Her fingers twitched nervously when they didn't find it and she sighed as she dropped her hand down.

"Is this thing ready to fly?" she called out. Cid poked his head around a wooden beam to look at her, his goggles down over his eyes. He slowly peeled the goggles upwards.

"We're not taking this ship out just to take you to Sherwater to get yourself killed. And what the heck are you wearing?"

"I had no intention of asking you to do that." She ignored his query about the suit. "I was simply asking if the ship is capable of flying, or if it's still awaiting parts or something."

"She's ready...apart from the balloon." He jabbed a spanner toward the folded balloon on the ground.

"Right. Good to know."

"Not that I'd take her anywhere unless the Professor was here to give the order himself."

"You did hear the Professor before I gave him the necklace last night, didn't you?" she asked in a measured tone. Cid didn't answer. "You did hear his declaration, that he would give me anything and everything I wanted in exchange for the stone?" She saw his jaw poke outwards as he crunched on his bottom teeth.

He had heard? Good.

"I'd say that gives me free rein over all the Professor's assets...even his employees, wouldn't you say, Mr. Mendle?"

"I don't think—" he began.

Larissa interrupted. "Like I said, I have no intention of taking this ship out for a simple trip to Sherwater. I just wanted to clarify our *situation*." She tried to stifle a grin at the air of authority she managed to develop in such a short time. "Do you want to come with me, Cid?"

"No." He plopped the goggles back over his eyes and returned to his work. Her pride disintegrated.

"How will I recognize the mercenary...Seren—um..."

"Serenia. She's not quite as tall as me, dark skin, dark eyes, shows too much flesh, got a head full of curls like you, except hers are brown and not natural. One would likely mistake her for a harlot."

"Sounds charming."

"Of course, you'd better not get confused with the actual harlots at the bar. You start asking one of them for *services* and you'll end up with a very different result."

"Marvelous. It would probably help my cause if you were with me. She might recognize you and be more willing to talk."

He threw his spanner down in frustration and leaned around the beam again. "First, I doubt she would recognize me, because she never took her eyes off the Professor the few times I was with him when he met with her. Second, she's a mercenary. If she doesn't like the look of you, she'll stick a knife in your eye. I couldn't charm a starving bird to eat a seed, let alone talk that woman into giving up information. Finally, if you're stupid enough to believe that waffle the Professor spun at you about promising you the world, then perhaps you deserve a knife in the eye. Maybe I should have left you to burn. This ship is grounded—indefinitely." He picked up a new tool and banged it loudly against something metallic.

As if Larissa's nerves weren't frayed enough at the dubious plan, now she felt her knees start to wobble. With a heavy sigh she turned on her heels and headed down the rope ladder and out the door. One final call from on deck pricked her ears.

"And don't forget your cat." Imago was already at her heel.

Outside, the snow storm had passed. The sunlight was strong enough to start melting the icicles that hung from the eaves of the surrounding warehouses; the melting snow rose up into thin steam clouds. As she reached the street corner she spotted a large cloud of smoke hanging in the air in the distance. The sound of a heavy engine chugging towards her made her smile; the trains were running again.

She reached Sallarium City Limit Station just as the steam engine arrived, the brakes screeching to a halt. The smoke cloud from the chimney stack surrounded the station, hanging low in the damp air and coating the snow with a layer of soot.

Larissa paid for a ticket with the money she managed to collect from her apartment the night before and headed to the platform. A rusty sign showed the stops along the eastern line, though most of the place names were obscured by a layer of snow. The last name on the sign was *Aditona*, the eastern coastal city and the largest port in all Daltonia. Though it was many hundreds of miles away, she knew it was at least the correct line to take to reach the nearby town of Sherwater.

After climbing aboard the train, she sat in the carriage and subtly eyed the contents of her purse, unsure if the meagre collection of coins would be enough to buy information from the mercenary. After all, there was no value in the information on the ominous price list she found in the Captain's cabin, which she had assumed the mercenary had written.

As the train moved off, the carriages lurched into one another. Imago sat on the seat beside her, his claws gripping the fabric to keep him steady.

"Just two stops," she whispered down to him. The carriage was pleasantly quiet, probably, she assumed, due to the bad weather. Perhaps nobody knew the trains were running again.

The city faded into the distance as the train raced cross-country. The landscape had turned to a blanket of pure white. Occasionally, the smoke plume would cover the window as the track curved, plunging the carriage into darkness. Larissa mindlessly rubbed the lockbox in her pocket, pondering the best approach to speak to the mercenary. She tried to ignore Cid's comment about her naivety, not to mention the fact that she was out of her depth with everything else.

The Professor wouldn't have gone to the trouble to pursue her if he hadn't truly been interested. What would be the point in theatrics if he didn't really care for her? And what of the airship? Surely such a romantic gesture as naming a beautiful flying machine after her meant something? She thought back to their first meeting, how nervous she was, how it had felt like fate had swept him into her path. Now she knew the truth, and it all seemed so false. She had acted like a fool and he had taken advantage. So why did she continue to put herself at further risk for such a man?

"Tickets, please," the Conductor called, making her jump out of her musings. The Conductor eyed her carefully as he clipped the ticket stub.

"If you haven't got a ticket for the cat, then it can't sit on a seat." He gestured to Imago with his thumb.

Larissa glanced around the carriage; she was the only passenger. The Conductor didn't seem to care, and rather than risk an argument she scooped Imago into her lap.

By the time they reached Sherwater it was past lunchtime and her stomach was growled furiously. Any energy she had from the meager breakfast rations had been expended in her nervousness. She held her breath as she passed rows of street vendors selling roasted chestnuts and fresh-baked breads. She didn't dare waste any coin that might be needed for the mercenary.

She found the bar tucked down a side alley. The buildings hung over the street at jaunty angles, blocking out the sunlight. A pair of grizzly looking men stood in deep discussion beside the entrance to the bar. Their conversation paused pointedly as she passed by. Imago didn't follow her inside, choosing to remain in the alley hunting rats.

Inside, the bar was lively, at odds with its appearance from the alley. Elaborate chandeliers dangled down from tall ceilings and pretty barmaids in skimpy outfits frittered between the tables serving the patrons. Larissa tried her best to look like she fit in, though she couldn't help but wonder how out-of-place the Professor must have looked in such an establishment. It was hardly the place for the aristocracy to frequent.

At the back of the room, a large figure stood behind the bar wearing a ghastly red corset that did nothing to hide her bulging figure. Along one wall, a staircase led up to a balcony where a line of scantily clad women stood. Larissa looked down at the grey boiler suit she wore and started to wonder if she should have just worn her tattered rags instead. She undid the first few buttons and wriggled the suit off her shoulders as she walked towards the bar. Somehow the small gesture worked to make her look slightly less out-of-place, although she still felt the back of her neck burning as though she were being watched.

"What can I get you, lovie?" The large barmaid beamed a warm smile. "Or are you looking for work?" The barmaid turned her gaze up to the women on the balcony, followed by a scrutinising look over Larissa's young form.

"I'm looking for someone," Larissa replied, scanning the room for anyone who might fit Cid's description. Her gaze settled on a dark, scraggly haired man sitting at the end of the long bar and dressed head to toe in black. He was too far away to hear her conversation, yet she was certain he watched her.

"Buy a drink first, then give me a name and I'll tell you my price," the barmaid said flatly.

"Oh?" Larissa hadn't accounted for having to pay out just to find out if the mercenary was in the vicinity.

"I'll have a glass of wine, please?"

The barmaid raised one eyebrow at her before turning to pull a dusty bottle off a shelf and pouring out a measure into a pint glass. Clearly, wine was not the usual choice in this venue.

"I'm looking for a lady named Serenia," Larissa said as she took the drink. She hoped that a direct approach would work best; she had neither the strength nor the will to start demanding things of people. The barmaid took a step back, placed the wine bottle rim under the ale tap, and proceeded to top up the bottle with ale. Afterward, she replaced the bottle back on the shelf.

Charming.

"Five gold." The barmaid's broad smile had faded and her face set in a hard stare.

"Is that for the drink or for the information?"

"Both."

"Fine." Larissa dug into her purse and produced five gold coins, presenting them to the barmaid. Larissa kept half an eye on the man at the end of the bar who now stared intently at her.

"Where's the rest of it?" the barmaid asked.

"You said it was for both?"

"Five for the drink, five for the information."

Dear Gods, if I make it out of here alive I'll certainly be broke...

She wondered if Cid knew of some secret money stash the Professor might have put in the airship for emergencies.

"Fine."

Larissa handed over five more gold coins; the barmaid raised both eyebrows in response.

"Serenia comes in every other evening. She usually only accepts work from men." The barmaid furrowed her brow. "She was in last night, so I doubt you'll see her today."

"Oh." Larissa's heart sank.

Two women on the balcony screeched obscenities at each other and the barmaid lobbed an empty bottle at them to break it up. The bottle smashed on the wall, scattering glass everywhere. The women stopped fighting and disappeared into separate rooms. Larissa's eyes grew wider as she wondered if perhaps this wasn't such a good idea after all.

"Listen, sweetie." The barmaid smiled at her again, this time rather more sympathetically. "I don't know what your story is, but I can tell you clearly don't know what you're doing."

"What makes you say that?"

"You never heard of negotiating?"

"Well, yes..."

"You never accept the first price. I tell you how much I want and you tell me how much you're willing to pay, and we meet somewhere in the middle, right?"

"Oh." The thought hadn't even crossed her mind. At her work, prices were set, no bartering allowed in such a fine establishment as Greyfort's Clothing Emporium. "I don't suppose you'd care to give me my money back and start again?"

The barmaid threw her head back and roared with laughter. Larissa felt her face burn red with embarrassment. "Listen darlin', if you're dead set on meeting Serenia I'll get one of the boys to send her a message. Maybe you'll be lucky enough to catch her interest. Not many people come asking for her by name, and never a woman."

"You'd do that for me?"

"Well since you paid me all this gold, it's the least I could do!"

"In that case, tell her I'm here on behalf of Professor Maximillian Watts. That should get her attention."

"Indeed it should." The barmaid raised both eyebrows again. "You take a seat, lovie. Enjoy your wine."

Larissa headed to an empty table at the back, choosing a good position where she could keep an eye on the doorway. Although the man at the end of the bar had disappeared, the hairs on the back of her neck did not settle. She tentatively sipped at odd-tasting wine and submitted to a long wait.

Chapter Seven

Only a day had passed, but the Professor suffered greatly. Due to the injuries he'd sustained in the explosion at the Hub and lack of medical attention, his health was failing. The visits to his cell were so frequent they had already established a routine. The Professor could endure around half an hour of torture before passing out, during which he would give them small pieces of information.

The woman, whose name he had forgotten, would sit neatly propped on a stool in the corner, scribbling notes. She stopped on occasion to peer at him over the top of her glasses while the *muscle* of the operation, Hans, would inflict some form of painful torture whenever he felt the Professor was withholding anything. It seemed Hans preferred the whip, although the Professor did not share that preference.

Doctor Orother visited frequently to check on the progress, followed always by the silent figure in the dark red robe who would stand nearby, watching. Orother now regarded the Professor as though he were visiting an exhibit in a museum. The Professor had tried convincing them that he would provide accurate drawings of his machine if only they would release him from his bindings. While the woman seemed to think this a good idea, Orother dismissed it when she consulted with him.

Deprived of food and water, the Professor found it impossible to stay focused and frequently lost consciousness. When he passed out, they left him alone. He would often be awoken by a bucketful of ice water thrown over his body, wrenching him back to reality.

His arms switched between tingling with painful pins and needles to being completely numb, as though they had been removed altogether. He could no longer will his fingers into trying to untie the knots in the rope; they had given up listening. His body was a mess of blood and wounds and unfortunate bodily functions which had passed beyond his control.

Above all else, he decided, he had to get down from the ceiling. If there was to be any chance of escape he would not find it by being so restricted, and if there was no chance of escape, he at least preferred to meet a grisly end in a position of his choosing.

Another bucket of ice water splashed across his torso. He gritted his teeth as the pain flowed through him like a wave, slowly ebbing away to a dull, constant ache.

"Professor, shall we resume?" the woman spoke, her voice never faltering in spite of the grim setting. He couldn't decide if she actually enjoyed this or if she was simply unaffected. Somehow the latter seemed more sinister than the former.

"We discussed the steam flow from the turbines to the condensers beneath."

How is she making this sound like a business meeting?

"However, I need more details on the void fraction values and the associated contributing factors. Can you please provide me with your calculations?" She dipped her quill into the inkpot and poised, ready to write.

"You expect me to remember complex calculations in this situation?" The whip crack echoed through the room and pain sliced across his lower back.

"I have low expectations of you, Professor," she retorted, adjusting her glasses. At that moment Doctor Orother entered, his fists curled into tight balls by his sides.

"Hans, you're required elsewhere."

"Doctor Orother." The Professor tried his best to sound calm and collected. "Your engineer, Miss Amaria, needs some calculations and I cannot focus in this position. If you would just let me down…"

"Yes, fine," the Doctor snapped and he waved an instruction at Hans.

"Make sure he's still bound and meet me in the control room."

The Doctor flew out in a rush, muttering something that sounded like *the engineer* and *the dirigible*. Had he been more in control of his faculties, the Professor would have congratulated himself for both remembering the woman's name and for talking the Doctor into letting him down. Instead, he merely grunted in exhaustion as Hans untied the ropes and he flopped to the floor.

Moments passed until he could focus again. Hans had bound his wrists behind his back with thick rope. He could feel the blood rushing painfully through his arms, causing his body to shudder, and his stomach lurched once more as he felt the floor swelling and dipping in an odd manner.

"The calculations, Professor," Amaria repeated, her voice terse and impatient.

"Yes, of course."

He relayed erroneous details, knowing they would figure out he had given them false information at some point. Maybe they'd work out the correct calculations themselves. It didn't matter; he wasn't about to give them everything, not after he'd worked so hard for so long. As he spoke, his eyes watched her fingers scribble furiously to keep up with him. The blood returned to his fingers, still tied behind his back, and he managed to wriggle them. It would take time and effort to escape the bindings, and he feared that time was not on his side.

He watched Amaria as she lifted her free hand to twirl her fingers around the thin gold necklace she wore, and his mind drifted to Larissa. Had she made it out alive? Was she now in trouble herself? He felt a deep twinge of regret in the pits of his stomach at the realization that he had dragged her into such a mess, and purely for selfish reasons.

Perhaps he should have listened to Cid's advice. Her face flashed through his mind—her soft jaw and innocent, blue-grey eyes. He remembered how she surprised him at her apartment, how close he came to giving in to his own carnal desires when she had shown such willingness. How differently things could have turned out if he would have just given up on that infernal machine for one damn night.

"Professor." Amaria peered over her glasses at him. "I hope you don't think that just because Hans is absent you can get away with sitting in silence?"

"Of course not. My apologies." Not realizing he'd stopped talking, he began again, relaying more false information. His hands curled into angry fists behind his back. It took a moment before he noticed he had regained full control of his fingers. It took a greater measure of control to still his lips from curling into a grin as he worked on loosening the ropes.

. . .

The winter sun glow faded swiftly from sight, and with the day's end more patrons spilled into the bar. Their raucous recreation provided an amusing distraction from Larissa's nervous thoughts. She had played the conversation over and over in her mind, trying to map out all possible questions she felt the mercenary may have and deciding on the most appropriate answers to each. Still, butterflies danced in her stomach, their constant fluttering turning into somersaults every time the door opened.

Nearby, another fight broke out between two *pleasure ladies* who argued over the custom of a handsome-looking young man in military attire. Larissa watched on for a moment, hiding her smile behind her drink when the gentleman decided to procure the *services* of both women at the same time.

"Well?" a sharp voice barked at Larissa from beside the table. She jumped and almost spilled her drink. "You're the one looking for me?"

A tall woman loomed over the table, casting a long shadow. Her dark skin made her stand out from the other pale-skinned people in the bar, and Larissa knew right away who she was. The mercenary was dressed just as Cid had described, as though she would fit in more with the harlots upstairs. The only exception was the belt laid across the top of her corset, which contained a selection of elaborate pistols and knives, on show for all to see.

"Serenia?" Larissa asked, her voice a squeak.

"Yes." Serenia's eyes narrowed and she placed her hands on the chair opposite Larissa, drumming her long, painted fingernails on the wood.

"It's a pleasure to meet you." Larissa found herself standing up, as though some form of formal gesture felt appropriate. "Can I get you a drink?"

"No," Serenia barked.

"Would you like to sit down?"

"No."

Larissa chewed on her lower lip for a moment, slumping back down in her seat. All her conversation planning flew out the window. She had assumed the mercenary would be at least moderately talkative, not monosyllabic.

"So, to business," Larissa sighed. She reached into her bra, pulled out the scrap of paper she had found in the Captain's cabin, and pushed it across the table. "Did you write this?"

Serenia glanced at the paper for a mere moment "Yes."

"And did you provide the rest of the report to the Professor?"

"I don't have time for inane chit-chat."

"Inane? A price list that includes interrogation, mutilation, and murder with my name on it might be inane to you. However, it's a little more than that to me."

"Are you going to get to the point this evening or should I come back tomorrow?"

"The point? Well, I need to know who else you sold this information to and where I can locate them."

"What makes you think anyone else would be interested? I could hardly believe the Professor had any need for such an…" Serenia paused, looking Larissa up and down, "…*average* girl."

Larissa gripped the paper in her hand, a hand that clenched into a tight fist, and sprang from her chair to lean across the table, bringing her face closer to Serenia. Her heart raced with anger and frustration, and the small voice at the back of her head screaming "Stop, you idiot, she'll kill you!" faded away into static.

"Listen, you can insult and belittle me all you want. I don't care. It doesn't change the fact that the Professor has been kidnapped by some maniac and I intend to rescue him."

She sucked in a deep breath. Was that what she intended to do? It seemed a far stretch now that she said the words out loud. After all, she was a clothing retailer, not some adventuring warrior. And as for the Professor, if it weren't for his strangely unwarranted attention towards her, she would be happily curled up in her apartment reading a book and enjoying a quiet weekend.

No, that Doctor would have still gone to your apartment looking for the Anthonium, *and you would have been there. Who knows what he would have done to you?*

"You? Intend to rescue the Professor?" Serenia snorted.

"That's what I said. Now, are you going to tell me what I need to know or not?"

Serenia straightened her back and looked Larissa over, giving her a thorough appraisal. "You'll get yourself killed."

"I am aware of the risks."

"Are you? I could kill you right now, you realize?"

"You could, though I doubt there would be any profit in that."

I hope.

"I could kill you and take all your money. That would be profit enough for the trouble I've taken to come down here."

Larissa sighed and slipped back into her seat. At least the woman was only discussing murder rather than enacting it. "I wonder," she began, an idea forming in her head. "If you did give me help, and I did manage to rescue the Professor, I'm sure he would reward you handsomely for your assistance."

"That's a lot of *ifs.*"

"Perhaps you'd like to join me? Come along and give your assistance? No doubt I'd have a much better chance of succeeding with someone of your caliber along." The thought of inviting this woman to come with her on an unplanned mission was almost as unappealing as the idea of trying to convince Cid to help.

"Twenty gold," Serenia said after a long and uncomfortable silence.

"For you to join me?"

"For the information you want. My assistance in your mission will cost you a thousand gold."

"I'll pay you five, and that's for answers to all the questions I have, not just one." Larissa arched an eyebrow at Serenia, hoping her first attempt at haggling would work.

"You'll pay me fifteen gold and I'll choose which questions I answer and which I do not."

"How about ten?"

"Fifteen, or I walk out of here and leave you stranded. Let's not forget who needs whom."

"Very well, fifteen it is." She pulled out the coins and held them in her hand, knowing that handing the payment over before getting the information would be a silly idea.

"Did Doctor Orother pay you for the same information about me which you supplied to the Professor?"

"Yes."

"Do you know where Orother has taken the Professor?"

"No."

"Do you know where I can find Orother?"

"He travels often. The last I knew, he was heading to Meridina."

"The mountain range?"

"Yes. Only extraordinarily wealthy people are permitted to visit the town, and only with a private invitation. The roads and trains are patrolled by guards, so unless you plan on robbing a bank or you manage to develop a keen knack for stealth, I don't expect you'll get too far in your endeavor."

"Perhaps I could get there without using the roads."

"It'll take months for you to walk there, across deadly terrain, in the middle of winter."

Who said anything about walking?

"You're sure you don't want to join me?"

"As amusing as it would be to watch you get yourself torn to pieces, I possess a sense of self-preservation and do not take on completely suicidal missions. Especially when there isn't much hope of getting paid at the end."

Larissa paused for a moment, considering what kind of work Serenia, as a mercenary, would usually accept. When she began questioning again, her voice filled with caution. "Did you leave the Doctor with the same price list for *further services* regarding me?"

"I did."

"And did he request further services?" A lump formed in her throat.

"He did."

"Which?" Her voice turned to a whisper.

"I think our time is up." Serenia stretched out her hand, awaiting payment, the fingertips of her other hand tapping against one of her pistols.

Larissa handed over the gold and watched Serenia snake her way through the throng of people in the bar until she finally disappeared through the exit. A clock on the wall chimed the hour and Larissa stood, heading to the alley to collect Imago. She hoped to catch a train back to the City as soon as possible, preferably without being murdered before she got there.

Chapter Eight

Cid sat on the warehouse floor, a large schematic of the dirigible laid out on the ground between his legs. In his left hand he had two pencils perched between his fingers and was busy chewing the fingernails of his right hand down to nubs.

"Stupid girl," he murmured to himself for the umpteenth time. "Gonna get herself killed." He did his best to focus on his work, on tinkering with the flying contraption, although his eyes flicked up to the clock at regular intervals.

The door to the warehouse opened inwards and Cid pulled a pistol from the hook on his braces, aiming it at the doorway. The cat came in first, the little black and white ball of fur stalking indoors as though he owned the place. Cid lowered the pistol and aimed it at the disagreeable creature.

"Cid?" Larissa called as her head of curls popped around the door. "Oh, there you are." She stopped in her tracks as she spotted his gun, which was trained on Imago. "Do *not* shoot my cat." She glared at him and set her hands on her hips.

"Fucking cat," Cid muttered and lowered the pistol. "You're still alive, it seems."

"Evidently." Larissa smiled to herself. Serenia's knack for short answers had rubbed off.

Cid rose to his feet and scratched the back of his head with the pistol. "And the mercenary?"

"We talked. She was informative."

"She...talked...to *you*?"

"Yes, and I managed to avoid the knife in the eye."

"Huh."

"I need to get to Meridina."

"The mountain range?"

"That's where I think Orother has taken the Professor. At least, it's a good place to start."

"Well...it'll take a few weeks by train. There's more snow on the way, so who knows how long the trains will be running. You'd best be on your way as soon as possible."

"I am not going by train."

"We've been over this. I have no intention of piloting the airship out of here on a fool's errand. Now, it's getting late and I need to get some supplies before the shops close." He grabbed an oddly shaped bundle from behind a cabinet and shoved it into her arms.

"These are for you. I'll be back in an hour or two. Here, take this as well." He laid one pistol on the bundle and pulled a large leather oilskin jacket over his shoulders as he left the building, quietly muttering curses to himself.

She carefully placed the pistol on the ground and unwrapped the bundle. Inside she found her old clothes; the corset had been haphazardly stitched back together with reworked boning; her boots were glued with new, practical, low heels attached; the singed edges of her skirt had been trimmed; and a new cream-colored man's undershirt added to the collection.

"Well, Cid Mendle, you're just the sweetest old sourpuss I've ever met." She immediately shrugged off the drab boiler suit, removing the lock box from the pocket. Then she kicked off the old boots and slipped the shirt on, cold air breezing over her bare legs.

As she began to fumble with the wrong-sided buttons, Imago let out an almighty yowl from beside the door, which slowly degraded into a low hiss. Larissa froze, her toes curling up on the cold concrete floor. She watched the doorway with wide eyes as minutes passed. When she was sure the door had not moved, she reached down to collect the pistol from the floor, gripping it limply between her shaking fingers.

Larissa chomped down on her teeth as she scanned the warehouse, fearful that someone had slipped in unnoticed. Imago still huddled into an attack pose beneath a table, facing the doorway, so she assumed no one had managed to sneak in past him.

"Imago," she called out in a half-whisper. The cat responded with a single flick of his tail, but his gaze did not drop from the door. Slowly, she tiptoed forward. Her fingers turned white as she gripped the pistol with both hands, aiming at the door.

Her breath pulsed in short, sharp surges through her nostrils. Visions plagued her mind of Doctor Orother standing behind the door, or Serenia, or some other burly character come to search the dirigible or to kill anyone they might find inside. Time passed and her breathing relaxed a little. With one long blow of air she stepped up to the door, pressing her ear against it; she heard nothing outside. Eventually, Imago sat back and scratched his ear with a back paw. After losing interest, he emerged from under the table to spring up onto the airship, his gaze turning upwards to the warehouse rafters.

"Fucking cat," Larissa muttered, for the first time agreeing with Cid's sentiments. Still, she felt the need to look outside. Carefully aiming the pistol with one hand, she turned the doorknob gently and pulled the door open a crack.

There was little light outside; delicate flecks of snow fell and a small breeze blew them into the warehouse. She pulled the door open fully and peeked out. She checked the building exterior in either direction, but there was nothing there. Several sets of footprints came to and from one corner, though it was impossible to determine if they were just hers and Cid's, or if anyone else had come along.

As the cold pricked at her exposed skin, Larissa stepped back inside and pushed the door closed. She grabbed a heavy table and dragged it across the floor to block the door.

"Cid will have to knock." She sighed and returned to the pile of clothes to get dressed, this time keeping the pistol within easy reach. Imago jumped down to join her as she finished tying the bow on her corset. She sat on the cold floor to tickle his neck.

"I need to convince that sourpuss to fly us to Meridina. He's such a stubborn thing. I don't even know where to start."

Imago stepped lightly across her legs and sat himself on the schematic of the dirigible still spread out on the floor. Larissa watched him thoughtfully for a while, lost in a daydream, her eyes wandering up to the wall to check the clock.

"I don't know what shops he's gone to. I don't know what supplies he's getting, and I don't know exactly how long he will be...so if you're thinking I can use the time to teach myself how to get this thing in the air, you are completely crazy. Mind you, I'm the one who's sitting here discussing utterly ridiculous, grandiose plans with a cat. So I guess I'm the crazy one."

Minutes passed. Imago curled into a ball and Larissa fiddled with one of her boot straps.

"It can't hurt to try, I suppose." She sniffed and scooted over to the schematic, lightly pushing Imago to one corner where the paper had a key detailing the structure of the semi-rigid keel. After spending a moment studying the page, she surmised that it was no more use to her than a blank sheet of paper. Instead, she headed to the large cabinet where Cid had found the strange yellow oil which had helped her skin to heal and she rummaged around.

"Ahhh!" she squealed when she found a large tome buried beneath a pile of wood shavings. It was entitled *The Dirigible – Manipulation Of The Apparatus Through Thermal Vicissitudes.*

She sunk back down onto the ground and crossed her legs to read the first chapter on the wheel and rudder operation.

. . .

The Professor regained consciousness once more. The room was lit this time, bathed in the warm glow from a burning torch in a corner. He was naked and curled into a ball, the hard floor sticking to his blood-soaked skin and his long blond hair stuck to the side of his face with thick sweat. Slowly, he rolled forward and sat up, his arms still bound behind his back. Thankful for waking alone for once, he took the time to assess his injuries.

Everything ached and throbbed. He looked down at his body, trying to focus on the bloody pink whip marks across his chest but his vision blurred around the edges. Awareness of how little time he may have grew and he willed himself to stand, his weight wobbling unsteadily on weak legs.

The Professor toppled forward and slammed against the cold wall. Desperation sank in as he could do no more with his body failing and his mind weak. He rested his forehead against the wall and through the corner of his vision he saw the green candle atop the table still flickering.

His chapped lips stretched into a weak smile, then he used the wall as a prop for his shoulder. Slowly, he dragged himself around the room towards the table, where he turned and lifted his arms to try to position the bindings above the flame. Through gritted teeth he let out a guttural shout of pain. His shoulders stung from the action and the flame burned his fingers and wrists as he struggled to keep them in place.

After a long and painful wait, the ropes finally began to burn and loosen. The Professor closed his eyes and pulled his arms apart, ripping the ropes before collapsing to the floor on all fours. The green flame wavered unnaturally and almost flickered out completely. The Professor's heartbeat pounded in his ears.

The sound of high-heels clacking along the corridor outside filled his heart with dread and he squirmed along the floor on his hands and knees, stopping to squat behind the door. A key turned in the keyhole and the door opened inwards. He held his breath, knowing he wouldn't get away with simply hiding behind the door.

The woman, Amaria, stepped into the room and the door clicked shut behind her. She bent her head low as she stared at the clipboard in her arm, and it took a moment before she looked up. The Professor couldn't see her expression, but he did see the backs of her calves stiffen underneath her beige stockings.

In one sharp pounce he lunged forward, throwing his arms around her neck and face. She squealed and bucked, and they toppled backwards, crashing to the ground together. He pinned her to him with all his strength, covering her mouth with one hand and squeezing her neck as tight as he dared with his other arm. After minutes of frantic kicking, she calmed.

"Now," he whispered in her ear, his voice hoarse, "it's my turn for questions. Where are we?" He released the fingers holding her mouth shut, retaining a strong grip on her jaw.

"You won't escape," she spat and he clamped his hand down once more.

"I didn't ask for your opinion, Miss Amaria. Let us try again. Where are we?"

"Why don't you go see for yourself?"

"Where is the Doctor right now?"

"Why don't you go see for yourself?"

He could hear the malicious grin in her voice as she repeated the spiteful suggestion. Inside he cursed her for choosing to show emotion now. He felt lightheaded with the exertion and bile tickled the back of his throat. His grip loosened, strength fading, and Amaria squirmed once more.

"No," he shouted at her, and with another surge of adrenaline he tightened his grip on her mouth and squeezed his arm around her neck as they wrestled. The ticking clock echoed in his ears. Amaria clawed silently at his arm and face, drawing blood with her long, perfectly manicured nails. Still, the Professor squeezed, a measured anger simmering below the surface of his psyche, until her fingers stopped clawing and her body fell limp.

The clock ticked past another minute and the Professor looked down at the woman in his arms, already knowing what he had done and already accepting the act with a cold indifference.

He pushed her body to the side and spent a few moments staring at her blank face. Her eyes had rolled up towards the ceiling. The Professor tried to search his thoughts for some pang of regret or distress at her demise by his hand. Instead, he found himself empty of emotion. He looked her over; her clothing was far too fitting and impractical to be of any use to him. Reaching into her coat pocket he retrieved the key and pulled the door open to crawl out into a short corridor.

Dimly lit lamps lined the corridor and a series of doors led to rooms on either side. He shuffled along, half crawling, half limping, tempted to test each door but unsure of what he may find inside. As he reached the corner, a sharp, cold breeze swept the hair from his face and he felt the floor dipping away beneath his knees, as though he were aboard a ship on a rough sea. He had felt the sensation during the torture and presumed it to be a symptom of the abuse. Now, he was certain the structure around him was moving.

He moved towards an ascending staircase. Flecks of snow fluttered through the opening at the top of the stairs and voices drifted through the air above; male voices speaking in relaxed conversation. The sound of heavy footfalls above made his heart jump and he gripped the banister for strength. A burly man marched past the stairwell opening, stopping just out of sight.

"She's down there now."

"You let her go alone again?" another male voice asked.

"She told me to stay away. She said he speaks better when they're alone."

"Ha, I'll bet. She probably gives him a nice little show in return for information."

"You think? That bitch is so uptight she probably hasn't seen her own tits for years, let alone shown them to anyone else."

"I bet I can get her to give me a show," a third man chimed in.

"How are you going to do that?"

"Pin her to the floor and rip her fucking clothes off."

The three men laughed and stomped off together, their footsteps fading from earshot. The Professor dragged himself up the stairs and peeked out. It was dark, cold, and open to the night air. He scanned the surroundings, careful to not let too much of his head poke out. A large canopy overhead blocked the view of the night sky above. His heart sank as he realized he was trapped upon an airship.

Dipping out of sight, he crawled back along the corridor towards his torture room, pressing his ear to each door and trying the handles as he passed.

The first room was filled with sealed boxes, stacked from floor to ceiling. The second door was locked; he tried the key, which worked. The room was much the same size as the others, though neatly appointed as a bedroom. He locked himself inside. A single cot occupied the wall joining the torture room. *Sickening*, he thought. Beneath the cot lay an ornate casket decorated in gold filigree. A small dresser and writing desk took up the back wall, and atop the desk he saw a jug of water.

"Thank the Gods," he whispered as he grabbed the jug and took long mouthfuls of water, choking as it hit the back of his throat. He poured the remains over his face to clear away the blood and gore. He caught a glimpse of his face in a small round mirror on the desk; the face that stared back at him was not one he recognized. He saw pale skin, greasy beneath bruises and blood, dull eyes sunken into the sockets, and a large laceration splitting across the left side of his forehead. The mere sight of it brought the threat of vomiting up the entire jug of water.

He laid his head on his arm and tried to force himself to stay focused. The sound of footsteps outside the room made his heart thump with fear. A swell of air caught the ship, causing it to rise and fall slightly. The rocking motion knocked the Professor to the ground. No amount of mental reasoning could keep him from slipping unconscious.

Chapter Nine

The book lay beside the dirigible schematic, propped open on a page entitled *Balloon Deployment*. Larissa had stopped watching the clock hours ago. Her eyelids felt heavy and her limbs protested the physical activity to which she'd been subjecting them. She worked on securing the final rope as the persistent hissing sound from the gas canisters echoed throughout the warehouse.

A large thump sounded on the door. Larissa looked up from the ship deck, a wrench clutched between her teeth and two ends of rope knotted through her hands. She had been attempting to tie her thirteenth stopper knot, following the directions on the ripped-out page laid on the floor between her feet.

"Fuck sake!" Cid's voice called through the door as he thumped to get attention. She clambered down, dragged the table to the side, and Cid stumbled in. He shoved her to one side and pushed the table back across the door. He then slumped against it, dropping a single shopping bag to the floor, and turned to face her. He was breathless and beaten, both eyes swelling up. A large cut across his arm bled through the slashed jacket.

"What—" Larissa began.

"We need to..." Cid paused and looked up at the dirigible. "Gods..." he muttered, "did you? How?"

The balloon no longer lay spread out on the floor but was now half filled with gas, slowly rising from the ship deck to take its place above. It had even been tied to the ship at all the correct anchor points.

"Cid," Larissa snapped, drawing his attention back to her. "What happened to you?"

"You were followed. We have to leave." He grabbed the bag, throwing it up onto the deck, then he marched over to the cabinet and pulled everything out.

"Who attacked you?" Larissa asked.

"Doesn't matter. We need to leave. Here, put these on board and get the rest. I need to check what you've done." He shoved boxes and books into her arms and climbed aboard the ship to take a look at her work. Begrudgingly, she did as instructed and collected everything in sight.

After Larissa grabbed the last two items, the schematic and book, she climbed aboard the ship. The balloon had filled completely and threatened to rip open the warehouse roof with the pressure. Cid ducked down into the engine room and started furiously shovelling loads of coal into the fire to power the propellers. Imago sat in the doorway, watching Cid intently.

Another large thump came against the door and Larissa spun so quickly she almost toppled over. More thumps sounded as she righted herself. The table buckled at another round of intensified pounding. Larissa stepped to the bow and raised her pistol, aiming at the door. Her hands shook with fear and tears spilled out of her eyes through uncontrolled, adrenaline-induced sobs.

"Cid!" she squealed. "Someone's trying to get in."

Cid appeared at her shoulder then scuttled backwards, grabbing a long pole with a hook on one end. He stepped up on the edge and stretched the pole up to the ceiling at an angle past the balloon, attaching the hook to a twisting winch. Larissa watched him without taking a breath, not sure what he was doing but silently praying he would hurry up.

The thumping and scraping at the door subsided into less frequent, heavier blows, causing the table to shift along the floor. Larissa's lower lip trembled and she wiped the tears from her eyes with the back of her hand.

With one final twist, a length of cable uncoiled and the roof peeled back in sections, folding outwards. Cid wobbled, the pole dropped, and the dirigible slowly rose into the snowy night air.

Cid tumbled back onto the deck and took up position at the controls. He flicked switches and pounded buttons, causing the two rotors at either end to splutter into life. Larissa gripped the rail with one hand to steady her feet as the ship lurched. They rose above the warehouse walls and she saw a line of large men standing outside the door.

Two men took a last run at the door, slamming into it with their shoulders and dislodging the table. Three other men had an array of pistols and shotguns, and a last man wielded a crossbow. As they saw the ship rising into the air, they readied their weapons and took aim.

"Shoot the one with the crossbow first," Cid called to Larissa. She turned to see him manoeuvring the wheel to turn the ship. "Don't look at *me*," he yelled. "Shoot that fucker!"

She turned back and tried to aim the pistol, squeezing the trigger. A shot rang out, the pistol recoiled, and a vibration shook through her wrist; the shot had no effect. Wherever the bullet had gone it was nowhere near any of the men below.

"Again! Shoot him. If he hits the balloon we're dead." Another shot rang out, this time from down below, and she felt air whip past her cheek. She squealed and dropped to the deck, aiming the pistol once again between the balustrades. A thump sounded behind her but she did not turn. Instead, she squeezed the trigger once more. A shot rang out and the man with the crossbow toppled backward, his arrow skittering off to the side.

More gunfire came from the men on the ground; bullets struck the keel, splintering wood in all directions. Larissa buried her face into the floor. The noise deafened her and she squeezed her eyes shut, waiting for a bullet to hit, waiting for the balloon to collapse, waiting for death.

Eventually the sounds from below ceased, replaced by the gentle, monotonous rotor noises.

Larissa lifted her head and chanced a look through the balustrades. They had risen too high to see much. The light from inside the warehouse made it impossible to focus on the dark streets outside. Frowning, she wriggled backwards and let out a yelp as her hip bumped into something. She turned over and found a pair of legs spread out to either side of her body. She looked up to see a long rifle, aimed over the side of the keel by thick, muscular arms clad in a short-sleeved black shirt.

She knew only one thing; it was *not* Cid.

Larissa lifted her pistol and aimed into the chest of the man who stood above her. As she squeezed the trigger he moved too quickly for her to react. One arm dropped from his rifle and snatched the pistol out of her hand, the motion continuing as he deftly spun the pistol around his finger and pointed it right back at her. She froze and held her breath, trying to focus on the shadows that danced across the features of the face above her.

"People who aim guns at me don't usually live to tell the tale," he stated, his voice deep and rough.

"Friend of yours?" Cid called over, though his focus was on working the wheel and rudder to steer the ship. Larissa did not answer; she was struck dumb. The man had not turned his gaze from her, and now he raised an eyebrow and stepped backwards, giving her space to stand.

"I..." She chanced a glance back to the ground. "Where—who-how?"

Her brain raced to piece together the puzzle, and most of all to place his face. His dark, tousled hair danced atop his head as cold wind whipped across the deck. Larissa tried her best not to notice how darkly handsome he was. He lowered the pistol, hooking it onto his belt, and set to reloading his rifle.

"Perhaps that *wine* went to your head," he said, flicking his eyes up at her briefly. "You were much more coherent in the bar." Then he turned his complete attention back to the rifle.

"You were there? Wait, are you a friend of Serenia?"

"No."

"You were watching me?"

"Yes."

"You followed me?"

"Yes."

The man sighed and slung the rifle over his shoulder and across his back, hooking it into a strap. Larissa let her eyes wander across his body; the black shirt and black trousers pasted him as a dark shadow in the dim lamplight on deck. She could see the outline of his figure and the bulging muscles of his arms and shoulders; the beginnings of a beard covered his chiselled jaw, and a strap filled with an array of knives wrapped around his waist. He raised an eyebrow as he noticed her lingering appraisal, and the flesh on her neck began to burn.

"How did you get on this ship?" she asked, attempting to cover up her ogling.

"He was on the roof," Cid chimed in, though his attention did not move from the controls.

"Who are you?" Larissa asked.

"My name is Holt."

"And you're here because...?"

"I'm looking for Doctor Orother."

"Oh." She looked over Holt's shoulder and exchanged a glance with Cid, whose expression was grim. He shook his head once.

"Well, Mr. Holt, it was nice to meet you and I wish you well in your endeavor. We'll drop you off now, I think." She marched past him, already certain that getting him off the ship wouldn't be that simple.

"You need me." His tone was dry.

"I do not need you. Seeing as I'm the one with the ship, I think you're the one who needs me, and this voyage is not accepting passengers."

"If it weren't for me, this ship would have crashed to the ground. You need me."

"You may have shot a few of those men, but we were pulling away and their gunfire merely poked a few holes in the underside. I shot the one with the crossbow. I do not need you."

"I shot the one with the crossbow. *You* shot the lamppost on the other side of the street."

"Oh." Her heart sank.

"An airship will get me to the mountains much faster than a train, it'll be much easier than trying to get past the security on the ground, and I can't fly it by myself. So, you are of some use to me, for now."

"Who says we're going to the mountains?" Cid asked.

"I do," Larissa and Holt answered in unison. Larissa rolled her eyes.

"Fine, you can come with us, but I need some assurance that you're not a psychotic lunatic."

"I am not a psychotic lunatic," Holt said.

"Wonderful, that's very reassuring," Larissa said, forcing her eyes to not roll a second time in as many minutes.

"I'll stay out of your way and take shifts at the controls."

Larissa regarded Holt for a moment. Now that he had brought it up, it did seem to make sense. If it were just Cid and Larissa, they'd probably have to land every now and then to rest, even if they took shifts. There was the furnace to feed, the tanks to control, and the navigation and steering to consider. It was too much for just a pair of people to do over any significant distance, and Meridina was a long way off. With Holt on board they would get there far quicker, and something in the back of her mind told Larissa that time was not on her side.

"Very well," she said to Holt and he nodded, heading towards the furnace to shovel coal. Larissa watched him leave, her gaze lingering even after he was out of sight. After a moment, she noticed Cid was watching her, a scowl etched across his face.

"I know this isn't what you wanted, Cid. You must understand you can't just hide away for the rest of your life. Don't you want to know what's happened to the Professor?" She laid her hand on his arm and he grunted, wrinkling his nose. He pulled on the wheel and the dirigible slowly turned in the sky, creeping along its new course.

"You should get some rest," he told her, pointing to the cabin up front.

"When you're refreshed, I want you to explain to me how the hell you became an expert on airship operation in such a short time."

70

Chapter Ten

An odd sensation tickled the hairs on the back of Larissa's neck. She had been in a fitful sleep; that much was easy to ascertain. Now, something dragged her back into reality. Her eyes felt so heavy that she struggled to will them open. As her mind slowly crawled back to awareness, she noticed something hot blowing across the side of her neck. Breath. Her senses snapped into focus but she kept her eyes shut. The hot breath moved from her neck down to her chest, and she couldn't ignore the sensation of someone leaning over the hammock.

Her mind raced with thoughts; what she should do, how she should react. Cid wasn't the sort to get so close, but the new guy—Holt. She had no idea what sort of a man he was. Despite his claim that he was not a psychotic lunatic, there really hadn't been any assurance. After all, mad people rarely introduce themselves as such. Something brushed her arm—a hand, snaking its way across her torso, not touching though close enough she could tell where it was. The slightest contact scraped across the flesh at top of her corset and she felt her skin breaking into goose bumps. After a moment the arm withdrew and the figure disappeared.

She sucked in a lungful of air, not realizing that she had been holding her breath, and she opened her eyes. It was daytime and lighter than she'd expected it to be.

"I wonder." A gruff voice came from behind the hammock and she jumped so hard that the hammock twisted and deposited her straight onto the floor with a heavy thump. She clambered to her feet and glared at Holt, who leaned against the wall with the lockbox in his hand, staring at it intently.

"What is in here?" he asked, looking across at her. When he saw her both his eyebrows raised.

"What kind of a man are you? You thief," she said, meaning to yell but instead barely managing a whisper. She patted herself down, catching sight of her own breasts as they threatened to pop free from the undershirt and corset. She shrieked and spun around to tuck herself back in. The entire top half of her torso, neck, and face burned with a blush; the whole embarrassing debacle made her sick.

"Give that back," she commanded over her shoulder to him.

"You're giving me orders?"

She spun around, stomped up to him, snatched the box out of his hand, and marched out to the deck to find Cid standing at the wheel. He wore a large coat with a dark purple scarf wrapped tightly around his neck and thick gloves. His bruised eyes had turned a mixture of colors and were sunken into the sockets.

"You look awful," Larissa said as she looked him up and down, clutching her cloak across her body in the cool daylight air.

"I'll survive." Cid caught sight of Holt emerging from the cabin and his brow furrowed.

"I didn't see him go in there. Did he...do anything?"

"No...it's nothing. I'm fine."

"He's dangerous."

"I figured that much out. You should get some rest. I can take control for a while."

"I don't want to leave you out here alone with him," Cid said quietly.

"It's okay. I get the impression we'll be all right as long as we're useful to him."

"And when we stop being useful?"

"I'll figure something out."

"Hmmm." Cid scratched his stubbly chin and gave Larissa an odd, appraising look.

"What is it?"

"I couldn't see it before...now I guess he was right."

"What?"

"The Professor never usually put so much effort into women. I asked him what it was he saw in you, besides the obvious."

"And?"

"Potential." Cid sniffed and gestured for her to take the wheel, launching into a lengthy description of how to operate the rudder, wheel, and controls, the significance of maintaining static-equilibrium and navigation via dead reckoning. Regardless of the fact that Larissa had already read about each topic in the book, she listened attentively. Eventually, after he let her take control for a time to prove she wasn't going to immediately crash the ship to the ground, he headed into the cabin for a rest, stopping only to mutter a brief comment to Holt as he passed by.

Holt stood opposite Larissa, leaning against the strut that held up the front rotor. He had donned a long black overcoat; she could see a slight glimmer of a knife blade resting against his chest just inside the coat, and he still had the rifle strapped across his back. Holt took out a small sheet of paper from one of his coat pockets. He eyed it carefully for a moment and then returned it to its place. Larissa noticed the action, making a mental note to ask him about it later. When Cid disappeared, Holt stepped forward.

"You need to shovel coal," she said before he had a chance to speak.

"I prefer to know a woman's name before I let her boss me about."

"You give me your name first."

"I gave you my name."

"You gave me part of your name."

"The only part I'm willing to give."

"Fine, have it your way. My name is Miss Markus."

"Miss Markus." He rubbed his hand across his chin, his cool blue eyes darkening.

"Larissa Markus?"

"What? How could you possibly know that?"

"Because you're famous." He stepped back and picked up a black satchel he had stashed behind a barrel, opened it, and pulled out a newspaper—the *Sallarium Express* with yesterday's date. He handed it to her, and one look at the front cover made her knees go weak.

Disaster at the Hub!

That was the headline. A rough sketch of the burning building with several city firefighters armed with fire hoses covered the front page, along with the beginning of a report at the bottom:

A large explosion rocked the heart of Sallarium City last night, tearing the Central Administration Hub to the ground. Several dead and many more wounded. Suspects Miss Larissa Markus and Mister Cid Mendle are being sought by city enforcers for questioning. Professor Maximillian Watts has also been reported as missing. Early statements suggest he has been kidnapped by Miss Markus and Mister Mendle for ransom or some other malevolent purpose.

She opened the paper with shaking fingers and read the report. It was filled with false information about the explosion; the scathing account painted her at best as a wanton harlot and at worst as a dangerous criminal. She handled the account as well as possible until the reporter mentioned her parents. Her dear dead mother...and the mere mention of her father's name in print was enough to push her over the edge. She slammed the paper shut and threw it to the ground, unable to read on. Hot, salty tears burst from her eyes and she gripped the wheel with both hands, attempting to stop herself from collapsing to the deck in a sobbing heap.

Holt looked on with an expressionless visage. After giving her a few minutes for composure, he spoke. "So, Doctor Orother took the Professor?"

"Yes."

"And you're running off to rescue him?"

"You already know all this. Can't you just leave me alone?"

Holt stepped closer, his tall, bulky frame casting a shadow across her features. "Is he your father?"

Something inside her snapped. In one swift motion her hand flew across the wheel with all her strength, aiming for Holt's cheek. Holt simply reached up and caught her wrist in his hand, the reaction requiring minimal exertion on his part, denying her the satisfaction for her effort.

"Sore subject?" He raised an eyebrow, although his face didn't quite crack into a smirk.

"What do you know about my father?" she spat through gritted teeth, trying to yank her hand away from his. His grip tightened, holding her fast.

"Not much, save for what is written in the article, and judging by how inaccurate the rest of the story is I can only assume the majority of their *facts* aren't worth the paper they're printed on. Still, I need to understand your reasons for taking this voyage, so I can decide on what to do with you when we get there."

"The Professor is not my father." She ripped her hand away and grabbed the wheel as they had started to drift.

"So, he's your lover?"

Larissa didn't answer; instead, she tried to focus on stilling her shaky breathing.

What answer could she give him? Could she really class herself as a lover after only three dates and one passionate kiss? After everything that had happened in the last few days, did the Professor really deserve to have her come and rescue him? She put so much energy into trying to figure out the *how*, only now, in the clear winter sky, hovering over fields and wastelands blanketed in thick pure snow, did her mind begin to question the *why*.

To clear your name, if nothing else.

She nodded to herself silently, though it seemed like a weak concession given the gravity of the task ahead.

"I know you won't want to hear this," Holt began after waiting in silence for a while. "A sweet little thing like you doesn't stand a chance against Doctor Orother."

"Sweet? Little? Gods you're an irritating man. Doctor Orother has already failed to kill me once. Twice, in fact, presuming those men at the warehouse were sent by him. He underestimates me. Everyone underestimates me." She sighed.

"So, you've escaped death twice. Though let's not forget the reason you survived the last attack. You couldn't hit the side of a stationary freight train with your aim."

"Right. I survived because some creepy guy came out of nowhere, hopped on my airship without a ticket, shot all the bad guys, and then refused to tell me anything about himself."

"Creepy guy?" His eyebrow rose again, and she felt an unexpectedly warm smile spreading across her face.

"You don't like my assessment?"

"I've been called many things in my time. I can't recall *creepy guy* ever being one of them."

"What do you expect? You stalked me all the way from Sherwater. You crept into the room while I was sleeping and tried to steal my Anthoni--uhh, my lock box, and you won't tell me anything about you. Ergo, you're a creep." She tried not to look at his face while a sense of unease at her own playful cheekiness skulked into her subconscious.

"I have answered several of your questions," he said.

"Oh. Well can I ask you some more?"

"There's nothing stopping you."

"Yes. Well, what do you want with Orother?"

"I want to kill him."

"Oh. Why?"

"Because he pissed me off."

"Does that piece of paper in your pocket have something to do with it?"

"Yes, it does."

"Are you always this irritating?"

"I could ask you the same question." As they reached an impasse, Larissa shook her head. He was far too distracting and unproductive. She just needed time to think and plan ahead.

"The fire's running low," she stated, not looking at him and hoping he got the hint.

"Are you dismissing me?"

"Yes."

"As you wish, Captain."

She beamed a huge grin as he stepped behind her, so quickly forgetting the utter despair she felt at the start of their meeting. A brief moment of silence was all it took for an idea to form in her mind, and she called back to him.

"When you're done, perhaps you could teach me how to improve my aim."

"Do you wish me to teach you?"

"Yes, although not now. I don't want to wake Cid."

"Is *he* your lover?"

"Gods, no!"

"So how did he come to be on this quest with you?"

"Don't be silly. He worked as the Professor's engineer."

"Hmmm, makes sense. Well, I could start by showing you how to throw with a knife. It makes much less noise and the principle of aiming is the same, though the technique differs, of course."

"Yes, I'd like that."

"As you wish." With that he disappeared into the furnace room and the air on deck instantly felt colder without his presence.

Chapter Eleven

The atmosphere in the room was antiseptic; the illuminated table, on which the captured Professor was securely bound, was the central focus. In his dilapidated state, he had been unable to fight when they'd found him in the room aboard the airship. He had barely registered the ship landing. His new prison could have been a hospital room, a laboratory, or even a morgue. From the vaulted ceiling, burning lights bathed him with ferocious intensity whereas the recesses of the room were dark with shadows. The Professor did not seem to mind the glare from the lamps, for he was lost, trapped within his subconscious mind in a world of days gone by. A moan or a whimper escaped him as his head slowly moved against the restraints binding him. Deep within his delirium he heard a soft voice speaking.

. . .

"You want to take me to dinner?" she said, her head cocked to one side.

He watched her eyes widen and her pupils dilate, as though she were a wild rabbit facing a farmer with a shotgun. It made his fingers twitch with excitement that he could affect her so. This was certainly the girl he had been looking for, the one he had tracked to Greyfort's clothing shop—Miss Larissa Markus. He'd visited the shop the day before under the guise of needing to purchase a new waistcoat. The girl had tried to hide the fact that she watched him in the shop, but he knew the look—one he had seen from many women. He found it all too easy to turn their heads. She would make an interesting conquest, a good sort of entertainment for the evening.

"It is the least I could do after I caused you such distress."

"I'm fine, honestly. It's...I just twisted my ankle. I should have been looking where I was going, anyway. It's my fault, really."

"I do have a reservation at *The Praze*. It would be a pleasure to have company for a change. If you're sure you wouldn't like to join me for dinner, Miss?"

"Markus, Larissa Markus."

"Well, Miss Markus, I'll bid you a good evening."

He turned, adjusting his hat and sliding his cane to the ground, making a satisfying *clack* against the cobblestone. He caught a glimpse of his own reflection in the smoky shop window beside them and chided himself at the smugness of his expression. Even so, the expression wouldn't fade, not when he knew all too well what was coming.

"The Praze?" she asked in a squeak. He forced the smug grin away and switched to a vaguely passive expression as he turned back.

"Have you ever been?"

"No, never."

"They make a delightful lamb terrine..." He watched as her face turned a beautiful shade of pink. He managed to keep his passive expression even as his mind roved, wondering just how much of her delightfully pale body he could make blush that shade.

"I like the sound of that," she said.

"So, you'll join me?"

"Yes, thank you, Mister?"

"Professor."

"Oh, I'm sorry, Professor." The blush on her cheeks turned a darker pink as she reached up and fiddled with the stone on the necklace. He chanced a smile, allowing himself the smug indulgence. While the *Anthonium* was the prize, why not go for the girl as well? The Machine was not yet ready for the *Anthonium*; he could afford to take his time and to feed his growing needs. He turned sideways and offered his arm, which she took with the softest touch, her shy eyes barely daring to look up at him.

"I think it's time to wake up now." A discordant voice echoed in his ear, he watched Larissa closely; her lips did not move. The sound wavered around him as he felt the biting chill of the early evening air creeping through his thick cloak.

He was sure he had spoken a coherent sentence, but all that actually emerged was a muffled mixture of consonants. The exterior of *The Praze*, the most exclusive restaurant in all Sallarium City, came into view ahead and then melted away into a white haze. As he turned to face Larissa, she dissipated into mist. Slowly, the surrounding city was replaced with nothing more than a feeling—a deep rooted fear mixed with dread as reality was rebuilt, block by block, brick by painful brick.

. . .

"Professor? I said it's time to wake up now." The thickly accented voice assaulted his senses, destroying the sweet dream and he opened his eyes. He immediately squeezed them shut again as his vision was greeted by a stark light, so bright it made his head throb.

He tested his arms and legs. Nothing moved. Slowly, he tried to open his eyes again, squinting until his vision adjusted. He lifted his head; it moved barely an inch upward as something prevented him from lifting further. He was laid out flat, pinned down at the shoulders, wrists, thighs, and ankles by thick metal braces.

He was dressed now, mercifully, in a white shirt and although he couldn't see further down he could feel a thin pair of trousers on his legs. His feet were bare.

"Ahh, there you are. It took longer than I'd anticipated to bring him round. Make a note to adjust the dosage next time."

The Professor could only utter a muffled groan.

"Now, not to worry. I don't need you to speak just yet. All you have to do for now is listen. Listen and understand."

Doctor Orother came into view, a dark outline against the backdrop of white light. He leaned over the table upon which the Professor was bound, his brown eyes so dark they looked as though there were no iris at all, just pure pupil. His mouth curved up into a permanently wicked grin.

"I apologize, dear Maximillian, for my original methodology. You must understand that I was keen to begin extracting information from you, and due to the necessity for travel, I had to resort to a somewhat primeval approach. Now, here we are."

Orother stretched out his arm and removed the bright light source, a series of pure-white gas lamps surrounded by mirrors which angled the light into one large domed mirror. This was aimed directly at the Professor's head. Once the light moved, he could make out his surroundings, at least immediately above and to the side. He was still unable to turn or lift his head to any great effect.

This new prison was cut from rock, the ceiling and walls consisting of rough, angled stone. The room was rather large; one end was littered with an array of medical cabinets and haphazardly positioned instruments hung upon a pole. The other end had a small gap in the rock by way of an exit, beside which stood a male dressed in a dark red robe and holding a clipboard in one arm. He furiously scribbled some notes, an empty syringe clutched between his teeth.

As far back as his restricted position would allow him to see, the Professor could make out some form of device—a large metal plaque riveted to the top with the letters M.E.C.U. stamped into place, and at the front of which a series of pipes protruded towards him. He furrowed his brow and felt an unnatural pulling on the skin of his head. Looking up, he caught his reflection in the metal side of the mirror and he saw the pipes of the device actually penetrated his skull. A glob of bile settled in the back of his throat.

"Unfortunately, as you disposed of my engineer, I have had to make some adjustments to my original plan. I was angry with you at first for causing such trouble. Luckily for us both, a solution is working its way towards us at this precise moment. Therefore, all I have to do is wait and prepare. All you have to do is...obey."

"Obey," the Professor found himself repeating aloud, the word sounding unnatural. His voice fell flat within the cave.

"It will take some time. I hope to have you suitably compliant within a few days. Much longer than that and you'll start to deteriorate beyond usefulness. The initial insertion and first connection to the Cleric's device was successful."

Orother stretched out his arm and patted the device. He reached up to the back of his own skull to pull out a single pipe from his head. The Professor spat up the glob of bile, and as it dribbled down his chin more threatened to follow.

"Really, Professor, I hadn't pegged you as being squeamish. You had better get used to it. I have connected you to the finest device I've ever commissioned; it's called the Memory Extraction and Conversion Unit. It has proven quite useful over the years, though the mortality rate for my subjects has been unacceptably high. It's taken a lot of work and quite a volume of failures to bring it up to scratch, where I'd risk using it on such a prized specimen as yourself. Though I would have hoped to hit upon a more useful memory in the first instance. Sadly, the Cleric and I haven't yet gotten it down to an exact science, at least not as exact as I'd like. Still, one can't appreciate success without experiencing failure. I'm sure you must have had a few failures with that machine of yours over the years?"

"Machine."

"Yes, good. Very good. Focus on that and we may complete this process much more quickly. I shall be pleased if that is the case. In the end, with the training I'm going to give you, you will wish for nothing more than to please me."

A feeling of dread settled in the Professor's stomach. He remembered hearing the reason the Counsel of Medics struck off Doctor Orother—for his unethical experiments upon the brains of beggars and harlots, whom he enticed away from a life of desperation and into his laboratory.

At once he knew there was no further chance for escape. He was trapped and doomed to become a puppet, and all because the Doctor wanted that damned Machine. His pride and joy, his life's work, had now become a noose around his neck.

As the Doctor repositioned the mirror, bathing him in that harsh and painful light, he knew he could not give in without a fight. He had to try and forget the Machine, to think about something, *anything* else.

As he closed his eyes, one picture entered his mind and the smallest smile touched the corner of his lips. Those beautiful, blond curls, tipping across pale shoulders and tickling the corset top. The shy smile and flushed cheeks. Eyes full of hope and wonder, and a mind sharper than anyone had ever given her credit for, even herself. Yes, she would do nicely. He vowed then to think of nothing else. Perhaps if he were lucky, Miss Larissa Markus would be the one to save him. If he were not lucky, at least she would be a beautiful memory to die to.

Chapter Twelve

Imago sat upright atop a barrel, staring across the ship, his tail flicking side to side. The cat had claimed it as his favorite spot over the last few days. The ship was silent save for the constant humming from the rotors until the quiet was pierced by a short *whoosh,* followed by a dull thud. On another barrel opposite Imago, the protruding handle of a throwing knife wobbled side to side for a moment and then stopped.

"Relax your elbow," Holt called, though he trained his attention on the rudder as he steered the ship away from a town that had appeared on the horizon. A great mushroom cloud of smog billowed into the air above it like an aura. Larissa stared at the barrel; the knife hit the center of the black dot Holt had painted on as a target. She wrinkled her nose and poked her tongue out at the back of his head as she retrieved the knife.

"Being juvenile won't improve your aim," he stated flatly.

"I hit the target dead on," she muttered under her breath, and made a mental note that this man seemed to have eyes in the back of his head.

"You did hit it, though it is stationary and large. The real skill comes from hitting a small and fast-moving target, and you won't achieve that if you don't relax your elbow."

"Fine. I bet I could still surprise you if I had a moving target to practise on."

"You could use the cat."

"What is it with people and my cat? He's the perfect companion, he never judges, criticizes, or complains, and he's much better company than you."

"If you say so."

Larissa lobbed the knife again and it smacked into the barrel side on, ricocheting across the ship deck and sticking into the bottom of Imago's barrel. The cat gave Larissa one long stare, jumped down, and headed into the cabin.

"Well, at least he's silent about his criticisms," she conceded.

"You should never throw or shoot in anger or desperation. Your state of mind affects your aim as much as a gust of wind or a misaligned sight."

"If I have to shoot or throw a knife at someone, it will be *because* I'm angry or desperate. I can't just turn off my emotions. We're not all born unaffected automatons, you know."

"All it takes is training."

"So you've had this training?"

"I have."

She gritted her teeth.

Cid seems like a fine conversationalist compared to this guy.

His inability to openly communicate was almost as annoying as his bulging muscular body. He had removed his over-cloak and stood in the cold air with the short-sleeved black shirt showing his bare arms. Every time he moved an arm, she surreptitiously watched the muscles flex, and when his head turned she could see the thick tendons of his neck working beneath the skin. It was an irritating, frustrating, and incredibly sensual sight. She cursed her aching libido for choosing to act up now.

"Hmm, where would a person get that kind of training? Were you in the army?"

"I was," Holt said.

"Not anymore?"

"Evidently not."

"Did you skip the training on basic communication?"

"I am well-versed in Tacit Code and Field Hand Signals."

"I meant conversation. Two or more humans speaking to each other. The sharing of information, thoughts, and opinions with others." She collected the knife and walked up to the other side of the wheel to stare up at him.

"I have never had a need to be well-versed in that form of communication," he said.

"Perhaps I can teach you how to hold a conversation in return for your lessons on how to kill people."

"What would be the point in learning that?"

"Well, to start with, it will prevent me from throwing this knife at your head. Your inability to talk is frustrating."

"If you threw that knife at me, you would not be successful." His stare grew dark, simultaneously goading and threatening. The hairs on the back of Larissa's neck pricked up and she felt a tingling shiver run down her spine.

Without pause to consider the madness of her intentions, she took a few steps back. The challenge given, she had wordlessly accepted. She positioned her feet into the correct stance, allowing her body to relax with a long exhale; her arm reached back, elbow relaxed. He watched her closely, examining her preparation, probably already thinking up criticism, she suspected.

Larissa frowned and looked out across the horizon, her eyes darting side to side as she tried to pinpoint her focus on one spot. From the corner of her vision she saw his head turn to follow her gaze, to see what it was that had caught her attention. Once she saw he had taken the bait, she took her chance.

Her focus snapped back and with one smooth flick of the wrist the knife released from her hand and turned over and over in the air, flying straight and true towards her target. The instant she let go she regretted it, for the briefest moment thinking her simplistic subterfuge would succeed. He turned, stumbling backwards, the blade disappearing from sight along with him as he fell.

The oddest sound emerged from Larissa, a sort of terrified squeal enclosed in an intake of air. She ran around the wheel and fell to the ground beside Holt, who lay sprawled on his side. She leaned over him, certain to see a gushing head wound and the knife protruding from his temple, but it wasn't there. Holt turned and rose, too fast for her to react.

In one move he grabbed her, flipped her onto her back, and pinned her down with the weight of his body. He brought the knife up under her chin, poking the tip of it into her neck. His face was calm and passively expressionless. Hers was filled with shock and concern as she had to physically squeeze her legs together to maintain bladder control.

"As expected, you were not successful, and you allowed yourself to become vulnerable."

"And you have taken full advantage of that."

"Not completely. But I could..." He leaned forward. The blade remained in place against her neck, her breathing shortened and skin erupted in goosebumps as his lips hovered inches above her own.

"Let her go or I swear to all nineteen fucking Gods I will blow a hole in the back of your skull." Cid's voice cut through the moment. Larissa watched Holt's jaw tighten in what she could only assume was some kind of emotion. Anger? Holt rose up, pulling her with him and lowering the knife as they stood.

"It's all right Cid. We were just, um, training." She walked up to Cid, who had his pistol aimed at Holt and didn't lower it.

"Is that what he called it?" Cid spat.

Larissa stepped to the side and looked at the two men, Cid with his pistol, Holt with the knife in his hand. His stance told her enough to know he was at the ready, and this was not a game she wanted to watch to the end.

The ship lurched as it caught a thermal lift and swayed off course. A flash of light on the horizon dragged Larissa's focus away from the two men.

"Umm, gentlemen? I think we have a more pressing matter to deal with right now."

"What?" Cid barked, refusing to have his attention drawn.

"I think we're being followed," Larissa stated as the blob on the horizon grew into the unmistakable shape of an airship. This time both Cid and Holt turned to look. Cid raised his hand to shield his eyes from the sunlight and squinted at the ship.

"Is that...?" Cid muttered.

"Pirates," Holt stated flatly. He grabbed the wheel and steered the ship back on course.

"Dear Gods," muttered Cid.

"Pirates?" Larissa half-sobbed. "What do we...how can we...will they…?"

"Catch us?" Holt interrupted. "Most likely. They'll have a gang of men to stoke the fire."

"What should we do?"

"We should prepare."

Chapter Thirteen

Larissa stood at the ship stern, a thin spyglass pressed to her eye as she watched the impending pirate ship gaining upon them. The ship looked old and battered, a poor comparison to *The Larissa*. The wood panelling of its keel was rough and silvery grey, and the balloon canopy above was made up of various patches of dark material. Two great masts stuck out either side of the deck, holding propellers, and another two protruded from the back end of the ship, giving speed to their advance. Two cannons reared on either side of the ship and one at either end; it was a ship prepared for a fight.

She could make out at least fifteen men on deck and didn't like to guess at how many more the hull may be hiding. Those in view were all armed with various weapons, and she had spotted one man stalking about the deck with a grappling hook, which he now loaded into a launcher. At the bow of the enemy ship stood a tall man who used a spyglass of his own to stare at Larissa, occasionally turning back to shout to the others.

She watched him closely. The crew seemed to look to him for instructions, so she mused he must be the Captain. He was dressed in a large, thick, fur-lined coat and had long grey-brown hair that mixed with an equally long grey-brown beard. Instead of a wearing Captain's hat worn by military ship Captains, a pair of goggles much like the ones Cid wore perched on his forehead.

Larissa turned around to look at Cid and Holt. They both faced her and waited patiently for her to speak. Cid had paused from shovelling coal, his sleeves pushed back to the elbows and the exposed skin on his arms and face black with soot. Holt's clothes were as clean as the moment he had joined them, despite all the times he'd spent shovelling coal as well. Both men appeared to be awaiting instructions.

Does that make me the Captain of this ship?

"There's at least fifteen of them. They're all armed and they have a grappling hook," she called to her crew of two.

Cid shook his head silently and disappeared back into the furnace room to resume shovelling. Holt turned back around and resumed steering. Larissa approached him, hooking the spyglass into a makeshift belt around her waist which also held one of Cid's pistols and a pair of throwing knifes donated by Holt.

"What should we do?"

"The mountains." Holt pointed ahead to the horizon. The beginning of a rocky, snow-capped mountain range seemed within reach.

"The mountains what? It's not like we can hide from them in there. You need to tell me what your plan is so I can—"

"So you can what? Get in the way? Get yourself killed or captured?"

"Help. So I can help. We can't expect to survive unless we work together."

"I don't expect you to survive."

"Charming." She stomped back to the stern and looked through the spyglass again, trying to ignore the thumping of her heart against her chest.

It was inevitable, she supposed. Holt had said right from the beginning that she needed him more than he needed her. Now she had become nothing more than a liability in his eyes. She had hoped to grind him down, work her way into his subconscious—to

92

make herself count—but their short moments of banter had been far too brief for him to build any emotional attachment.

At the bow of the pirate ship, the Captain waved his hands. Larissa thought he signalled to his crew at first, but eventually she realized his signals were directed at her.

"Holt!" she yelled. "They're sending us a message."

Before she'd even finished the sentence he was at her side and slipped the spyglass from her hand. At first he just watched. When the message stopped he sent a simple response back with exaggerated hand motions. She watched the exchange in silence, chewing on her bottom lip until it ached. Holt handed the spyglass back to her and headed toward the wheel in silence.

Larissa rolled her eyes. Any grandiose notions she'd had of being the Captain dissolved. She walked over to Holt again, unwilling to give up just yet.

"Look, I know you don't need me, I know I'm a burden, and I know you don't care if I live or die, but that doesn't mean you can't give me something. Just share some small amount of information. I promise I won't get in your way if you have a plan to escape or survive by yourself, just tell me what they said, or what's going to happen. Please."

"They want us to surrender."

"I suppose I could have guessed that. What will happen if we do?"

"They will take what they want," he paused to give her a long stare, "anything of value."

"And what will happen if we do not?"

"They will take us by force, and take what they want."

She huffed a laugh. It was inane, and he hadn't told her anything she didn't already know. Nevertheless, he was at least talking and that was some progress—just a little too slow for her liking.

"What did you say to the Captain?"

"I told him I understood his message."

"Just that? It seemed like a lot of signals for just that."

"Irritating."

"What's irritating? Me?"

"Yes, you. You're damned incessant."

"You mean I'm irritating because I figured out you're holding something back? Please, Holt, *just tell me*."

"They said they'll let us go if we hand them what they want. Who they want."

"Who do they want? You?"

"No."

"*Me?*"

"No."

Larissa's brow furrowed and she looked over at Imago, who was lying on his favorite barrel. She shook her head and dismissed the thought, and after eliminating everyone else she realized the answer just as Cid stepped out from the furnace room.

"Well, what the fucking hell is going on?" Cid barked.

"Cid," Larissa said softly. "So, if we give them what they want they will let us go?"

"I've never known a pirate to keep to his word."

"And what did you tell the Captain?"

Before Holt could answer the sound of gunfire pierced the air. Larissa and Cid ducked while Holt did not flinch.

"Are they trying to crash us?" Larissa asked.

"That was a warning shot. They won't want to destroy something as valuable as this ship unless they really have to." Holt turned the wheel and steered the ship around a jutting rock face as they drew alongside the rising base of a mountain. Without warning, he released the wheel and grabbed his pack and a length of rope.

"You're running away? That's your big plan?"

"I don't know what they want with your friend. You can come with me if you wish. He cannot. They are unlikely to chase after the two of us across the mountains."

"I'm not just going to leave Cid to his fate," Larissa said.

"Wait, what do you mean, they want me?" Cid asked, clearly affronted. Holt ignored him and tied the rope to the ship rail.

"I had a feeling you wouldn't leave him. Don't shoot them or fight, there are too many. They'll just kill you. If you're lucky, they'll only spend a day or two raping you, then sell you to the nearest merchant as a slave."

"If...I'm *lucky*? So that's it, you're just leaving, like some coward?"

"This isn't my fight. Goodbye, Miss Markus."

With that he slipped over the edge and descended to an alcove in the rock just below the ship. As Larissa turned to Cid, a large shadow came over the deck, blocking the sun; the pirate ship drew alongside them and the weathered faces of the men on board came into view. The pirates stood with weapons at the ready, trained upon Cid and Larissa. The man with the launcher fired the grappling hook, which slapped onto the deck beside Larissa's feet. The hook retracted and caught against the side rail, and within moments the two ships had pulled together. A handful of men jumped aboard, accompanied by their Captain.

"Take the wheel, Jameson," he commanded, his husky voice peppered with a more musical accent than Larissa had expected. He pointed to the furnace room and two other men followed his wordless command to take over stoking the fire. The remaining men who had jumped aboard searched the ship.

Another man boarded; he was distinctly different from the others, who all wore rugged old clothes, with dry, cracked skin on faces full of scars and facial hair. This new man was tall and strong, his clothing clean and neat, with short-cropped hair. He stood beside the Captain, who scratched at his beard and addressed Cid and Larissa.

"Well, all good so far. Cid Mendle?"

"Who the fucking hell are you, and how do you know my bloody name?" Cid yelled in the Captain's face. The man with short hair nodded once.

Crack

The sound echoed in Larissa's ear before she even registered what happened. Cid collapsed to the floor in a heap, and the Captain holstered the heavy pistol that he'd just used to knock Cid out cold.

"Take him below deck and secure him."

Two men scooped Cid up and dragged him to the other ship. The man with short hair followed with a sickening smile on his face. Larissa stood on wobbly legs. She didn't try to hide the tears in her eyes; there was no point.

"And what to do with this one?" The Captain rocked back and forth on his toes. "You got a name, girl?"

Larissa didn't answer.

"Never mind. Not like we need a name. Not for what I'm going to do to you." He reached out and grabbed her by the arm.

Her reaction came as naturally as a peaceful slumber. She grabbed a knife from her belt and in one swift movement rammed it forwards with all her might, plunging the blade through his coat and deep into the flesh beneath. As the blade cut through him it squelched, like slicing raw meat, she pushed it in as far as it would go. The Captain lurched, grunting heavily and stumbling onto her.

His grip on her arm grew tighter and he reached up with the other hand to grip her other shoulder.

Time slowed, tears flowed down her face in fear, and she watched the Captain's eyes as they glistened with painful realization. Her aim was good, too good. The Captain's eyes lolled to one side and his body followed. He pulled her down with his weight and they crashed to the deck together.

"Captain?" a man on deck asked as, one by one, the others realized what had happened. Larissa pulled the blade out of his chest and scuttled backward on her backside, her arm coated in bright, fresh blood.

"Fuck...Captain!" One man rushed to the body. The sound of feet pounding on the deck echoed around her and Larissa's vision blurred around the edges.

"The girl!"

More voices called to each other with obscenities, threats, and prayers to the Gods. She couldn't focus on any of them as she felt her limbs go limp. A strange tingling sensation tickled the back of her head and everything faded to black.

Chapter Fourteen

The light burned. The pain burned. The memories came in fits and starts, oddly disjointed and rarely useful. The Professor had lost track of time; he could have been there for months or just hours, it was impossible to tell. Between lengthy replays of his past he found moments where he was aware of the present, the cave, Doctor Orother, and the device attached to his brain.

Those fleeting moments were cruelly shattered by shocking pain, sent like a bolt from his head down to his toes. He screamed often, and when his screams subsided he listened to them echoing inside both the cave and his own skull. It was agony, pure hell. The only release came when he found a memory that Orother liked—and the Doctor only liked memories that were recent, or that involved the Machine. Those short moments of release from the pain felt euphoric, and it became harder to fight against it.

He thought of Larissa often, her shy smile and pretty laugh. Every time she flashed through his mind, a deep sense of shame and regret followed—how callously he had manipulated her. He had exploited his wealth and position to charm such a sweet girl, and that selfish charm had now destroyed her. He dared to imagine she'd played dead as he instructed, and escaped the fire at the Hub.

Perhaps she'd returned home and resumed her life as before. Yet deep down he knew that wasn't the case. She was most likely dead, or blamed for the fire. He tried not to think of her as destitute, alone, and cold, living like a beggar or locked away in some darkened jail. Still, the bleak thoughts plagued his mind, along with the ultimate realization that he could do nothing about it. Another shock of pain coursed through his body and he let out a pitiful yell, sounding like an abused dog.

"The machine, Professor," Doctor Orother said for the hundredth time, his voice calm and measured.

Larissa.

Her name hung in his mind; he repeated it over and over, desperate to remain focused. He felt the familiar sensation of regressing inwards, slipping into a distorted memory, powerless to stop it.

. . .

"It's not a problem," Larissa spoke, looking at her feet and clutching her cloak around her body.

"I could still take you out." He reached up to gently brush his knuckles across her cheek. She looked up at him, her eyes full of desire.

"Or you could stay here with me..."

He watched as she allowed her cloak to fall open and slip from her shoulders. The thin straps on her silk shirt cascaded down next. His mind raced as he imagined the vision that was to follow. Oh, how he desired to let it continue, to let her bare herself to him. Better still, to grab that shirt and rip it down. To take control, to push her to the ground and bury his face in her cool, pale flesh, to run his tongue up and down every inch of her body. Instead, he stepped inward, clasping her shoulders to prevent the shirt from falling completely, cursing inwardly for the choice.

He ran the tips of his fingers along the chain of her necklace, tracing his nails across the skin behind the silvery-white stone at the end of the chain. His fingers roved down the front of her chest until he realized she held her breath. He bent forward, bringing his mouth close to her lips.

Control yourself, Max.

"Miss Markus, I cannot recall a time when I have been so easily seduced."

He felt an unpleasant twitching of his erection as his body physically protested this decision to take the moment no further. The Gods were cruel, he mused, that they would give him such a malicious choice—the chance to make love to a beautiful young woman who clearly wanted him, or the chance to finish the Machine and finally see all his effort and work over the years come to fruition.

Perhaps I can still have both. The night is young.

He reached down and collected her cloak from where it had pooled around her feet, then brought it back up around her shoulders as he focused on the monumental task of trying to draw the blood back up into his brain.

"I'm afraid I do need to stay close to the Hub this evening. It is a critical time...perhaps you'd like a personal control-room tour?"

The cloak slipped from his hands and fell to the ground. Larissa said something in response, though the words were jumbled. He felt an odd pain shoot across his face and the scene before him dissolved into pure bright light.

. . .

"Not this again," Doctor Orother screamed manically through gritted teeth. The pain shot across the Professor's face again as he realized he was being punched, though the light kept him from actually seeing anything. He grunted and tried to move away, but to no avail; he was still pinned tightly. The light disappeared as

Orother pushed the mirror away but the Professor's vision remained blank.

"I am sick of seeing that stupid girl. I don't know what you ever saw in her. You should have ripped that stone from her neck the day you found her and left her in the street. The machine, Professor. Maximillian. I implore you. The pain and suffering will only increase until you submit and give me what I want."

"The girl is the key to the source." His words were rough, barely audible. A small voice at the back of his head screamed for him to stop, yet the break from the pain was too sweet a moment to lose.

Orother frowned and removed the pipe from the back of his own head, then crawled onto the table to perch on all fours above the Professor.

As the Professor's vision returned, he saw only an outline at first. After a moment, the features of Orother's face fell into place; a soft, disturbing smile danced across his lips.

"Oh? Do tell me. How is the girl the key to the source?"

A second face came into view above him, though the man's features were obscured by a dark red hood—the Cleric. The Professor had been aware of the man's presence from the beginning, though the Cleric had stayed out of view and hidden in the background until now. A pair of green eyes pierced into his soul with an unnatural intensity.

The Professor opened his mouth to speak but no words came out. He lay in silence, his mouth opening and closing like a mindless fish trapped in a bowl.

"Silence, Maximillian? That's fine, no need to talk. Just think of it..." Orother softly stroked the Professor's face.

The Professor's first instinct was a feeling of disgust and fear. As the soft strokes slowed his pounding heart and replaced the aching pain in his body, he understood the depressing truth; he had already succumbed to the 'training'. The pleasure he experienced at seeing the Doctor pleased with him was just as intense as the pain he experienced when the Doctor was not happy. Now, he felt a burning desire to remain that way, in comfort and at rest.

Orother stopped stroking and climbed down from the table. The Professor let out a whimpering noise. The small voice within him, calling for him to fight, to not give in, faded to nothing more than a whisper.

"Show me how the girl is the key, and I will release your legs."

The Professor watched as that sickening grin on the Doctor's face spread from ear to ear. The Cleric backed away from view and Orother's grin twisted and faded into the background, replaced by a large bookshelf. The Professor found himself within an older memory, one he had hoped never to share with this maniac.

Chapter Fifteen

The first thing Cid became aware of was the thumping pain behind his eyes and a ringing in his ears. It felt as if his entire brain had been pummelled to mush with a club. He kept his eyes squeezed shut and opened his mouth to swear. That was when he noticed the unmistakable metallic taste of blood. His stomach lurched and he spat a great globule of bloody spit across the floor. His tongue protested with a bolt of pain, and as he sucked on it he realized there was a chunk of tongue missing.

"Mmmm, fuck it."

Cid opened his eyes and found the room appeared sideways; his brain tried to un-jumble the mess and he realized he was laying down. He tried to sit, lifting a hand to the greatest source of pain on the side of his head. The tender lump that had formed on his temple screamed out when he touched it and he collapsed down onto his back.

He spent the next few moments listening to the ringing in his ears, and as it subsided he heard a dark chuckle coming from somewhere nearby.

"Mr. Mendle, you awake?" a male voice filtered through the ringing sound. It was not a voice he recognized, although he didn't need to know who the speaker was to determine that he was not a friend.

"Fuck off," Cid spat. The words came out in a lisp and slur.

"Captain hit you hard."

"Tell Captain to fuck off."

"Captain dead."

"Good." Cid didn't open his eyes. Instead, he tried to remember precisely what had happened and where he was. He felt a knot in the wood beneath him—the ship. He tried to place a Captain—the pirates. Then he tried to place himself in context and instead remembered the girl. His eyes snapped open.

Above him stood a man whose head almost touched the ceiling, which must have made him at least seven feet in height. They were positioned within a small room, bare save for a few boxes stacked in a corner. A lantern hung from the wall provided the only light. Cid's captor had short-cropped hair, an excessively muscular build, and attached to his belt was a long, thin, leather whip.

"I am Hans. Doctor sends regards," the man said. If his accent hadn't given away his foreign origins, his lack of grammatical accuracy would have sufficed.

"Tell Doctor to fuck off."

"You tell him yourself soon. First, you tell me where *Anthonium* is."

Cid replayed the last few days in his head, winding the clock backwards to piece it all back together. Had this man been in the Hub? Was he the one who searched the girl's apartment looking for the stone? Did Orother think Cid had taken the *Anthonium*? It didn't make as much sense as he'd hoped, though now he knew what they wanted and that he'd left the *Anthonium* with the girl. It was only a matter of time until they found it.

"How the fuck should I know? The last time I saw it, it was in the machine. The machine that your Doctor burned to the ground."

"The machine was searched. *Anthonium* was not there. You are lying. I will find the truth, either from you or from the girl."

"Where is the girl?" As soon as he'd asked he regretted it, seeing the grin grow on Hans' face.

"She killed Captain. She is being punished...I will show you."

Hans leaned down and dragged Cid to his feet to march him out into a hallway. As Cid followed, he realized this was not their ship; this interior was different. The slatted wood along the corridor walls was old and faded to pale grey with signs of rot, and the entire place smelled like a beer barrel. A line of matching lanterns lit their path along the hall. They turned a corner and found a collection of men huddled around an open doorway, their faces sullen. Their expressions did not improve when they saw Cid.

Hans pushed past the men, pulling Cid along with him.

"Oi, mate, what makes you think you can push in?" one man barked as they moved past. A few others muttered amongst themselves.

As they reached the doorway, Hans pushed Cid into a small storage room which was haphazardly dotted with irregular boxes, and between the boxes stood clusters of men, each of them looking down into one corner. Their path forward became blocked by male bodies that refused to move and Cid could not see past them. In his peripheral vision he caught sight of a flash of purple, and as his attention was drawn he saw a bundle of clothing stashed beside a box. The purple material of Larissa's corset was torn to shreds and spread across the bundle.

A muffled cry from behind the wall of men drew Cid's attention away from the clothes. The sound was followed by the unmistakable thud of a fist connecting with bone and the cry disappeared.

Cid trembled. He could not see what was going on so his mind decided to fill in the blanks, and he stood helpless and useless to change anything. Unexpectedly, a gap appeared and a man emerged with a smug expression plastered across his face. As the man pushed past, Hans charged forwards, dragging Cid with him.

"I will use the girl, now," Hans stated.

"Like hell you will. You got your *prize*, the rest is ours. That was the agreement, mate."

As Hans argued with the other men, Cid's attention fell to Larissa. She was naked and curled into a ball in the corner. She'd buried her face in her hands, her pretty blond curls matted and tainted with her own blood over cuts on her head. Her shoulders shook with silent sobs. Cid looked over the line of her body; her pale flesh was dotted with vicious cuts and bruises, and he found his heart aching to scoop her into his arms and carry her away from all the madness.

Somewhere in the mess of events he had come to develop such a deep affection toward her, one he'd thought himself incapable of feeling. He inched closer as the men behind him argued. Larissa sensed someone moving toward her and she shuffled backwards into the wall, squeezing her legs into her chest and bringing one arm down to cover her breasts. She kept the other hand across her eyes. Cid immediately stepped back, wanting desperately to shout at her that it was him and that he didn't want to look at her body or touch her like that. Not like these other fucking pigs.

"Brennan," a voice called from the corridor, "Jameson says he's having trouble with the other ship."

"Damnit. All right, everyone up on deck," Brennan said to his men, and turned back to Hans. "You can have her for however long it takes us to sort this out. After, we'll get right back to it. We're not done with this little bitch, not until every man here has had a piece of her. When we're done, we're gonna climb as high as the ship will go and push her over the side, see if she can fly. If you get in the way of that then the good Doctor's money won't save you from the same fate. Come on, you lot, I said up on deck."

The rest of the men filtered out one by one, grumbling amongst themselves until finally Cid and Larissa were left in the room with Hans.

Cid looked the man up and down. Cid was not a fighter, and had never claimed to be a brave man, though he was smart enough to know a losing battle when he saw one. Hans was a behemoth; he stood well over Cid's initial estimate of seven feet, and his shoulders were wider than the doorframe.

If Hans were similar in size and stature as Cid, he might have tried his luck and attacked, though with this huge brute Cid didn't even know where to start.

Hans bent over and grabbed hold of Larissa's wrists, dragging her along the floor and forcing her to stand. He reached out and grabbed a thick length of rope from a box and swiftly bound Larissa's wrists. He threw the rope up through a rusty old hook hanging from the ceiling, leaving her dangling there. Hans pressed his fingertips between her legs, into one of her thighs, and proceeded to drag his fingers upwards, scraping his nails through her blond tufts of pubic hair. His fingers traced a line up her pale stomach, pausing as he reached her breasts. He flashed a dark glance at Cid, who watched in sheer horror. Larissa whimpered through tightly pressed lips and tears spilled out the corner of her closed eyes, rolling down her puffy face to leave tracks in the soot and blood-soaked skin. Hans lightly ran his fingertips across one of her nipples. Cid looked down at the floor, a feeling of utter shame folding over his mind like a darkened veil.

"You will look at her, or I will make her suffering worse," Hans stated plainly, and Cid forced himself to watch again.

He slumped against a box as his head throbbed with pain. Larissa kept her eyes squeezed shut, and Hans pulled the whip from his belt. Cid squeezed his own eyes shut, instantly forgetting the threat. It was too much to bear to see her so abused and fragile, and the thought of having to watch her suffer further punishment sickened him. His mind turned to dark thoughts and he chanced a glance around the room, looking for a knife; if not to kill Hans, perhaps to kill the girl, put her out of her misery. She faced death anyway. Could he bring it upon her sooner?

"Where is the *Anthonium*?" Hans asked Cid, though Hans' gaze was trained upon Larissa.

"I don't know," Cid sighed.

Hans took one step backward and flicked his arm, bringing the whip down in one smooth motion straight across the front of Larissa's body. She screamed and bucked against the rope, a thin pink line immediately emerging across her chest.

Cid collapsed to his knees.

"Please, stop. It's...I think it's in her cloak. There's a lockbox." Cid waved to the bundle of clothes.

"You find it," Hans ordered, and Cid crawled to the bundle to search frantically for the lock box. After a few minutes he found nothing and his stomach lurched with despair.

"Well? Where is box?"

"It's not here," Cid whispered as his voice threatened to break into a sob. He looked up and found Larissa had opened her eyes and was staring down at him. In that moment he felt pure hatred for himself, that he had let her get into this predicament. He had let her down, and he hung his head in shame.

"Holt," Larissa whispered through shaky breaths.

"That fucking bastard," Cid spat.

"What, who is Holt?" Hans asked as he twitched the whip in his hand.

"The man who got off the ship at the mountain."

Cid sputtered through gritted teeth. A quiet pause filled the room as Hans, Larissa and Cid all passed uncertain glances at each other. The quiet was filled with shouts and calls from above. Hans stared up at the ceiling, only inches from his head; he let out an odd growl of frustration and turned to Cid.

"You, get up there. See what happening and come back. Bring Brennan with you, he's the new Captain."

Cid stood up again, his legs struggling to find balance. He looked at Larissa and all she could do in return was look back, her face blushing pink as she did so, and he didn't need to ask her why. He felt the same flush of embarrassed shame.

"I will not hurt her while you are gone, though I *will* hurt her if you don't go. Go, now!"

Cid stumbled out into the hallway and lurched in the direction the other men had gone. As he turned a corner he found a stairwell and he crept upward, still moving on uneasy legs. He paused as the door opened out into the world above.

"Tell him to come around starboard side and we'll go over to check it out," the new Captain, Brennan, called out to someone. Cid chanced a glance up on deck; the majority of the men stood along one side, looking out across the sky.

"Something's wrong, Brennan. Jameson's dropping," one man called.

"What? Where are the others?"

"Dead. He says they're all dead."

"What the fuck? Tell him to just hold it in the air and we'll come him."

Cid emerged from the stairwell and stood beside a mast pole; everyone else was too busy to notice him. He craned his neck to see between the heads blocking his view, and he spotted the Professor's ship, *The Larissa*. As it slowly lost altitude, one man stood at the wheel frantically trying to control the entire thing by himself. Cid spotted the problem before anyone else had seemed to notice; there was a large hole in the tip of the canopy fabric which flapped in the wind. It was more of a slice than a tear—a deliberate act caused by a knife.

"Vent some hydrogen. We need to lose some altitude to get to him." Two men scuttled past Cid, disappearing into the bowels of the ship to follow orders, and moments later everyone on board felt their stomachs lurching as the ship dipped in the air. Within minutes the two ships were at the same height and closing toward one another.

"We're too close to the ground. You boys need to get on board and find out what the fuck is going on. Get him up high or we'll crash. That ship is worth a fucking mint and I don't wanna lose it," Brennan called, his voice reaching a frantic pitch.

Some men at the side scuttled backwards at his orders, cursing and shouting. The Larissa came into full view and Cid's jaw dropped as he saw the ship hull swinging out of control and lurching straight toward the pirate ship. He grabbed the mast pole and braced for the impact. Seconds later it came, a gigantic thumping crunch that rippled throughout the ship as the two wooden structures knocked together, throwing bodies left and right. The cracking sound continued on, as wood panels buckled and bowed in reaction, floorboards popped away, shedding nails. The force of the hit sent both ships plummeting off at odd angles.

Cid watched on helplessly, gripping the pole as he saw Jameson's body aboard The Larissa fly through the air. The man wasn't moving due to the impact, though. Instead, he soared through the air with blood pouring from his slit throat. The downy hairs on the back of Cid's neck prickled and his breath caught in his lungs when he saw a black-clad figure sprinting across the other ship's deck, closely followed by a slim-lined, black and white cat. The two creatures reached the edge at the same time and simultaneously jumped through the air toward the pirate ship. As *The Larissa* bucked and rolled over on its side, cascading downward at an unstoppable rate, the cat landed on the rail with grace. The figure in black disappeared out of view beneath.

Cid forgot himself and ran forward, gripping the rail to look over. As he reached the edge he saw the last of *The Larissa* crashing into a rocky mountain ledge, his heart pausing as he waited for the inevitable—the furnace explosion mixing with the leaking hydrogen. It ignited as predicted and, at first, the explosion echoed in a low rumble from within a deep orange flash. The blast finally released, piercing the air and forcing a fireball up in a great plume. The heat singed Cid's knuckles and face, and the force pushed him onto his backside. A shudder ran through the entire ship.

His body tingled all over, the experience more intense than he'd expected, and he was left once again, helpless and useless. Voices around him infused the air with cursing. He looked up to the pirate ship canopy and rolled onto his side to find the cat, *her* cat, staring at him with the kind of impassivity only a cat could pull off in this circumstance. The cat slowly curled its neck to look at the rail and Cid unwittingly followed its gaze. He saw it, for just a split second; a hand reached up and grabbed the rail, then disappeared from sight. He turned to find Imago had disappeared as well, and his heart sank as he was brought straight back to grim reality.

Chapter Sixteen

The Professor stared at the bookshelf. He found himself in the odd position of realizing this was a memory, not a real experience. He tried to wiggle his fingers, expecting to feel the table beneath him and his arms pinned. Instead, he found his fingers would not respond to any amount of coaxing; the memory was fixed and he was trapped within its confines. On some conscious level he was grateful to at least be free from pain for a while.

"If you're looking for the map, it's not there," a male voice called behind him as footsteps sounded on the tiled floor.

The Professor sighed and turned, expecting it to take a bucket-load of charm to extract information from the fellow approaching. And if not charm, perhaps a bucket-load of gold.

"And who said I was looking for a map?"

"Everyone who comes to this section of the record library is looking for the same thing, and they all leave disappointed. Nonetheless, if you don't believe me, feel free to see for yourself."

The man was shorter than he'd imagined, a pair of oval spectacles perched on his oversized nose and a few strands of grey hairs dotted through his slick black mop. He looked older than he should have looked for his age, with dark circles around his eyes and a dowdy brown corduroy suit that fit poorly.

Perhaps it will take only a small bucket of gold.

"So, where is the map?"

"You mean you're not going to deny that you're after it?"

"What would be the point in denying it?"

"Most folks do. They just grumble under their breath and leave, or spend hours looking over the place, trying to prove me wrong. Then they grumble under their breath and leave."

"Well, let's say I am looking for it. Can you tell me where I can find it?"

"Nope."

"Ah. So what can you tell me about it?"

The man tipped his head and peered over the top of his glasses at the Professor.

"Who are you?"

"I am Professor Maximillian Watts." The Professor extended his hand, which the other man stared at blankly for a moment. Eventually he reached out and shook the Professor's hand with a grip limper than a newborn babe.

"Ah, I know you. It's not often we have an aristocrat visiting the archive. I'm Jon Field, Clerk of Geological and Archaeological Records."

"A knowledgeable fellow, no doubt. Fine subjects of study."

"Indeed, indeed."

"I am looking for Professor Markus. He and I were friends for a time at University, and I've been meaning to search for him for a number of years."

"Wait, you mean you're not looking for the-I mean...you knew Professor Markus?" Jon's eyes lightened and his demeanour shifted visibly.

The Professor clicked his tongue behind pursed lips. He wasn't accustomed to making up such flawed lies on the spot; it seemed as though the trail to the *Anthonium* ended here, and so he reasoned it was worth the risk. All he could do was hope this man couldn't piece together the age difference between the two Professors, that

Markus was almost ten years older than himself and that he had clearly never met the man.

"I did. You knew him, too?"

"I worked with him," the man replied. "On the same expedition that...well, that is to say, I was one of the last on our team to see him before he disappeared."

"Ah, so you may be of more use to me than the map."

"If only that were the case. I'm sad to say I have no idea where he went when he disappeared."

"All the same, I'd like to hear about it. You were supposed to be searching for some artifacts, I believe?"

"Yes. President Hague Senior was in power at the time and he had a penchant for old imperial items. I think he fancied himself an Emperor, and as Professor Markus was famed for his success in finding Emperor Dynestis' burial chamber, the President commissioned an expedition. The Professor was delighted and hired an entire team of assistants, myself included. We travelled the world with him and did well for a number of years, until something changed."

"Oh?"

"It all started with that woman. Why is it always a woman who ruins things?"

"Fascinating creatures. They can distract the most dedicated men from their undertakings at times," the Professor said with a smirk.

"She was just a pretty girl and a new assistant on the team. Professor Markus was smitten from the start. We all knew what they were up to. Quite out of the blue he married her, and the next thing we knew he shipped her home to Sallarium City." Jon fiddled with the rim of his glasses before continuing.

"I heard she had a baby a few months later, but I never saw her again. Good riddance, too. That was when he really changed. He started having mood swings. That quiet, clever man became violent and distracted. He lost all sense of time. Our discoveries had dried up and we followed empty trails to dead ends, failing to find even the corpse of a rat for months on end. Eventually, President Hague grew weary, and as his party sought re-election he started to analyze his spending. Of course, he could no longer justify frivolous ventures such as archaeological expeditions, especially those that had ceased to produce results."

Jon sighed and adjusted his glasses once more. The Professor watched him silently, he hadn't expected to get this much information from the man without either paying or pressing him for it. He pushed away the niggling feeling of guilt that prodded the back of his mind; he wasn't about to fall to pieces over taking advantage of a lonely man's need for conversation.

"One day, Professor Markus had a visit from some men. I have no idea who they were, but they looked like Foreign Government types. He stopped talking to me about such matters when that woman came onto the team, and he didn't see fit to resume his trust in me after she left. The map showed up out of nowhere and he would disappear with it alone for weeks or months at a time.

"He would come back looking years older, suffering from dehydration and exhaustion. He started to fire us, one by one, dismissed us without warning or explanation, until I was the only one left. I tried to speak with him, to see if he would listen to reason. All I could get out of him was some rambling madness about..."

Jon had been staring off into the distance and now his attention snapped back to the Professor. Jon looked him over with a scrutinising gaze, and the Professor maintained an impassive expression—one he'd mastered over the years. That look would stand him in good stead if he ever developed a taste for poker.

"*Anthonium*," Jon finished.

"The element?" the Professor asked, his voice quavering slightly on the word.

"Don't tell me you don't know anything about it. If you knew enough of the story to come looking here, you must have known about it. Gods, even the bloody press had heard the rumours when they started reporting on his disappearance."

"Yes, of course. I just didn't want you to think-"

"That you were after it? Everyone is after it—the world's rarest element, so valuable with all its magical powers." Jon wiggled his fingers and made a face as he spoke the word *magical*.

"So you don't believe he found it?" the Professor asked, no longer bothering to hide his interest.

"Oh, he said he found it. He even showed it to me."

"Oh?"

"During our last talk. He was barely coherent. All he had was a lump of silvery stone. They've given me the geology section to maintain, yet I don't know the first thing about it. Rocks and stones only ever serve as inconvenient obstacles to great treasures and historical artifacts. There was nothing at all remarkable about the stone."

"So, he kept it?"

"Oh, no. He bade me send it to his *darling* wife with an incredibly paranoid list of instructions for what she should do with it. Mustn't hold it for any length of time with bare hands, must keep it in a lead box, shouldn't expose it to heat, blah blah. Once he finished rambling, he went ahead and fired me."

"A shame."

"Indeed. After that, he disappeared, and no one has seen him since."

"So, you sent it to her?"

"Hmm?"

"The wife, the stone?"

"Yes. For all the good it would have done her. Poor woman was left destitute. With no income and no one to claim him as dead, she probably ended up in some workhouse, or goodness knows where. Serves her right, if you ask me."

"And his instructions?"

"Hmm?"

"Did you give her the instructions for how to care for the stone?"

"Don't be ridiculous. He was a jabbering idiot at that point. Why would I give credence to such nonsense?"

"Because, my dear fellow, you may well have fated the woman to her death."

Jon stared up at the Professor, blinking.

"Did she have a name? Besides Mrs. Markus, of course?"

"Did you even know him at all, or was it just a ruse?" Jon said as his face sunk into a scowl.

"What does it matter? You've done the man a tremendous disservice."

"What? I've never been so insulted. How could you say such a thing?"

"If he left behind a wife and child, you should have been man enough to care for them in his stead. You should have at least looked out for them a little, put aside your disgust for the woman. Even if you did not believe he truly found the *Anthonium*, you should have considered the safety of those to whom you sent the stone. No wonder he fired you. You were a poor and disloyal employee."

The Professor sucked a deep breath in through his nose and glared down at Jon, who muttered incoherent sounds of protest to himself. He pushed the man to one side with the edge of his cane and strode toward the exit, feeling simultaneously glad for a new path to follow and angry at Jon Field's behavior.

As he reached the glass doorway the sunlight assaulted his senses, and as he stepped through the door his arms stuck in place. The world toppled over and he was once again back in the cave with Doctor Orother.

. . .

For a while everything remained silent and bathed in harsh light. The silence ended when Orother spoke, his voice soft and melodic.

"So that is how the girl came to have the *Anthonium*? I suspected she may have had a piece but wasn't entirely sure until I learned you had taken an interest in her. How fascinating. I recall going to that library myself to search for the map. Never chanced upon that fellow, though. Not that it would have mattered. Eptoran maps are virtually unreadable. The only shard I've come across is of no use to anyone. Is the mother dead?"

"Yes." The Professor found his voice. It was small, meek, and too quick to provide answers.

"You think the girl may know where her father is?"

"Yes."

"And you never asked her?"

"No."

"No, I'd have seen that memory by now, seeing as that girl is all you've shown me. You are a stubborn thing." Orother turned away to address his assistant.

"James, send a message to Hans. Tell him to collect the girl along with the engineer and the *Anthonium*. It seems we have a use for her, as well." Orother pushed the light to one side and reached across the table to unlock the braces pinning the Professor's legs.

The Professor tested each leg in turn, twisting his ankles around and raising his knees. The freedom of movement felt exquisite.

"As I promised. This should provide more comfort. Continue to comply and I'll be more generous. If you revert to fighting, I shall lock you back up again. Eventually, we will come to a mutual understanding and I will allow you to wear simply this."

Orother lifted up a metal collar. Under normal circumstances the Professor would have been disgusted by the concept, but now he felt almost euphoric at the idea of wearing it. The notion of gaining a small measure of freedom, to stand and move around, to avoid the light, the memories, and the pain, made his breath catch. The Professor's mind played back through the words.

Orother had spoken to one of his assistants. *The engineer*—Cid? *Collect the girl*—Larissa? His heart jumped into his throat as he considered the notion of Larissa, or even poor Cid, his faithful engineer, being subjected to Orother's cruel and painful torture. He knew at once he had to do something to try to prevent that from happening.

"So, back to your machine. Will you now show me how to build it?"

"Yes."

A final tear of defiance trickled down the side of his face as he watched Orother head towards the Memory Device. This time he would not fight. Orother had to believe he was defeated, and the only way was to give him everything he desired, to give up his Machine. And he would do it...for her.

Chapter Seventeen

Holt held onto the curved underside of the pirate ship. He gripped the wood with his fingertips, bracing his body, and balanced on the edges of his feet. The cloth on his back burned from the ferocious heat within the downed ship's plume of smoke. He had to take short breaths to prevent coughing and risk giving himself away. As the pirate ship turned from the wreck below and the heat and smoke dissipated, he focused on listening to the voices above.

In the measured chaos of his last moments aboard *The Larissa*, he had failed to determine the exact number of men he would have to face on the pirate ship, though his estimate was at least ten on deck.

The voices above barked, filling the air with expletives and threats. He closed his eyes. The more people up on deck who paid attention to the downed ship meant less people below hurting Larissa. Unfortunately, having them all on deck was not ideal for his predicament.

Moments passed and he had determined eight distinct voices. He had also concluded Cid was still alive and being dragged back down below. He wasn't sure if Cid's survival was good news or not, as he'd already threatened him once and Holt usually didn't let people live after the first threat. After a few more moments he heard one man express his keenness to "get below and finish with that girl". Part of him felt relief at knowing for sure she was still on board and still alive. Another part of him knew all too well what lay in store for her. He felt the anger rising in his blood. If he had to slaughter a ship full of pirates, then so be it.

When the voices disappeared Holt climbed. Inch by inch he crawled up the curve, taking care to test each new contact point for weakness before he trusted it to hold his weight. When he finally reached the top, he chanced a glance over the edge. Only three men remained on deck, one at the wheel and two others busying themselves with work.

The ship gained altitude again, and he surmised there must be at least one man at the hydrogen tanks and another two in the furnace room stoking the fire to climb at such a pace.

A man headed toward him carrying a bucket. Holt dropped one hand down to his belt and unhooked a knife, holding it loosely between his fingers. A cold breeze rushed past his head, blowing his scruffy hair out of place. He sucked in a calm breath as the man approached the ship edge, just above his position. The man placed the bucket on the deck and picked up a handful of loose nails, dropping them in the bucket as he stood.

Holt pushed off with his toes from his wooden perch and launched up, grabbing the man by the shoulder with his left hand and plunging the knife into his neck with his right. Holt slipped back down below the guardrail, pulling his target overboard. Before the man had a chance to register what was happening it was already too late. His body tumbled over the rail and fell through the air without so much as a scream escaping his severed vocal chords.

Holt chanced a look up again. The man at the wheel did not look in his direction; he launched over the rail and ducked behind a thick mast pole. Taking a moment to assess the situation from the new angle, he was still equally aware of his exposed position and that it wouldn't be long before someone realized his first victim was missing.

Muffled shouts came up from below deck, telling him that time was running out fast. He needed to act quicker. He sprinted across the deck and grabbed the man at the wheel, latching his hand around his mouth. His target was too confused to react and far smaller in build, giving Holt barely any fight. He dragged him across the deck and turned the man over the side with one lift.

The second worker came up the staircase nearby and headed toward the empty bucket. He pulled a finger from his earhole and stared down at it as he walked.

"Hey, guys, you should hear that lot down there. They're having a right shouting match...hello? Anyone?" The man turned around in circles, frowning at the unmanned wheel and rudder. "The fuck is going on?"

Holt left the last man on deck and dipped into the furnace room, swiftly dispatching the two men inside, and finally he took care of the man at the tanks. On deck, the last man still stared back and forth between the abandoned bucket and empty wheel, scratching his head. Holt considered him for a moment when a short, shrill scream came from below. Holt froze in place, his heartbeat quickening. His calculated approach shifted to something more panicked. He abandoned the last man on deck, gliding past his line of sight, and headed down the staircase towards the sound of angry voices.

The corridor was tight, an uncomfortably enclosed area for fighting a ship full of angry pirates. Holt felt a slight irritating twinge of regret at crashing the other ship, which had been far better designed despite being much smaller.

He reached a junction in the corridor; a group of men huddled around a doorway up ahead, and just past them the corridor disappeared down another turn. They trained their collective attentions inside the one door, so he straightened his back and walked past them, hiding in plain sight with silent footsteps.

As he passed he caught a glimpse into the room; the image of pale flesh, bound and beaten, flashed through his vision with such speed that it barely registered. No one noticed his presence as he slipped around the other corner.

"We need to find this man, Holt. He has the other item the Doctor wants," a thickly accented voice boomed out.

"I keep telling you, mate, that's not my fucking problem. He wanted the engineer and he's gonna have him. We've lost a Captain and several other men to this mission and now we've lost a hell of a payday with that ship. These men want vengeance and I intend to let them have it. Now, hand the girl over or I'll string you up right beside her."

"Breeeenan..."

Holt watched, peering around the bend, as the last man from the deck came trotting down the corridor towards the others as he called out in a panic.

"What now? What the fucking hell do you want, Grubbs?" Brennan emerged from the room and all the men turned their attention to Grubbs.

"It's the others, uhhh…Sir, they've gone."

"Gone?"

"Jim and Derek, they was there one minute, then gone the next. And then there's Gibbsy and Bates and Hook Nose."

"And they're gone, too?"

"No. They're dead."

"Fuck. Wha-who's flying the ship?"

Grubbs shrugged and Brennan shoved him into the wall as he pushed past, hurrying down the corridor. More men followed without needing command.

"Lock that fucking door. I don't want those bastards going anywhere," Brennan called back, and as the last man exited the room he slammed the door shut and locked it. Grubbs was ordered to watch the door, leaving the corridor empty save for Holt and Grubbs.

Holt watched Grubbs for a while, his hand twitching beside one of his throwing knives. It would have been an easy shot, perhaps too easy, but some part of his subconscious warned against killing him. If Holt successfully rescued both Cid and Larissa, the three of them were not enough to fly a ship this size all the way to their destination and land safely. Even if they were all in peak physical condition, they would need help. Perhaps this man could be persuaded.

Grubbs resumed the exploration of his earhole with a finger and slumped against the wall. Holt smirked as the man unwittingly turned his back to him. When Grubbs pulled his finger out and looked down to inspect whatever he'd found, a blade slipped silently along his throat. Holt pushed his chest against Grubbs' shoulders. The man instantly trembled as the blade dug into flesh, drawing a thin trail of blood.

"Shhh," Holt hissed in Grubbs' ear. "Who is still inside the room?"

"The, uh, girl and the engineer man, and the tall matey."

"The tall matey?" Holt stepped backwards along the hall, forcing Grubbs to back-step with him.

"Hans, he's called. Works for that Doctor. He's a damn big bugger, though. You probably wouldn't be able to get your knife around his throat as easy as you have with mine. Take it easy, yeah, mate?"

"When I'm done, you'll have a choice. Work with us, or die."

Holt turned the far corner and ducked into an empty room, releasing Grubbs from the knife, spinning him in one motion; his fist met the man's jaw. Grubbs collapsed in an unconscious heap, and Holt headed back to the locked room.

He bent down on one knee and pulled a set of lock picks from a back pocket, making swift work of the padlock. He pressed his ear to the door; inside, quiet male voices exchanged muffled words. The voices did at least give away the speakers positions and Holt tried to rebuild the brief glimpse of the room in his mind. A pile of upturned boxes bundled along one wall, presumably displaced by the earlier impact; Larissa, hung up in the middle like a piece of meat at a slaughterhouse.

He blinked away the narrative and pictured the two men on either side of her. The voice on the right sounded closer to the ground. Sitting? Kneeling? The other rested at normal height. He trusted his instinct and took a step back, lightly gripping a throwing knife in each hand and relaxing his stance. He lunged for the door, barging through with his left shoulder and instantly spinning to release the blade in his right hand. It flew through the air, turning end over end and finding its target, though not in the throat as Holt had hoped. The man was far taller than he'd anticipated. Instead, the blade sunk into the tall man's chest, failing to penetrate deeply as it hit breastbone.

Hans stumbled backwards and grunted. Holt released the second blade with his left hand, though his aim was not as true from that side and he'd already lost the element of surprise. Hans turned, lifting his arm, and the blade sank into his bicep instead of hitting his face.

Holt charged forward, pulling another knife free as he reached the taller man. Hans was already prepared. The giant allowed Holt another strike, turning his torso as the knife swung across, slicing him instead of penetrating. The knife clattered to the ground and Hans took full advantage, swinging his fist straight into Holt's cheek. Holt's face rippled with the sheer force and he flew backwards into the wall.

Holt sunk to his knees, making himself a small target as Hans brought an onslaught of punches and kicks. Holt was surprised when the beating ended abruptly. He chanced a glance up and watched the heavy man lurching over, his face contorted with agony. He emitted a high-pitched, quiet sort of squeal. Holt stood up and spotted the cause.

Cid bent over behind Hans, his hand gripping the blade that Holt had dropped earlier; the sharp end of the blade had been fully inserted into Hans' groin. Cid pulled the blade out in one swift movement and Hans toppled over, clutching himself and squealing. Holt bent over and pulled his knives out of Hans' chest and arm. Then he stalked around the room and swung a blade across the rope that bound Larissa to the hook in the ceiling. Her body collapsed and he caught hold of her, scooping her into his arms and striding towards the doorway.

"Lock the door behind us," Holt half-whispered to Cid over his shoulder as he carried Larissa back to the room where he'd left Grubbs.

Holt carefully laid Larissa's limp body on the floor and she curled up, shying away from him. A barrage of thoughts flashed through his mind, but they would all have to wait. He still had work to do. He removed his coat and placed it over her. Cid entered the room and sunk down to his knees beside Larissa.

"Who the fuck is that guy?" Cid whispered, pointing at Grubbs.

"A recruit. We need workers. If he stirs, hit him. Keep him out cold until I return. I will bring others."

"Wait, what are you going to do? There's too many to tackle by yourself."

"Are you volunteering?"

Cid frowned. Holt waited. Eventually, Cid shook his head and turned his attention to Larissa. Holt gave her one last glance and was perplexed to find her looking up at him with bright blue-grey eyes. After what she'd just been subjected to, he had not expected her to look so clearheaded and alert.

"I will return," Holt stated, answering an unspoken question, and he headed through the door.

Back in the corridor two men marched towards him, weapons at the ready. One carried a pistol and the other wielded a short sword. They paused to check the lock on the door.

"Where's Grubbs gone?"

"Probably dead, fucking dumbass idiot."

Holt flattened himself to the wall around the corner, a knife at the ready in each hand and one gripped between his teeth. As the footsteps came close he stepped out, flinging the first knife at the man with the pistol; it struck him directly in the neck. The second man shouted an expletive and lunged forward.

Holt blocked the sword with his second blade, though the sword bit into the skin on the back of his hand, cutting deep into flesh. Blood spilled from the wound, but Holt did not stop as his opponent tried to swing a punch with his free hand. In one swift twist, Holt turned and buried the knife between the man's ribs. The man let out a yell of pain. Holt silenced him, taking the last knife out from his mouth and shoving it into the soft flesh beneath his opponent's chin.

After letting him fall, Holt retrieved his knives from the men as they breathed their last, cleaning the blades on their clothing. He collected the pistol and the short sword as well. He ripped a chunk of material free from one man's shirt and bandaged the wound on his hand as he headed back to the stairwell, determined to finish the task.

Three men were visible on deck—Brennan at the wheel and two others flanking either side of him, alert and clearly on watch for trouble. They had armed themselves with rifles. Holt climbed the last few steps and appeared on deck, no longer attempting to hide himself.

"There he is," a man shouted, aiming his weapon at Holt. Brennan's grip on the wheel tightened.

"You have two choices," Holt spoke clearly and loudly to ensure the other men, who had emerged from their stations, could hear.

"You can try to kill me, and wind up dead, or you can stay alive and remain on board as crew."

"Well, there's seven of us, you fucker, and one of you. Your odds don't look too good to me."

"There were two ships and twenty of you to begin with and only one of me. My odds have been improving markedly for a few hours, though my patience is running out."

"Finish him off," Brennan barked.

Immediately, the two men beside the wheel fired their rifles and the air filled with the smell of gunpowder. The shots missed their target, as Holt had rolled backwards down the stairwell. As he reached the bottom step he righted himself on one knee and fired his pistol at the first person who appeared. The body bucked and tumbled down, stopping just beside him. Two more appeared and fired weapons. Holt had already ducked around the corner, and once their shots were spent he popped back out and released two knives. Another pair of bodies tumbled down the stairs.

"Take the wheel," Holt heard Brennan barking at another, and Holt stepped backwards along the corridor, waiting for Brennan to show up.

"You gonna fight me like a man, you bastard?" Brennan called as he reached the bottom.

"As you wish, Captain." Holt straightened his back and readied the short sword. Brennan turned the corner with his own sword drawn, his teeth bared and face red with anger. Brennan leapt forward and Holt parried, the clang of metal echoing along the corridor as their swords clashed. Again and again Brennan attacked, his pace relentless and his skill much more advanced than Holt had originally anticipated.

They bucked and jabbed at one another, thrusting and blocking, swords splintering wooden panels as they wildly caught along the walls. The sweat poured down Holt's face and the injuries he'd sustained previously shouted out in protest. He took another step backwards and stumbled, twisting to the side; Brennan took advantage and threw a punch that caught Holt in the ear.

The pain shot through his head and his legs gave way, bringing him down. As Brennan swung down toward him, smiling into the final blow, Holt accepted the grim reality of his failure.

Brennan's blade came down and bounced against the wooden board beside Holt's head. The movement above ceased and Holt looked up just as Brennan toppled over backwards, the handle of a knife protruding from his eye socket. Holt craned his neck behind to see Larissa, standing at the other end of the corridor. His black coat hung loosely from her shoulders and her arm lowered down to her side. He stared at her in silence for longer than was necessary.

Her face was blank as she glanced down at him.

"I relaxed my elbow," she said.

"I can tell. Though I'm grateful your target was not moving."

Holt rolled over and stood up, bending down to retrieve the blade from Brennan's face only to find it so tightly wedged it would not budge. Cid emerged from the room to stand beside Larissa, closely followed by a confused-looking Grubbs.

"Are they all dead?" Larissa asked.

"There are two more on deck. They will be the weakest and they may be persuaded to remain working on board for us in exchange for their lives."

"Good. I will talk with them." Larissa strode forward, her naked legs and bare feet stepping over Brennan's body. After a pause Holt joined, walking at her side, and the others followed closely behind.

"Are you sure you're up to this?" Holt asked, failing to hide the incredulity in his voice. She was proving far more capable than he'd credited.

"Quite sure, Holt. Thank you."

Chapter Eighteen

Larissa stood at the pirate ship bow, staring across the mountain range. Between two large peaks on the horizon the sun was setting in a glowing orb and the sky sang with a deep orange shine, fading to pinks and purples. Small dots of starlight pricked through the farthest reaches of the blackening space above. A thin wisp of freezing air bit at her cheeks and disturbed her curls.

A heavy, waxed coat covered her body from shoulders to feet; the garment had been purloined from a dead pirate by Cid. Behind her the men worked. Three new, rather reluctant recruits including Grubbs were busy with their assigned tasks of maintaining the furnace and removing the dead bodies. Cid manned the wheel, and Larissa had no idea where Holt had disappeared to.

As she watched the sun's edge dip behind the mountain ahead she sighed. The pain of her injuries had reduced to a dull ache, scabs had already formed over open wounds and the bruises seemed to be fading quicker than usual. Her mind felt numb; the stress and shock of the last few hours had become too much and some part of her conscious brain was acutely aware that other parts of her mind had shut down.

She thought of the men that Holt had killed, the ship wood turned red with spilled blood, the sound of gunshots and swords clashing and splitting flesh ringing in her ears. Before, she would have been disgusted and shocked—perhaps she would have vomited at even the thought of it. Now, there was nothing, no pity, no sadness, no sense of satisfaction that they'd gotten what they rightly deserved. No feeling at all.

She wondered if something inside had broken forever, if some part of herself had snapped—irreplaceable, irreparable. She played the moments in the room below over and over, the men attacking one after the other, the shouts and calls from their comrades, the sense of fear and desperation that smothered her.

Like a thick blanket wrapped too tightly, it stifled her. She recalled how quickly she'd wished for death and wondered now if death might have been the preferable option. What was the point in continuing on after such chaos and such a loss of identity? How could she possibly hope to save the Professor if she had failed so miserably to save herself?

"Training," Holt's voice interrupted her vein of despairing thoughts.

"What?" she replied, not turning to look at him. He appeared at her shoulder and matched her gaze toward the horizon.

"You said I was an emotionless automaton and I told you all it takes is training. I believe you've had your first lesson." He lightly gripped her hand and placed the lock-box into it.

"Why did you take it?"

"They would have found it and known it was something of value. I didn't want to give them another reason to hurt you."

She blinked at the box, processing his words, and then placed it into a coat pocket.

"Well, you can keep your lessons. I've learned quite enough."

"No," he said.

"No?"

"There are more lessons to come."

"For you, perhaps. I will get off at Meridina and go..."

"Go? Go where? You're giving up?"

"I can't do this. I'm a sales clerk. Nothing more than a silly little girl with stupid, naïve dreams."

"You are much more than that."

Larissa turned to face him and found his gaze fixed firmly, awkwardly, dead ahead. "Because I killed a man?"

"Two men, I believe the count is, although I distinctly recall telling you not to kill anyone. Had I known the first thing you would do would be to stick a knife into their Captain, I might have amended my plan."

"Your plan? I thought you'd abandoned us. Why didn't you just tell me what you were going to do?"

"You had to believe that I'd abandoned you. Otherwise you may have acted as though you expected to be rescued and they would have paid more attention to me."

"Well, why didn't you just abandon us? Why bother to come back at all?"

Holt fell silent, though his face was tense and the tendons on his neck jutted out as he chewed on his teeth.

"Holt, I asked you a question."

"You may not like the answer."

"You're concerned you'll hurt my feelings? Just answer the question."

"I was not equipped for the journey across the mountains during winter."

"I see. Why did you think I wouldn't like that answer? Did you think I expected you to tell me you wanted to be the hero, save the damsel in distress so we could fly off into the sunset together and live happily ever after?"

"That's exactly what I thought you wanted to hear."

Larissa puffed a laugh through her nostrils, though it was more a reflex than an actual feeling of amusement. Hours ago he would have been right, she would have imagined that was his reason. She would have entertained fleeting romantic intentions and been disappointed to discover that was not the case. Now his actions and his reasoning for them simply made sense.

"A stupid, naïve girl, just as I said. Two seconds ago you said I was much more than that."

"You are becoming much more." Now he turned to face her. "The pain will fade. The memories will stay and you will find a peace within them. The scars will recede and you'll be no more aware of them than you are of your skin. And before we reach our destination, you will have thought of a plan for how to save your Professor."

"See, I knew you could do it."

"Do what?"

"Have a conversation." Her face refused to break into a smile as she spoke.

"Hmm. Don't get used to it."

"Holt?"

"Hmm?"

"I do need to know one more thing."

"And what is that?"

"Uh, excuse me, Miss—umm, Captain 'Rissa." Grubbs scuttled along the deck and stood below Holt and Larissa, wringing his hands together and looking down at his feet.

"It's the big fella, the Doctor's man. He's still alive and we was wondering what we should do with him?"

"He's alive? Where is he?"

"Still in the storage room. We went in there and found him. He's bled quite a bit, though not dead. When we saw he was alive we shut him back in and came up here to see if you wanted us to finish him off like?"

"Thank you, Grubbs. He may actually be of some use," Larissa said.

"Right you are, Cap'n." Grubbs and the other man who'd been following him headed back below deck.

"Did he just call me Captain?" Larissa asked, turning to Holt, and for the first time she saw his lips had curved into a genuine smile. He passed a glance at her as she frowned up at him, and they set off together towards the stairway.

The door to the storage room was still locked. Grubbs and his mate leaned against the wall opposite, staring at the door as though they expected it to grow legs and walk off.

Larissa tried to hide the shudder that coursed through her body as they approached. She'd hoped to never have to go into that room again. The dungeon, her chamber of torment, and the monstrous beast of a man whom the room now contained, were more terrifying to her than any of her worst nightmares. Grubbs pushed off the wall and brandished the key to the padlock at Larissa as she approached.

"Thank you, Grubbs." She pushed the key into the lock as Holt drew out a pair of knives. The other man behind them muttered to Grubbs, "Bloody hell, you got a *thank you*, and she remembered your name."

Larissa made a mental note to try to remember the names of the other men they'd acquired as crew, especially if they were going to regard her as their Captain—though she couldn't quite fathom why they'd assume she was in charge instead of Holt.

Holt pushed the door open; at first there was no sign of anyone inside. The severed rope still hung from the rusty hook in the ceiling, swinging to and fro with the ship's movements; a lump caught in Larissa's throat as she saw it. Behind a stack of broken boxes the floorboards were stained red with blood and she wondered at how much of it was her own.

As they moved forward they found Hans slumped over behind a box, clutching his groin with both hands, his head hung low. Trails of blood leached out of the wounds on his arm and chest and leaked into a pool on the floor. He did not acknowledge their presence; his chest still rose and fell with slow breaths. Holt pushed in front of Larissa and bent down to collect the broken piece of rope. He kicked Hans' leg and the large man lolled over, bumping against the wall. His eyes were closed and sunken into their sockets, and he let out a low groan.

Holt bent down and pulled Hans' arms out from beneath him, binding his wrists in one motion, and dragged Hans onto his back. Then he pinned his arms to the floor behind his head. The bigger man did not protest, though his eyes did open and his gaze fell directly onto Larissa, who had inched closer. She felt an extra boost of courage with the protection of Holt at her side.

"Is he dying?" she asked Holt, though she knew the answer.

"Yes."

"Will it take long?"

"Many hours."

"You hear that, you disgusting brute?"

"Unnhuh," Hans grunted, his eyes rolling.

"That means I only have one thing to offer you—a swift end in exchange for some information."

"Ju vihiduos," Hans muttered in his native tongue. Larissa didn't need to speak the language to understand that it was not a message of compliance.

"Very well." She marched towards the door and Holt followed, understanding her plan. It wasn't until the door was slammed shut and the padlock jingled loudly enough to sound as though it were being locked that Hans called out, "wait!"

The hint of a smile threatened the corner of Larissa's lips and she pondered whether *satisfaction* qualified as an emotion. They returned to the room to find that Hans hadn't even managed to move his hands from where Holt had left them.

"You changed your mind?" Larissa asked.

"Give me your word," Hans said.

"What?"

"That you will end it, quickly, no more pain."

"I give you my word, you bastard," Holt chimed in.

"I don't trust him. I want your word."

"Very well, you have my word. Now you will answer my questions. Is the Professor still alive?"

"Last I saw him, he was...alive."

"Where is Doctor Orother taking him?"

"He has a mansion at Meridina, on Clockman Peak."

"What did he want with Cid?"

"Professor killed his engineer."

"Oh." A small sense of pleasure tickled the back of her head at the thought that the Professor had disrupted Doctor Orother's plans. Though as the first real emotion seeped in, it threatened to open the floodgates and send her tumbling into a sobbing mess.

"How many guards at the mansion?" Holt asked when Larissa had fallen silent. Hans did not answer.

"How many guards?" Larissa repeated.

"Five." Holt and Larissa exchanged glances. It was a rather obvious lie.

"What will Orother do to the Professor?" she asked, instantly regretting the question. What had she expected him to say? That the Professor would be well-tended? Treated to three hot meals a day and given steaming baths?

"He will be trained." Despite his dilapidated state, Hans still managed to crack a sickening smile.

Larissa stared down at the man at her feet. The room fell flatly silent as the conversation reached its obvious end. She had killed twice already, but this felt different. This man, however awful he was, lay at her feet waiting to be put out of his misery. She'd given her word on it. She ran it over and over in her mind—who would know of her broken promise besides Holt if she just walked away and left Hans to bleed to death? She figured Holt would understand and not even judge, but could she forgive herself? Did the cruelty of this man justify her turning into a cruel woman? Hans stared up at her. The look was not pleading, though there was a question in his eyes, a question that demanded an answer.

Larissa held out her palm towards Holt. Without a word he handed her a knife and took a few steps back toward the door.

Hans bent his head backwards, opening a target on his neck, and Larissa knelt down beside him, bringing up the knife. Movement in the doorway caught her eye.

Holt lunged forwards but he was too slow. Hans whipped his hands up, catching Larissa's wrist and pulling the knife free. Then he rolled over, pushed her to the ground, and pinned her with his weight.

Excruciating pain shot through her shoulder as Hans plunged the knife straight through until it stuck in the floor. She let out a blood-curdling scream. His body, hot and heavy, heaved across her torso, his salivating lips drooling onto her face.

Holt reached them, throwing himself into Hans to push him off. Holt ended the trauma, stabbing Hans in the throat over and over until the gurgling and spitting of blood ceased.

Larissa closed her eyes, her body trembled, and for some odd reason she felt her toes tingling. Within the blackness that threatened to swallow her whole, she heard Holt cursing. Finally, a sense of calm spilled over her mind again like a cool summer breeze.

Chapter Nineteen

Larissa stared up at the dark wood ceiling in the pirate Captain's cabin. It was an unpleasant, dingy place that smelled of damp and tobacco ash; nothing like the refined cabin on board *The Larissa*. She'd been laid out atop the Captain's desk, charts and trinkets scattered across the floor beneath. A set of Emperor playing cards spread haphazardly across the desk's surface.

Holt and Cid were nearby, making some sort of preparations and arguing amongst themselves. Imago appeared and jumped up, depositing himself upon her chest. She reached up with her uninjured arm to scratch the top of his head, somewhat confused at how he'd managed to get aboard and survive the carnage unscathed, yet certainly grateful that he had. Imago purred and curled into a ball as if to sleep.

"Fucking cat. Get off!" Cid yelled, marching over. Imago immediately jumped down and scurried away.

"Cid..."

"No, don't you *Cid* me. You're injured. You don't want cat hair getting into the wound. I'm going to fix you up."

"We've discussed this. I will do the stitching." Holt followed, depositing a tarnished silver plate containing gauze, a needle, and thread.

"I don't trust you," Cid said.

"I came back and slaughtered a ship full of pirates to save the pair of you."

"To save yourself, more like."

"Bring the water and the liquor."

"Piss off. I'm not your serving girl. Go get it yourself."

"You keep talking to me like that and I'll cut you into a serving girl."

"Gentlemen," Larissa interrupted, "as amusing as you two are to watch, I'd really appreciate if we could get this over with."

"Sorry," they answered in unison. Cid disappeared to the back to collect the water and liquor, and Holt leaned over Larissa to pull open her jacket.

"This needs to come off."

She nodded and closed her eyes. Larissa usually avoided being nude even when alone in her bedroom. Now it seemed to be a frequent occurrence in front of strange men.

At least these two don't want to beat me to a pulp and rape me.

"What the fuck are you doing?" Cid's voice reached a pitch that usually would have required a kick in the groin. He slammed the bottles on the desk.

"I can't stitch the wound if the garment is in the way."

"Well, just cut a hole in it around the shoulder. You don't have to get the poor girl nude."

"There are other wounds that need tending."

"So? Come back to them after. She's been through enough of this shit, for fuck's sake."

"Cid..." Larissa's voice was calm and quiet. "I need someone to keep an eye on the others."

Cid's mouth dropped; it was a dismissal, albeit a polite one. Larissa expected him to argue further, but he simply hunched his shoulders, passed Holt a dark glare, and slammed the door shut behind him.

"I'll have to apologize to him for that, later."

"A Captain shouldn't apologize to his...her crew. Orders are orders."

"And is that what I am? The Captain?"

142

"So it would seem." Holt leaned over again and opened the jacket. Larissa closed her eyes once more, instantly feeling the cool air trickling across her hot flesh. The other side opened and she was bare to the world, bare to him.

A thought hummed at the back of her psyche; a comparison between the shame she'd felt when the pirates had ripped the clothes from her body and the experience she was having now. It was as though her brain tried to express emotion, but whatever part necessary for that was still shut down and numb.

"Gods." Holt's voice wavered in the air above her. She wasn't sure if he was shocked at the beaten state of her body, or perhaps simply reacting to her nudity—and she wasn't sure if she wanted to know which it was. She kept her eyes shut and tried to suppress the fact that she could feel her nipples hardening in the cold air.

An eternity seemed to pass where nothing happened. She strained to hear him moving; he had a knack for stealthy silence. Larissa shivered at the anticipation of his touch against her flesh, but it didn't come. Just as she toyed with the idea of opening her eyes for a peek, she felt him slowly easing the jacket off her wounded shoulder. It hurt, as though a hot poker peeled away broken flesh, and she winced, biting down on her bottom lip to keep from shouting out.

"Gods," Holt said again, this time more pronounced.

"What is it?" Her eyes fluttered open and she looked at his face. He looked confused, rubbing a hand across his stubbly chin. His gaze moved over every inch of her body, running up and down, again and again. She tried not to imagine the horrific sight he must have seen—bruises of every color, crusted blood, and Gods only knew what else.

"Is it really that bad? Why aren't you sewing me up?"

"No need."

"What?"

"See for yourself."

Frowning, she lifted her head to look down at the shoulder wound, expecting to see a great, gaping hole dripping with blood and gore. The blood and gore were there, although instead of a hole there was a fresh layer of scar tissue, pink and clean, a perfectly straight line in the place where the blade had penetrated.

She pushed up on her elbows and looked down to the rest of her body. There were bruises and cuts, though they were light and fading. The heaviest bruises had turned to faint yellow patches, each cut replaced by another fresh, pink scar. She looked as though weeks had passed since she'd suffered the abuse, rather than mere hours.

Larissa sat for a time, propped on her elbows, assessing her body with a newfound interest. Holt did the same; his fascination was such that he even reached out to lightly prod at a scab on her belly.

"You know, I usually prefer to know a man a little better before I let him get me nude on a table to poke at me."

"Hmm," was all he managed by way of retort, and his physical exploration continued across her chest.

"I suppose my injuries weren't as bad as I'd first thought, though I was sure that knife went straight through."

"Your injuries were significant. You should be in extreme pain and several of these should have only just scabbed over. There should still be a large hole in your shoulder." His fingers explored up her belly, over her right breast, onto her shoulder and there he pushed at the fresh scar.

"Ouch."

"Sorry." Despite the apology he did not stop prodding. She sat up fully, turning to the side.

"I don't understand."

"How long have you had the *Anthonium*?"

"The stone? My mother died two years ago. She left it to me."

"Stored in the lock box?"

"No, that was Cid's idea. It was a necklace."

"And you wore it?"

"All the time."

"Ah. That probably explains it."

"It does? Wait, how did you know it was *Anthonium* in the box?"

"You told me."

"I did?"

"When you called me a *creepy guy*."

"Oh." A familiar feeling came over Larissa, and she realized she was blushing. Head to chest her pale skin tingled, feeling like she'd been burned by the sun. As though she had just woken up from a dream, she became aware of her nudity and the fact that she'd turned to face him, her legs dangling off the desk edge with him positioned in between. As she tried to shy away, scooting backwards across the desk, he gripped her arm and his examination moved across her face, where she'd taken several blows to her chin and cheek. She tried to reignite the conversation, to talk through the embarrassment.

"So, *Anthonium* has healing properties?"

"*Anthonium* has many properties, so they say. It's so rare that people don't really know much about it, except..."

"Except what?"

"That long-term exposure is deadly."

"Oh." Her head sunk down as she thought of her mother, suffering on her death bed from some disease they couldn't name, and too many painful truths became terribly clear. She felt a need growing inside, a need for comfort, for something warm and safe, for something powerful and emotional. Holt lifted her chin with his finger and looked her directly in the eye, his gaze intense behind a blank expression.

"Perhaps two years is just enough exposure to be beneficial."

Her lips parted and a hot breath escaped. Something unnameable settled between them and her nudity seemed oddly appropriate. Holt inched backwards, dropping his hand.

"Holt..."

"It seems the ability to heal quickly will be a great aid to you in finding your Professor."

"He's not *my* Professor." She gripped his hand and pulled him back, and he did not resist. Slowly, with a slight tremble in her arm, she placed his hand upon her breast. They stayed still, in perfect tableau for a moment, her heartbeat echoing in her ears. The burning across her skin intensified. His expression softened and he leaned down, pushing his lips onto hers. She reciprocated, their kiss hungry with unexpected desire.

Holt bent over, pressing her back onto the desk, and his hands explored her body now with renewed purpose. She reached up and knotted her fingertips through his hair and he moved downwards, planting a line of hot, rough kisses along her chin and neck. His hands swiftly unbuttoned his shirt, and then he sat back on his heels atop the desk, flinging his shirt to the floor.

Her gaze darted across the breadth of his torso, bruised and covered in cuts from the fighting. Beneath the cuts and aged scar-lines was firm, taut skin, bulging with hard muscles. A line of black hair stretched from his navel to his trouser top, which he now unbuttoned, too.

A dark thought threatened as the Professor flashed through her mind. How many nights had she spent dreaming of him in this position? Was this an unfaithful act? Was she even ready for this kind of intimacy with a man she barely knew a thing about so quickly after the horrific events she'd just experienced? As Holt removed his trousers, she closed her eyes, the thoughts of the Professor and her insecurity threatening to bring tears. Her mind began to second-guess the moment, but her body begged, screaming for it to continue.

Holt brushed his thumb down her cheek and her eyes opened again. A tear had escaped.

"We don't have to..." he said with a furrowed brow.

"Please." The word emerged as a breathy whisper and she hated the sound of it. It sounded weak and pathetic, as if she were begging. She sucked in a deep breath and forced aside the plague of doubts in her head. She wanted this, needed this, and nothing was going to stop her from getting it.

"Don't stop," she said, voice strong and determined.

"You're sure?" Holt's eyes wandered down her body, the appraisal sending a spark of heat between her legs. For the first time she looked down and saw him, how close he was, and how ready he was, his erection poised between her legs. She tucked her arm between their bodies and gripped him gently, choosing to answer with action.

Holt squeezed his eyes shut and let out a deep moan. She studied his reactions, as slight as they were. The mere thought of giving him pleasure brought her close to the edge of orgasm. The ability to strip him of the façade, even for a moment, made her feel more powerful than anything. He bent forward, capturing her lips with a rough and needy kiss. Then he moved down, trailing his lips along her neck, placing kisses down her chest, pausing at her breast with a long lash of his tongue across her nipple. His hand reached up and lightly gripped her throat as he moved across to offer the same treatment to the other side, adding a slight nip with his teeth. His attention sent bolts of pleasure throughout her body, every inch of her flesh coming alive with sensation. He dipped to the side and hooked her knee across his shoulder as his lips moved downward even further.

She let out small moans of delight before he'd so much as begun, the anticipation of his attention rattling her. As he bent down to kiss between her legs, she lost focus. No matter how hard she tried to concentrate on each stroke of his tongue, each movement of his fingers, her efforts failed. Breathing became effort between deep gasps and quiet moans of pleasure, and as he slipped his fingers in deep, a final flick of the tongue over the most sensitive spot, her back arched away from the desk. The world disappeared in a bundle of sensation. Her legs shuddered and her lungs screamed for air and new tears escaped her, but for a very different reason.

Holt settled her leg back down and climbed back onto the desk. His hands clasped her hips, pinning them, and she reached out to grip onto the sides, digging her nails into the ridges of the wood. As they came together, it didn't matter that her notions of romance were abandoned. She didn't care that they hadn't said those precious words to one another. All she could do was focus on the intensity of the moment; the heat of their bodies and the rhythm of their joining. The air in the cabin turned from stale and cold to hot and dense. The sound of the propellers on deck were drowned out by their relentless movements; flesh against flesh, sharp breaths and restrained moans of pleasure. The heavy desk shifted reluctantly with their ferocious actions.

"Please," she cried between breaths. His pace increased and she felt the rush building again within her core.

The tips of her fingers turned white as she sharpened her grip upon the desk and squeezed her eyes shut. She imagined screaming, shouting his name, begging for more, pleading for it to never end. The world disappeared into a blur of red lines and white heat as her senses came tumbling back all at once. She let out a cry of pleasure. He gave out a moan, their passion descending into nothing more than heavy breathing and thumping hearts.

Holt bent forward to rest his forehead on her chest, and she let out a final shudder of pleasure. For all her doubts, she knew this had been what they both needed.

She reached up and knotted her fingertips through his hair once more, gripping him as though he were some precious thing she daren't let go of for fear of losing him altogether. They lay together, their slowing breaths filling the space as minutes slipped past. She mindlessly scraped her nails across his scalp. His lips brushed against her stomach before he climbed off the desk and dressed himself.

She watched him in silence for a moment, studying his body as he moved. He didn't look at her, and she wasn't sure if he intentionally avoided doing so, or had just slipped straight back into Mister Indifference. She wanted so much to understand him and read him correctly, but it was an impossible goal. She wished for a moment that she could be as aloof and hard-to-read. Not an easy task for a woman burdened with a blushing affliction.

As he attached the final button on his shirt and she swiftly covered her body with her borrowed jacket, there came a determined knock at the door. Seconds later the door opened and Grubbs strode in.

"Ah, yous all fixed up, Cap'n Rissa? Holt do a good job on you?"

She bit her tongue.

"You know, it's customary after knocking to wait for an answer before you open the door," she said.

"Oh, 'tis? Sorry about that. Only Captain before you liked his food, ya see, and he always wanted to know the minute dinner was ready."

"Dinner? *You* made dinner?" Her tone was harsher than she'd really meant for it to be.

"Yes, Sir, Miss, Cap... That's why they call me Grubbs. It's nothin' fancy, mind, so don't get your hopes up."

"This should be an experience," Holt said quietly.

"Seems to be a day for experiences."

Larissa and Holt held each other's gazes for a millisecond before they both followed Grubbs towards the smell of baked pork and apples.

Chapter Twenty

Larissa was perched atop a barrel on deck, her legs curled up and crossed beneath her body. Pale light from a swinging oil lamp nearby bathed one side of her face in an orange glow. She stared across the black horizon as it skittered by sideways, dotted with distant mountain peaks—the clear and cold night sky, outlined by starlight. A plate of food rested on her lap. Imago sat beneath the barrel, looking up at her expectantly, and she tossed him a small chunk of baked pork.

"You almost look like a Dolanite Priestess at meditation," Cid mused as he approached. "If you weren't stuffing your face with that Gods-awful slop that Grubbs made, of course."

"It's not that bad. And I didn't really take you for a religious man, Cid."

"Well, I am. I missed prayers today. It's Saints Day, you know."

"Is it really?"

"Young things like you don't bother with it all that much, I suppose."

"I'm not that young...and you can't be *that* old." She stared up at him, wondering if he would take the hint and offer up his age. He only seemed oblivious to such subtleties.

"How old are you, Cid?"

"Fifty-two."

"And...the Professor? How old is he?"

"You never asked?"

Larissa felt the familiar rush of blood to her cheeks. Now that she thought of it, there were an awful lot of things she should have asked the Professor before she had let her heart be so overcome by him. She shook her head at herself, and then looked up and shook her head at Cid.

"He's forty-five."

"Forty five," she repeated, testing the number out loud. It seemed a little absurd, perhaps even obscene, compared to her mere twenty-two years; he was indeed old enough to be her father.

"And he's never married?" She looked at Cid and his expression had shifted as though their conversation now tread on shaky ground.

"Perhaps you should have asked him these questions."

"No doubt, and if he were here I would. But he's not here, and all I have is you. You aren't betraying him anything, you know. I'm sure I could check out some tome on the family lineage of the aristocratic line of *Watts* to find the answers, only there doesn't appear to be a library nearby."

"Fine. He's never married."

"So why—"

"Do you want the truth?" Cid blurted. Larissa blinked up at him, stunned yet intrigued.

"Yes, of course."

"He's never married, though don't think that means he hasn't been with women. Many women."

"Oh."

"They come and go. He does whatever he wants with them and sends them on their way. They're nothing more than a momentary distraction from his work."

"Oh."

Long minutes passed by in silence; even her mind fell quiet, as though she had indeed been thrown into some form of meditation. Nearby, two of the new crewmen broke into snorting hysterics over some menial jibe. As they realized how much noise they made, they looked up at Larissa briefly and bowed their heads back down to recreate the quiet. She didn't even need to speak a word, hadn't so much as scowled at them.

What an odd crew this ship has...

"If I was just to be another worthless conquest, a distraction, why did he ask you to name his fine airship after me?"

"Changed."

"What?"

"He asked me to change the name of his airship. It was called *Carise* before I think, and *Rebecca* before that. Then there was *Jemima*—Gods she was a lovely one. Great big—"

"All right, stop. I get the picture." Larissa sighed and unfolded her legs, placing the plate on the floor and leaving Imago to devour the remaining food. She headed towards the wheel where Holt stood steering the ship.

"If it's any consolation," Cid called to her, "I don't think he ever promised any of the others all the things he promised you."

"You said I deserved a knife in the eye if I was stupid enough to believe that tripe."

"Perhaps, though he'd never been as keen on the others as he seemed for you. Spoke very highly of you once or twice."

"Once or twice? Gushing praise, indeed. Are you trying to console me, Cid?"

"Bah, I dunno what I'm trying to do. I don't know the first thing about you women. Gods know what's in your brains, but I'm damned sure it isn't cogs and gears, otherwise I could figure you out in no time."

Larissa passed Cid a sideways smile and resumed her approach to Holt. She stood beside him for a moment, looking across the horizon, trying to figure out if he saw anything different than her untrained eyes could spy. Holt unexpectedly broke the silence first.

"You said he was not your Professor."

"I did...he's not."

"And yet."

"What? And yet what?"

"You are upset to learn of his womanizing."

"Womanizing? What—how did you hear our conversation from all the way over here? It's not even like we were downwind."

"I have good hearing."

"No shit."

"Cid's bad language is rubbing off on you."

"Why do you even care? What difference does it make if I love the Professor or not? What does it matter to you if I start to swear like some common pirate?"

"It...doesn't."

"You're right it doesn't. Just because we... Gods, I don't even know your first name. You haven't told me anything about you, like how come you're out of the military, or what's on that piece of paper you keep checking when you think no one is looking, or why you're so hell-bent on killing Orother, or anything at all."

"William."

"What?"

"My name."

"Oh. William." His name sounded odd.

"Call me Holt."

"Oh. Holt."

"And don't tell anyone else."

"Like a secret?"

"Can you keep a secret?"

"Well I wasn't planning on telling everyone about what we did in the Captain's cabin earlier, so I think I can manage to keep your name private as well."

"Your cabin."

"My cabin."

"Where you should be."

"And why is that?"

"To rest."

"Oh. Are you dismissing me? Are you dismissing the Captain from the deck of her airship?"

"Suggesting. I'm suggesting a possible course of action to the Captain."

"And if I were to ignore your suggestion?"

"I would become more persuasive."

Larissa laughed, a full-bellied, deep, and refreshing laugh that lingered in the air, and everyone on deck turned to watch.

"Perhaps you're right. I will rest. How long until we reach Meridina?"

"At this pace we will arrive some time tomorrow. Do you have a plan yet?"

"No. No idea. You?"

"Other than going in and killing everyone who gets in my way?" Holt said with a smirk.

"Yes, other than that."

"No."

"Well, let's call that plan B. Goodnight, Holt."

"Goodnight, Captain Markus."

She carried a lantern back to the cabin. Long, dark shadows danced off the silvery, wooden wall panels as she walked along the corridor. A shudder wavered down her spine as she passed the storage room and she tried not to wonder whether the men had disposed of Hans or not.

The cabin was still an uninviting place despite the nicer memories it invoked. In the husky dark of night, the creaking of old wood and metal seemed much more pronounced than during the day. With every delicate step she took inside, scrapes and cracks echoed within. Her body responded as though someone drew long fingertips across her shoulders, teasing the downy hairs on the back of her neck. The lantern light wavered as she placed it atop the desk and reached into a drawer to look for candles, anything to help illuminate the darkness.

Once Larissa lit every candle she could lay her hands on, extinguishing virtually every shadow within the cabin, she began to relax. The papers and trinkets had been replaced atop the desk. She pulled the lockbox containing the *Anthonium* from her coat and rolled the dials over with the pads of her thumbs, running through the code in her head just to be sure she could remember it.

Finally, she placed it back into her pocket. The pirate Captain's cabin had neither a hammock nor static bed in which to sleep. Instead, a large reclining chair had been pushed in a corner with a smelly old blanket laid across it. Larissa sighed and tucked herself into the chair, pulling the blanket up to her neck. The smell of yeasty ale and old cigar smoke assaulted her senses and the candlelight danced with the airship's movements. Creaks and groans from the wood turned to background noise.

Larissa stared at the large wooden desk and mindlessly rubbed at the scars on her stomach, thinking how much better Holt's touch had felt. The propeller sounds faded into the distance. Imago walked between her legs, dragging his tail across her ankles, and then he left her in peace.

Chapter Twenty One

Cid stared out at the black horizon, gently guiding the wheel through his hand and tugging on the rudder to steer their course. The ship was quiet, yet the atmosphere aboard did not feel peaceful. Cid leaned forward, resting his weary head against his arm, taking slow and measured breaths. He figured a little meditation wouldn't hurt as the course ahead was clear for now. His mind settled somewhat as he methodically ran through everything that had transpired.

It was crazy—the whole thing nothing more than a bloody, crazy mess. The sort of mess he'd managed to avoid for all these years. He'd known the risks the Professor took with the Machine, though he wondered now why he hadn't given it more thought at the time. All this could have been avoided, or at the very least his own part in it.

He thought of Larissa. Vivid images of her abused body danced across his mind and he found himself squeezing his eyes, brow furrowed, trying to force the images away. The vision shifted to another image of Larissa the night he'd first met her, sprawled out in the Hub, threatened by fire. He'd acted on impulse to scoop her up and drag her out of there. If he hadn't, she'd have died then and there and all the chaos over the last few days could have been avoided.

He played it over and over, trying to decide which outcome was better, or perhaps which was the least bad. When he exhausted all reason and argument, his mind went blank, entering into a blissful indifference over the whole thing. Imago appeared in his line of sight beneath the wheel and Cid let out a guttural grunt at the cat.

"Fuck sake, animal, can't a man have a moment to himself?"

As Cid looked up, he flinched and tugged on the wheel. The ship swung to the side, narrowly avoiding a large tree jutting from the mountainside. Imago padded over and jumped onto the rail beside the tree, watching it as they passed by.

"If you think I'm going to thank you for that, then you're mistaken," Cid said to the cat. "Why don't you go and bother Holt?"

As soon as he'd spoken the man's name he started wondered where Holt was. Cid thought he might be sleeping soundly, perhaps even soundly enough to not notice someone approaching. This was his chance to bring an end to the madness. Without Holt at her side, Larissa might think better of continuing on with her mad mission, especially after she had already suffered so much.

There was the Professor to consider, of course, but Cid knew their chances of actually rescuing him and escaping alive were slim. Holt had saved them from a dismal fate, but Cid couldn't bring himself to feel graciously about the man. A strange thought crossed his mind and Cid looked to Imago.

"Where is Holt?" he asked.

Imago flicked his tail and dropped from the rail, padding along the deck quietly. Cid took a long look ahead, this time taking extra care to be sure there were no obstacles in their path, and when he was satisfied he followed after the cat with light steps.

Imago stalked around the furnace room to the stern of the ship and there, hunched in a ball on deck, lay Holt. The back of the ship was poorly lit and Holt's black clothing blended into the dark surroundings. If it hadn't been for Imago, Cid probably would not have spotted the man at all. The cat walked up to Holt and Cid silently waved his arms, mouthing expletives at Imago. Somehow, the cat seemed to take his meaning and backed away.

Cid stared at the sleeping ball of the man he contemplated killing, then edged towards him. How ironic—if their places were switched, Holt probably wouldn't hesitate. He'd doubtlessly have no trouble sticking a knife into Cid's throat, or perhaps simply throwing him overboard. Yet Cid could not so easily reconcile the contemplation into actual action. It would be cowardly, he mused; not that he'd ever considered himself a brave man, but what if this was his only chance? Could he forgive himself later if everything went to hell and he'd let go of this opportunity to end it?

"Make your move," Holt spoke, and Cid physically jolted backward.

For a while everything was silent, save for the pounding of Cid's heartbeat inside his own head. Holt didn't move, his body still curled into a ball. Cid wrung his sweaty fingers behind his back and cleared his throat.

"I just came to see if you'd agree to take a shift at the wheel. I could use a rest," Cid said.

A moment passed before Holt uncurled himself and stood up, his facial features obscured by the darkness of the night. Neither man spoke, though Cid was sure Holt passed some dubious contemplation through his mind. Eventually, Holt headed to the wheel.

"I was also thinking," Cid called to him, "that it might be nice if we could do something...for the girl."

"Such as?"

"No idea. What do girls like?"

"Clothes."

"Yes. I'm sure that'd make her happy," Cid said.

"I don't know of any clothing retailers in the mountains."

"Good point. I'll think on it, perhaps ask the others."

Holt gave him a terse nod and then disappeared from view. Cid let out a long, shaking breath, and Imago padded around to stand at his side. He wasn't sure if Holt believed his innocent intentions, but the fact that he was still alive was a good sign. He contemplated sleeping where Holt had slept and then changed his mind, instead heading to one of the rooms below.

. . .

When her eyes opened, the cabin was bathed in daylight. The candles had all melted into waxy blobs. She rubbed her eyes, trying to bring the room into focus. Something was different. In the middle of the room stood a large tin bucket, and a sizeable wooden box had been placed beside it.

Larissa frowned and sat upright, expecting to startle Imago until she realized he wasn't there. Tossing the blanket aside, she walked over to the bucket; thin wisps of steam rose up from the hot water inside as heat travelled into the cold morning air. She bent over and lifted the box lid, finding a soft towel, folded neatly, and bar of soap perched on top. Beneath the towel there seemed to be endless reams of thick, red, velvety fabric, edged with black lace.

Larissa set the towel and soap down and pulled the fabric out, holding it up. To her shock and mild delight she found it to be a dress. The skirts were knee-length and the dress had a stitched-in bodice. It was a little too low-cut for her liking and seemed as though it might be better suited to a serving wench at a brothel. But it was, at the very least, far more beautiful and presumably more comfortable than the oversized jacket. She figured it would help to make her feel less shambolic.

Larissa shrugged the jacket off her shoulders, her skin instantly pricking up in goose bumps, and set to giving herself a much-needed clean. She made sure to take extra care with each new scar. The bruises were gone, and as she worked down her body the grime and dried blood disappeared. Finally, she flipped her head over and dipped her entire mop of curls into the bucket, scrubbing furiously with the soap to clean off the muck. After towelling dry, she pulled on the dress. It was a size too big and didn't quite fit right, though the fabric was lovely and thick, with long sleeves to cover her arms. It was heavy enough to wear out in the winter air.

"Where the hell did they get this from?" she mused aloud as she fiddled with the waist, trying to twist it into her body shape. She looked down to the bucket; the now cold water was murky with blood and soot.

"And which of them arranged all this? Surely not Holt."

"Why surely not Holt?" Holt's voice travelled across the room. She spun around so quickly that she tumbled backwards and landed on her backside. Holt stared, his arms folded across his chest, his shoulder blades pressed against the far wall with a grim expression.

Larissa scrabbled to her feet. "How long have you been there? Were you watching me bathe like some pervert?"

"Which question would you like me to answer first?"

"You were watching!"

"If you had checked the room prior to disrobing you would have seen me. You need to become more wary of your surroundings. Always check for threats. A cunning enemy will find the best hiding place."

"Don't change the subject and try to pretend like you'd planned this as a lesson."

"I did not intend to watch you. You awoke before I left the room. I expected you to see me, and when you didn't—"

"You stood and watched anyway."

Holt pushed off from the wall and stepped in front of her, a frown on his face. "My apologies."

She sighed, not quite sure why she berated him for watching, especially after what happened the last time they were in the room together. Usually she would have craved and appreciated such avid attention from a handsome man.

"So, you did this? For me?"

"It was a team effort."

"Really?"

"Goodson knew there was a dress in the storage room."

"Which one is Goodson?"

"The youngest."

"Ah."

"Cid suggested the water and soap, and I delivered it all."

"And why does a pirate ship have a dress, soap, and towels on board?"

"You...might not like the answer."

"Oh, let me guess, prostitutes?"

"It is commonplace."

"Charming." She looked down at the dress, now feeling foolish in it.

I hate this stupid dress.

"I look like the ship's harlot."

"No you don't."

All right, perhaps hate was too strong a word.

"You're sure?" She asked.

"It suits you."

I meant like. I like this dress.

She smiled to herself. A small amount of time spent thinking about clothing, fashion, colors, and fabrics made her feel at home. However, it was a fleeting thought as she realized it was morning and they would reach their destination at some point during the day.

"Has everyone else rested?"

"Yes, we took shifts."

"Good. We should go up on deck." She reached into the discarded large jacket to retrieve the lockbox and collected a chart from the desk as they headed out.

On deck, Cid was once again at the wheel and the others kept themselves busy. The sky was bright and the breeze felt fresh, no longer bitingly cold. Far below, the rocky terrain was less pronounced, and snow-tipped trees dotted the terrain now between the lumpy boulders.

"Morning, Cap'n Rissa." Grubbs emerged, his eyes glowing as he caught sight of her new outfit. "You like the dress, Cap'n? Goodson remembered we had it and remembered where it was, didn't you, Goodson?"

"Yes. Thank you, gentlemen. It's much appreciated, Goodson." The youngest crewmember, Goodson, blushed beneath his tanned skin and bent his head forward. His long mop of dark blond hair flopped over his face. Larissa smiled. It felt nice to find someone else who suffered from the affliction of blushing.

Cid wore a new pair of goggles over his eyes, making it difficult to discern his expression as she approached.

"Come on, girl, we'll be there within the hour," Cid started. "What's the big plan?"

"Well, has anyone here actually been to Meridina?" The question was answered with silent shaking of heads.

"It's a private town for rich aristocrats. No one gets in without an invitation," Holt reiterated.

"So access by rail is restricted?"

"Yes."

"I imagine the security will also be watching the skies, specifically for pirates?"

"That would be a sensible deduction. Considering the wealth of the residents, Meridina must be a frequent target for pirates."

"And seeing as we're clearly flying a pirate ship, we may draw attention to ourselves before we can even get close. I don't suppose any of you gentlemen were aware of your previous Captain's plans to deliver Hans and Cid to Orother?"

Another round of head shaking ensued. Larissa paced up and down for a moment, muttering half-thoughts. Eventually, she uncurled the chart of the area that she'd picked up from her cabin and knelt down to spread it across the deck. The others leaned over to look.

"We can't risk flying directly into Meridina. That would be stupid. We'll have to land as close as possible and trek in on foot. Hans said Orother has a mansion on Clockman Peak, but it's not marked on this chart, so we'll have to find someone to ask."

"Interrogate," Holt said.

"Not necessarily. I could try asking nicely."

"That's not usually effective."

"Maybe not for you. You don't exactly give off an *easy going* vibe." A couple men chuckled under their breaths, though the laughter was cut short as Holt passed an icy glare their way.

"And when we find this place? What next?" Cid asked.

"I will go in," Larissa stated.

"No!" Cid and Holt shouted in unison.

"Now, now, gentlemen, it's the logical choice. Orother is expecting Hans to bring him Cid, and I have no intention of putting you in harm's way, Cid. Orother already has the Professor and he doesn't know Holt is involved. I'd prefer to keep you as a surprise. I'm the only one he doesn't want at all, but I do have the

Anthonium. That is in a lockbox, and I'm the only one who knows the code to open it. If he wants any hope of getting at the stone without destroying it, he shouldn't kill me straight away. I can sneak in, find Orother, and negotiate with him, buy some time for Holt to find the Professor."

"Find the Professor?" Holt asked.

"Yes."

"That is your mission. Not mine."

"Oh."

Minutes ticked by in silence. Larissa scratched at her temple, digging at a particular spot on the skin. Her hopes that Holt would come around to her plan and help out with finding the Professor faded away as time ebbed by.

"There." She jabbed her finger into the chart. "We're approaching from the west, aren't we?"

Holt grunted in agreement.

"So, we should see Meridina as we pass between these two peaks. We can fly in the shadow of that mountain and land somewhere around here. That should be close enough."

She looked up, expecting someone to argue or disagree or tell her she was being ludicrous. Instead, the men silently nodded in agreement. She rose to her feet and the men resumed their duties. Imago padded over and sat himself upon the chart. It wasn't the most grand and elaborate plan in history, but it was better than nothing.

Larissa looked out to the horizon once more, wondering if she could ever settle back into her old life again after such an adventure. Given that they managed to survive. Then again, if they did survive and rescue the Professor, what would happen if he still wanted her and resumed his promises of affection? What if her silly heart couldn't say no to him, even after everything she'd learned? What about Holt? Her gaze met with Holt's; he gave her a careful, contemplative look as he walked away.

If I don't go back to my old life, what the hell would I do instead?

Chapter Twenty Two

The pirate ship perched atop a smooth plateau in the shadow of the last mountain beside the private town of Meridina. Cid had landed the ship well. A pair of skids had been deployed on either side for the landing, as the keel was curved to allow for ocean crossings as well as air travel. Cid was noticeably proud of his skill at landing such a cumbersome ship in rugged terrain.

Larissa, Holt, Cid, and Goodman headed across the rocky terrain, the other two men remaining behind to try to repair the damage the ship had sustained in the crash with *The Larissa.* They had to get the ship as ready to take off again as possible, should the necessity for a speedy departure arise. Larissa had tried to tell Imago to *stay*, though she wasn't sure if he'd understood. The cat had never quite gotten the hang of learning commands. She couldn't see his furry little outline following behind, so she assumed he remained upon the ship and hoped he would be safe there.

Holt led the group, a pack of supplies on his back and an array of weapons across his chest. He picked his way over perilous, snow-covered rocks, and the others followed in his wake, trying to mimic his movements. Larissa wore a belt across her waist, a pair of throwing knives and a pair of light pistols slotted through the leather. The others had weapons too, purloined from the ship's storage room. They looked ready for a fight.

Their journey across the snowy terrain passed in relative silence due to the perilous route. As the pirate ship disappeared behind them in the distance, the terrain levelled out and they could finally walk side by side.

Ahead, the mountain town of Meridina grew before their eyes. Tall buildings stretched up to the heavens, carved from the mountain rock, each one designed with precise symmetry. Large, arched windows adorned every structure with ornate stained glass set into the frames. It looked to Larissa like a town from the fairy-tales her mother used to tell her as a child.

As they drew closer they tried to disguise their approach by creeping between jutting stone spires. Eventually they reached the edge of a road, which was fairly busy and bustled with traders and clientele walking to and fro. The roads appeared spotless, clear of all traces of snow. Men strutted the streets in smart suits, top hats, and thick over-cloaks. Some carried fine canes with bejewelled tips, others wore monocles or fur collars. One man stopped nearby to check his pocket watch; it was the finest timepiece Larissa had ever seen, polished gold with diamonds embedded around the face.

The women all dressed in elaborate costumes, flashes of lace and velvet, shining silks and thick fur linings. They tied their feet up in expensive winter boots and adorned their heads with artistic hats. It was a town full of excessively rich citizens, the reserve of the aristocracy. Larissa turned to look at the men with her and then glanced down at herself.

"We clearly don't fit in here. Cid looks like a filthy furnace worker. Goodson, no offence, but you look like a pirate. Holt looks like...uhh...some kind of assassin. I may have managed to pull off *respectable* in this dress in Sallarium City, but amongst these people even I look out of place."

She noticed that, dotted in between the fine, expensively clad people, stood guards. The burly men were dressed in plain, dark navy uniforms, though not quite the same as the military style. Some guards walked along with the rich folk, others stood at

168

various entrances to buildings. All of them watched their surroundings carefully.

"We'll get rounded up the moment we set foot out there," Cid grumbled.

Larissa scanned the street, desperate to find a sign of some cleaner or boot polisher or something. She couldn't imagine the rich folks sweeping the roads themselves.

"There must be workers," Holt said, as though he had read her mind, or at least he shared the same thoughts.

"I don't see any."

"They're probably only allowed out at certain times, expected to remain hidden away during the day. Rich folks don't like to see the poor people who clean up after them."

"That's awful," Larissa said.

"That's the kind of life you were agreeing to with the Professor, you know," Cid chimed in. "All haughty and arrogant, worried about what the neighbors thought of your new outfit and if you had a large enough jewelry collection or not. Never mind the riff raff staff, the poor folks should be grateful to have jobs. At least, that's how the aristocracy behave."

Larissa wrinkled her nose at the thought, wondering if she would have so easily succumbed to the decadence of it all—if she would have been blinded by pretty dresses and charming parties and never given a thought to the people who did all the hard work.

"Even if we tried to pose as misplaced workers, I think we'd raise suspicions as a group, and I'm not willing to split us up yet."

"Sewers," Holt whispered, dragging Larissa back behind the stone spire they had been using as cover. He pointed to a grate nearby.

"Oh, charming. How will we even know where it comes out?"

"We'll have to chance it. We'll go along until we find an exit in an alleyway or something." He was already lifting the large cover, and as soon as it was off the smell assaulted their senses. Larissa gagged.

"If it smells this bad up here, I don't think I can manage to cope with that stench up close."

"You have a better idea?"

Larissa chewed on her lip for a moment. Her fingers twitched up to her neckline, searching for the necklace, and then dropped back down to her side. She shook her head at him.

"You'll acclimatize." Holt disappeared down the hole in one bound. Goodson followed wordlessly and Cid crouched beside the hole, offering Larissa a hand to help her down.

As she found the rusty rungs to climb down and began the descent, her hands scraped against the slime-covered brick walls. The stench intensified and her stomach churned. At the bottom, the space opened out into a wide-arched stone corridor, dimly lit from the grate above. Her feet landed in a puddle of sludge that slowly made its way downhill. Goodson stood further down the sewer, and Larissa could see the fading bob of Holt's figure ahead.

"He's gone to take a look-see," Goodson whispered, shadows dancing across his face. Larissa wanted to answer him but she was too busy pinching her nose and covering her mouth, trying to only breathe through the smallest gap in her lips. Cid bumped her out of the way as he came down the ladder.

"Fucking hell, it's rough down here," Cid muttered, covering his mouth with his forearm. Holt returned into view and they watched as he marched straight past, seemingly unaffected by the stench. He gave a slight wave of his hand and indicated they should follow.

They walked for ages, heavy footfalls landing in depths of sludge and muck. There was no ledge to protect them nor any obvious exit points. The sewage leached out great green plumes of steam, which intensified in the poor streams of light from a few holes in the ceiling. Larissa wretched several times, bile catching in her throat.

Eventually they came across another set of rusty rungs leading up. Holt disappeared up the ladder. The others stood in silence, their faces long and drawn as the effects of the rank air took its toll.

"Come up," Holt called down, though his voice was soft. Larissa followed first; she'd never climbed a ladder so quickly in her life.

They emerged from the sewer directly into a building. The walls were built from aged red brick and reached up into a tall, cramped room. Streams of light poured in through a singular stained window above, a curved half-pipe leading from a grated gap in one wall to a hole in the ground beside the sewer entrance. As the others emerged from below, the small room turned into a tight squeeze.

Holt pushed through to the door, drawing his finger to his lips to keep them quiet. Behind the single wooden door they could hear footsteps echoing toward them, then fading away as the person walked past.

"Where do you think we are?" Larissa whispered to Holt.

"A Dolanite Citadel." The answer came from Cid. His eyes were turned up to the window and he appeared to be studying the picture in the stained glass, that of a white cloaked-figure reaching up to the skies. "The Saint of Purification." He pointed to the character in the window.

"You're sure it's a Citadel?"

"I spotted the building on the approach to the town. I hoped I might get a chance to visit, though I didn't expect you had allowed recreation time in your plan."

"You're right. I didn't. Sorry, Cid. Do you think we could walk around here freely?"

"Unlikely," Holt said.

"We may be able to disguise ourselves as priests, though. That way we wouldn't look so suspicious elsewhere in town," Cid suggested.

"Fine. I'll go and grab three men and a woman, knock them out and tie them up, we'll take their clothes—"

"Gods, no!" Cid interrupted Holt. "You'll curse us all."

"Curse?"

"You might not be a believer, but I am, and I won't have you going around like some common thug, bashing priests over the head and stripping them naked."

"Cid, keep your voice down," Larissa chided. "I agree that it's not the best plan. As soon as our captured men and woman are found, we'll have people looking for us."

"They won't be found quickly if we dump them in the sewer," Holt said.

"Gods! I'll have no part in this."

"So come up with a better solution." Holt folded his arms across his chest. The small room fell silent and their faces turned blank.

"I could..." Cid started, "see if I can, um, find their sleeping quarters. They must keep spare robes about."

"You think you can manage to stumble across sleeping quarters, find robes, and come all the way back here without being detected?" Holt asked with one eyebrow raised.

"I can find the rooms easily enough."

"How?"

"All Dolanite buildings have the same layout," Cid said, "and there will be references to each of the nineteen Gods in the architecture, carved into the doors and suchlike. The Goddess of

Harmony will be depicted in the resting areas. How do you not know all this? Are you all unbelievers?"

"Well, my mother would take me to the festivities each year, and I had some classes in school. Sadly, other than that..." Larissa shrugged at Cid. Goodson hung his head in silence and Holt simply continued his icy glare.

"Well, at least let me try. Give me some time before you go assassinating everyone in sight, would you, Holt?"

Holt looked at Larissa and this time her eyebrows rose. Was he asking her to make the final choice? She chewed on her tongue for a minute, mulling it over. While Holt's plan would certainly be quicker, it would give them less time in the long run, if—or when—the kidnapped priests were found. Not to mention she'd likely lose Cid's support by agreeing to such a plan.

"All right, Cid, we'll wait. Please hurry back. I'm not sure how long we can stay in here undetected, and I'm not sure how much longer I can hold onto the contents of my stomach being this close to that smell."

"Will do, Captain." Cid nodded and Larissa couldn't help but smile.

Chapter Twenty Three

Doctor Orother leaned back in his favorite wingback chair and laid his fingertips on the patchy, grey material of the armrests. He scratched at the fabric three times, admiring the grooves he worked into the material and padding beneath. It looked as though some wild cat had dragged its claws down the sides.

He leaned forward and grasped a jar on the desk in front of him, turning it around slowly. Inside the jar the liquid contents stirred, and as it turned a pair of eyeballs rolled around within the liquid. Beside the jar lay a collection of discarded medical syringes. Leaning back once more, Orother turned his head slightly to admire his other, most recent, piece of work.

The Professor stood still, staring at the jutting edges along the cave's ceiling. He was barefoot and his toes repeatedly curled and uncurled, dragging along the sharp edges of stone beneath his feet. He had given Orother enough information for now, and the Doctor had released him from the table and moved him into his personal work area, still within the cave confines. It was a spacious room with various tables, machines, and artifacts, none of which the Professor could reach. He was bound by a thick metal collar around his neck, which was linked to a chain firmly secured at one end to a wall. The chain was short, preventing him from reaching anything in the area, and so he was left to stand or sit at his leisure and do nothing more.

The Professor looked as though some part of his broken mind tried to grasp the edges of reality—to piece back together his soul, like attempting to fix a priceless vase that had shattered into a thousand tiny pieces. But he had neither a reference image to work with, nor an adhesive to make the pieces stick. Orother decided the

Professor looked well and truly fucked up, and that was a most satisfying result.

"Maximillian," Orother called out, and the Professor curled his neck down and around to look at him, his eyes sunken into their sockets. Orother gave him a broad smile, baring his teeth. "I've had a letter about you. I thought you might like me to read it to you."

Orother picked up the thick, expensive, watermarked paper from his desk and ran his thumb through the red wax seal that had somewhat reattached itself. He ambled down the sloping cave floor toward the Professor, stopping just in front of him. With a smirk, he waved the letter in the air. The Professor tracked it with his eyes, a look of mild intrigue on his face. Orother opened it and read the letter out loud.

"Doctor Orother,

I was very encouraged by your latest missive on the progress of our mutual friend, Professor Watts. It has been frustrating for me these past few years to know that the gentleman was in possession of such powerful knowledge. Yet he was foolish enough to request permission to build it as a private enterprise, with the short-sighted intention of harnessing its capabilities for power production.

I am still dealing with the destruction he brought upon us by secretly building that thing in the Hub. Now that you have the knowledge, I wish to know how quickly you can build a new Machine with the adjustments we discussed. Our Eptoran enemies are growing restless, and the shores of Daltonia are threatened with war. I must have a working weapon ready, post haste, though we have still not located the source of Anthonium. *Please continue to update me on your progress at regular intervals.*

Your good friend,

President Henry Hague Junior."

Orother stood looking at the Professor, trying to gauge his reaction. There seemed to be no reaction at all; the man's face was a dull blank, and he mindlessly scratched at the white linen fabric of his trousers. Orother scrunched the letter in his hand and threw it at the Professor, the paper bouncing off the man's shoulder and landing between his feet. Though the point had been to mold the man into a compliant instrument, he had so enjoyed tormenting him, and now it was frustrating to see the poor creature so utterly destroyed. It felt like he'd broken his new favorite toy. Orother stood tapping his index finger against his lip, the two of them staring at one another in silence.

"You know, Hans will return soon, perhaps today or tomorrow. He'll be bringing Cid with him, and that girl of yours." Orother watched as the Professor's eye twitched ever so slightly. He chided himself for not thinking of this approach first, and continued on with the torment, in truth he had no interest in the girl, save for wanting to get at the information in her head.

"I haven't yet decided what I'm going to do with her. Perhaps I'll simply attach her to my device and extract the information I require that way. I doubt she'll fight as hard as you did. She's such a flimsy little thing." The Professor's hands curled into fists and his jaw clenched. Orother laughed at him.

"Of course, once I'm done with her, perhaps I'll get to enjoy her. Pick up where you left off, so to speak. Perhaps I'll make you watch as I take her over and over again, make the little wretch scream and beg for me to stop."

The Professor launched forward, his teeth bared, growling like a feral animal. The chain reached its limit, wrenching his neck back as he tried in vain to lash out at Orother.

"Ha, Professor, you *are* entertaining. Though as much as I've enjoyed your company this morning, I have other things to do today."

· · ·

Once Orother left the room the Professor collapsed to the ground. He sat for some time, rocking back and forth, his shoulders shaking violently though no tears fell. When he calmed down, he resigned himself to the fact that he was stuck there and could do nothing about it.

He reached up to scratch at his head. He had discovered four distinct, small holes in his skull—one above each ear and two further back, each one edged with a metallic rim and all put there by the Doctor for direct access to his brain and memories. He pulled at his long, white-blond hair around the edges of the holes; it was shaved off in patches, though the remainder was still as long as ever. He resolved to cut it short if ever he escaped this hellish existence.

Vivid images flashed through his mind of Larissa pinned to the table, having holes drilled into her head just like his own. Orother forcing her memories to replay for him, raping her mind and laughing through the torment. Worse still, he couldn't stand to see her broken body destroyed by whatever means Orother could concoct.

The Professor buried his head in his palms, squashing the heels of his hands into his eyeballs until they burned in complaint. As he released the pressure and opened his eyes, it somehow seemed to work. Dark and sparkling spots danced across his vision until they dissipated and he returned to the room, his mind calmed.

The Professor looked down at the scrunched-up paper Orother had thrown at him. He picked it up and unfolded it, smoothing the paper out with his fingers. The letter was handwritten, the President's signature clear as day. It was incredibly incriminating, to the point where the Professor almost laughed out loud at the audacity of it. He stuffed it into the shallow pocket in his trousers just as the sound of high heels clacking against the rock floor towards the room reached him.

A guard entered, followed by a tall, dark-skinned woman. The Professor regarded her through squinted eyes; it took a moment to register who she was.

"The Doctor was here a moment ago," the guard said. "Wait here. I will find him. Don't touch anything and stay away from that." The guard pointed at the Professor.

When the guard disappeared, the woman stepped forwards, thick curls of hair pinned to the top of her head in a fancy manner. She wore a short black dress with puffed-out ruffle skirts that revealed her ebony legs, and her shoes were shiny patent black with ridiculously high heels.

"Well, hello, Professor." She smiled crookedly at him.

"Serenia."

It was all he could manage to say the mercenary's name. His mind raced with a thousand things. He wanted to shout at her and curse her to hell for selling him out, now that he knew she'd been involved with Orother all along. His mind flashed with images of her splayed out beneath him, his pale white hands gripped around her dark brown throat, watching the blood rush to the whites of her eyes as he choked the life out of her body. He felt his eye twitch as she stepped a little closer.

Almost, just a few inches more.

"I'm sorry, Professor. I didn't know he'd do this to you. You must understand it was just business, and he paid a far larger sum." Her eyes widened as she looked him up and down. If he didn't know better he might have actually believed she felt remorse. Still, he was unable to speak, his mind locked away by Orother's cruelty.

Serenia leaned in slightly and the Professor's palm twitched. The chain attached to his collar was no longer stretched out fully. If he could move swiftly enough he could lash out, grab hold of that obscene mop of hair and yank her to the ground. His heart raced at the thought.

"Ah, Serenia!" Orother returned to the room and she stepped back out of reach. The Professor's heart sank.

"Doctor."

"Do you have some news for me?"

"Yes, although it's not quite as you'd hoped. Do you want to discuss it in private?" She nodded towards the Professor.

"No, it's fine. I have him under control, my dear. Besides, he may like to hear your news. Do tell."

"We have located the pirate ship Hans chartered."

"Oh?"

"A guard spotted it approaching over the mountains. It's landed and the occupants have entered the town."

"They entered the town?" Orother asked, frowning. "Hans was supposed to have them land here. I arranged clearance."

"That's the problem. I sent some men to retrieve the ship, and they're bringing it here as we speak. We won't be able to ascertain what has transpired until the ship is brought in. Perhaps the pirates have broken their word."

"Fucking barbarians. Tell the men to kill every pirate on board when they arrive...no, wait. You said some occupants have entered the town?"

"Yes, that's what the guard saw, though he said he lost their trail."

"How many did he see?"

"Three men and a woman."

Orother looked at the Professor, who had been watching the conversation in silence and with a blank face, hiding the seething pit of fury and fear that bubbled beneath his skin. Orother smiled, that sickly, toothy grin the Professor had come to know was a bad sign.

"Secure the ship and bring it onto my grounds. Bring any remaining occupants directly to me. I shall discover what has happened and what their devious little plans are. Either way, I do believe I'm about to meet your young lady, Professor. What a delight!" Orother placed his arm around Serenia's shoulder and guided her out, leaving the Professor alone with his darkening thoughts.

Chapter Twenty Four

Cid poked his head around the door to look about. Outside was a long hallway, their room opposite a junction where the hall split into three directions. The ceilings were excessively high and a line of small stained-glass windows ran along the highest point of the ceiling in all directions. The various pictures on the glass were painted with blues, greens, and yellows. The walls had been cut from the mountain stone in which the building was embedded. The stone had been carefully smoothed back, which left the walls with an eerie shine.

To the right and the left, the corridor curved around a bend, reliefs of the Mountain Goddess—a buxom, nude woman with a bald head—cut into the stone at periodic intervals. Straight ahead, the corridor stretched on, sloping upwards and obscuring the view beyond. Pictures in the stained glass above showed the Spirit of Beasts, a creature with one head of a bull and one head of a fish, the legs of a horse, and the tail of a peacock.

Cid turned back to glance at the others one last time.

They looked like a dishevelled bunch of misfits. Even Holt, who usually managed to not get a speck of dirt on him, had bags under his eyes and his unshaven stubble was fast growing into a beard. If they were discovered, the priests and priestesses would doubtlessly raise the alarm immediately rather than taking pity. Cid tried to suppress the thought of Holt mercilessly slaughtering anyone unlucky enough to come across their hiding place; the man still made him nervous and he hated leaving Larissa with him.

She looked up at Cid with anticipation, as always. Once again he felt the need to do his best to live up to her expectations. He'd spent the majority of his working life working for the Professor.

They'd become so accustomed to each other while building the Machine that they'd gone for days without talking, and Cid hadn't felt the need to impress anyone with his skills. He wondered how Larissa had managed to bring about such a change in him so quickly.

He nodded tersely, slipping out into the corridor, and headed down the hall straight ahead. Each Dolanite place of worship was designed with a specific section dedicated to each of the nineteen separate Gods, Goddesses, and Spirits. Every section had either a central hall or chamber for the specific worship of the Deity to which it was dedicated. Often, in the smaller places of worship, several Gods were crammed together into one room, which was then split into sections for the sake of efficiency. Cid was used to those much smaller places; they felt homely and comfortable, and most importantly he could get all his praying done in a few hours.

The far larger buildings were always more daunting and people were expected to spend a significant amount of time in each section to justify the extravagant rooms. This particular building was far larger and more opulent than any Cid had ever visited before. It would probably take an entire day, maybe even two, to get around the whole place. Ordinarily, that would have made him feel apprehensive, but this time he was incredibly grateful as he wound his way through long corridors without bumping into a single soul.

The pictures of the Spirit of Beasts in the glass windows above turned ever darker in theme as he walked along—images of animals ripping apart human bones and feasting on young babes as they were wrenched from their mothers' arms. The glass coloring turned to red, casting an eerie light down the corridor. Cid hung his head, avoiding looking at them. Usually the images were just symbolic, to bring the worshiper into the correct state of mind, to respect the animalistic nature of beasts. Yet there was something about the walls turning to deep red around him that made the hairs on the back of his neck stand on end.

Eventually the upwards slope evened out and he came to a large, black, metal gate that stood partially open. Cid stopped and looked between the bars. On the other side of the gate was a large room with plain wood benches around the sides, the ceiling even higher here than in the hall. The room appeared to be empty. Cid scrunched his nose up and tapped mindlessly on the gate, trying to figure out what it was that stopped him from just entering, especially as the sleeping quarters should be the next section along.

"Lost your way, my son?"

Cid spun around and stumbled backwards, his shoulders crashing into the gate which rattled on its hinges. The sound echoed throughout the chamber and down the corridor. A priest had crept up behind him, dressed in a long, grey robe. The plump, elderly man stared at Cid with an odd grin on his face, though the smile was almost obscured by a frizzy, greying beard that covered the lower half of his face.

"I...uhhh, sorry, Friar. Yes, I'm a little lost."

"You do look out of place."

The priest looked Cid up and down, his bushy eyebrows dancing across his forehead in a whimsical expression. Cid looked down at himself; his clothes were tatty, his hands and forearms covered in burns and scabs and soot. He imagined his face looked just as bad, if not worse. Compared to the pristine rich folks they'd seen on the street, he looked like some sort of filthy, escaped convict.

"I wanted to say some prayers. I know my kind isn't usually welcome here, but I figured it looked pretty empty, so I thought I'd chance my luck."

Oh Gods, I'm lying to a priest. I'm going to burn for this.

"Your kind?"

"I work the furnace at Clockman Peak." He just about prevented himself from cringing at the awkward lie.

"Do you, now? What made you come all the way down here?"

Cid's mind fell blank and his face gave him away. He wasn't used to making up lies, let alone needing to do so in a holy place of worship. He mulled over the idea of just telling the truth, seeing if the priest would take pity and help. Perhaps if he could take the man back to Larissa, she could talk him into helping. She seemed to have a gift for it—that was, of course, if Holt didn't just slash the poor man's throat. The priest sighed and waved his hand apologetically.

"You must work for that awful heathen, that *Doctor* Orother. Felt the need to escape as far down the mountain as you could, hmm?"

Cid's face turned askew and he found himself nodding, dumbstruck.

"I'm not surprised, though I'd like to know how you got here. The guards don't usually let the workers walk the streets."

"I was...discrete."

There, that's not really a lie is it?

"No doubt. The sewers may be discrete, but you can catch all kinds of diseases from wandering around down there."

"How did you...?"

"The smell, my son. Well, this is the quieter time of day, so I think we can make an exception, though if you come across any of my brothers or sisters they may not be so forgiving. So make it quick."

The priest stepped past Cid, pushed the gate open, and nodded as Cid entered the room. The priest pulled the gate closed behind him and disappeared back down the corridor, muttering to himself.

Cid stood in the chamber, subtly mulling over the interaction. Usually he would have trusted the word of a priest without hesitation, though after the events of the last few days he had grown wary and mistrustful of even his own mind. He sighed and slumped down onto a bench, knowing full well that he didn't really have time to sit around praying.

"Old habits die hard," he said aloud. "Spirit forgive me, purge my soul, accept my penance..." His prayer continued on, the words so ingrained in his psyche that they rolled off his tongue with natural ease. By the time he finished he felt the familiar ease of rest wash over him, as though a great weight had been lifted from his shoulders. He hadn't even noticed that his eyes had fluttered closed.

"And Gods grant me the strength to survive this adventure, and place in my hands the courage to save the life of the Professor and the girl."

His eyes opened, and breath caught in his throat. Sitting in front of him, plain as day, he saw the little black and white ball of fur—Imago.

"Where the fuck did you come from?"

The cat turned its head to look at a different entrance gate. Cid's mouth dropped open, astonished that the cat was here, had followed them, and seemed to be able to understand him.

"Don't be fucking stupid, Cid. The fucking cat can't fucking understand you. And stop fucking swearing." Imago flicked his tail as a sign of impatience.

"Right. Well, I can't sit around here all day. Bloody Holt will be itching to fling a knife at some poor bugger before long."

He paused, trying to figure out if he was talking to himself or to the cat. Unsure which answer would make him sound crazier, and equally unsure what difference it made either way, he settled on the

185

idea that perhaps, just perhaps, the Gods had answered his prayer—perhaps Imago was there by divine providence. He was, after all, in the chamber of the Spirit of Beasts.

"Let's go find some robes."

Imago stood with Cid and followed close behind him as he made his way to the sleeping quarters. Once he had completed the task, he made his way back to the room where the others waited. Imago followed silently at his heel along the way.

Chapter Twenty Five

"I wonder how the others are getting on with repairing the ship," Larissa mused, though she kept her voice low. She sat cross-legged in one corner of the small room. Goodson sat opposite, mirroring her position, and Holt sat beside the door, his legs pulled up to his chest. He'd spent the time periodically looking out the door and shushing Larissa's attempts at passing the time with idle conversation.

"If we are successful in our task, and manage to get in and out of Orother's place alive, I doubt the ship will be where we left it," Holt answered.

"You think it will be discovered?" Goodson spoke, his voice was even softer than Larissa's.

"Discovered or taken," Holt answered.

"Taken?"

"By the men we left behind," Holt said.

"They assured me," Larissa began.

"They are pirates," Holt interrupted. He pulled the door open slightly to search the corridor once again, raising his hand to indicate the others should stay quiet. When he closed the door, Goodson spoke up.

"We are good men, Mr. Holt, better than you give us credit for."

"While those *good* men may not have been in the storage room with the others when I took the ship, you mustn't forget that they were waiting for the others to finish with you." Holt addressed Larissa, ignoring Goodson. "They would have had their turn beating and raping you, given time. Even this one." Holt pointed his finger at Goodson.

Larissa looked at Goodson, who glared at Holt, though his expression softened and his gaze dropped to the floor when he noticed Larissa watched him, too. Larissa sighed, wondering if life would become less complicated any time soon.

"Cid's returning," Holt said as he rose to his feet.

Larissa pressed her ear to the wall, straining to listen. She could hear some distant footsteps, though to her they sounded exactly the same as every other person who had passed by.

"How can you tell?" she whispered.

"His gait is unique."

"Really? Could you tell if it were me instead?"

"Yes."

"Really?"

"Yes."

"So what does my gait sound like?"

"Soft."

As she was about to press him further on matters of stealth, there came a soft tap on the door and Cid's voice muffled in the room as he spoke into the wood.

"It's me. Don't kill me."

Holt opened the door and Cid stepped inside, carrying an armful of robes. Imago followed him into the little room.

"Cid, thank goodness," Larissa squealed, stepping forward to hug him, having not seen the cat. Instead of reaching Cid, she trod on Imago's tail. The cat shrieked and jumped onto Cid's shoulder, then Cid tumbled forward and crashed into Goodson and the bundle of robes flew through the air.

Eventually, the momentary chaos settled, allowing them to regroup. Larissa spent an inordinate amount of time fussing over the cat, to the point where Holt resorted to clearing his throat loudly to distract her.

"Orother's house is up the mountain," Cid said as he tried to adjust the ill-fitting robe across his chest.

"How do you know that?" Holt asked. He'd already donned the robe, which not only fitted him perfectly, but somehow made him look like he had been born into the priesthood. Cid wrinkled his nose in disgust just as Goodson unintentionally jabbed his elbow into Cid's ribs as the young boy fought to get the robe over his head in the restricted space.

"The priest told me," Cid replied.

"You spoke to someone?" Holt's tone turned dark.

"A priest, yes. Don't worry, I didn't tell him anything."

"He is aware of our destination."

"But he thinks I work there. He doesn't know about the rest of you or what we're up to. Honestly, Holt, you're far too paranoid."

"Unless the man is a complete moron, he will know something is amiss and he's likely to report it to the guards, or to Orother himself."

"Listen, you." Cid took a step closer to Holt and raised his hand, brandishing a finger in Holt's face. Holt's eyes darkened.

"Gentlemen, please. We just need to get going. There's no point standing around arguing about things that can't be changed."

She tipped her head sideways and tried to squeeze herself in between the two men to diffuse the situation, though she was significantly shorter than the pair of them. Holt looked her over; she wore a man's robe that was incredibly bulky over the top of her dress, and she looked like an overweight monk.

"You should keep the hood pulled down over your face, or someone will question why a woman is wearing a man's robes," Holt said, then pulled the door open and stepped into the hallway, waving for the others to follow.

"We need to get out of here and back to the town," Holt said to Cid, effectively asking him to take the lead.

"Fine, just follow me." Cid tucked his arms beneath the robe sleeves and bowed his head, moving along the corridor in slow and measured strides. Holt followed next and Goodson and Larissa came last, walking side by side, Imago joining at Larissa's heel.

For the most part their journey was uninterrupted. Larissa watched their surroundings from the corner of her eye, admiring the carvings in the stone and beautiful colors of light streaming through the stained-glass windows in the ceiling. They entered a large chamber with sparkling crystals embedded in great rows along the walls, jewel encrusted benches and golden statues of a male in various sanctimonious poses. Larissa caught sight of Goodson, whose head had lifted from the pious bow. His jaw dropped and his eyes darted around the enriched surroundings.

"I believe it's the God of Ore," she whispered to him. "Even a priest-in-training would be used to the sight."

Goodson forced his mouth shut, cleared his throat, and resumed the bow. Larissa caught sight of Holt, who had turned just enough to watch their exchange; his sullen expression did not improve.

It'll be a miracle if he doesn't murder Cid or Goodson before this journey is over.

"I believe the exit will be beyond this chamber," Cid whispered.

"Good," Holt said. "We should hurry. We're being followed."

The two men turned on their heels and headed towards the opposite exit. Larissa and Goodson followed as the sound of feint footsteps echoed down the corridor behind them. Larissa felt her heart pounding in her ears and her feet tripped slightly as the pace quickened.

They entered yet another corridor in the maze-like structure, the steps of their pursuer growing louder as they rounded through twists and turns. Larissa kept glancing behind, expecting to see someone catch up to them. She smacked face-first directly into the thick, itchy robe of whomever was in front of her.

They had stopped, the footsteps behind them had stopped, and in front a figure blocked their path—a plump, elderly priest with a fuzzy grey beard that covered the majority of his face. He stood with his arms crossed and hood folded down, glaring directly at them. Larissa stepped to one side, trying to get a good look at the man while attempting to keep her face hidden.

"That one is a woman," the priest stated clearly, nodding in her direction, though the statement seemed to be directed at Cid.

"The young lad is a pirate," the priest continued, nodding at Goodson, "and that one is...an assassin? Or something in the military, though this is most certainly not a military operation."

Larissa heard the slightest metallic sound coming from beneath Holt's robe—a blade being drawn. She reached out and placed her hand on his arm, silently pleading with him to wait.

"You can try to stab me if you wish, my son, but I am under the protection of the God of Order and you will not succeed. I am here to offer you aid in your quest."

"My apologies, Friar," Cid said, bumbling somewhat. "It was not my intention to lie to you. We mean you no harm, we just need to get through the town discretely."

"To Doctor Orother?"

"Yes," Cid said.

Another metallic sound came from Holt's robe as he drew a second blade. Larissa tightened her grip on his arm.

"If you intend to infiltrate his operation there are a few things you should know. I would be happy to offer you some information, only I'd prefer to not have a knife at my throat, if it's all the same to you. I am Friar Narry. Have you all eaten recently? I have some cold meats and bread in my room if you'd like to join me."

"I don't mean to sound ungrateful, Friar," Larissa said, "but we don't have a lot of time."

"Ah, much more than just a woman, I see. You're the leader. Hmm, that's interesting. Well, I will escort you through the town. We can discuss along the way, save the food for another day."

Goodson groaned.

"Thank you. We must get out of here as soon as possible. I'm sure we were being followed," Larissa said as they started along the corridor once more.

"I was following you," Narry said.

"Really? So how'd you end up in front?" Goodson asked. The others all stared at him. He'd barely spoken two words this whole time, and it seemed an odd moment for him to find his voice.

"It is quite a skill to master, one of many I possess."

"Magic?" Goodson said, his voice almost a squeak.

"That's not how we refer to it, young man. They're called skills and illusions."

Narry led them around yet another bend into a large foyer with four blazing fire pits at each corner and an excessively ornate door at the opposite end which led to the outside world. They followed in silence through a gathering of people at the citadel for afternoon prayers, and emerged into the crisp winter air.

After walking the streets in silence for a while, the crowds of people and their accompanying guards thinned and Larissa thought it safe enough to speak.

"So, Friar Narry, you said there are things we should know?"

"The priests and priestesses in this order of the Dolanites have been aware of Orother's questionable activities for some time."

"What sort of activities?" Holt interrupted.

"Many people enter his property under guard and few of them are ever seen leaving."

"What kind of people?" Holt asked.

"Mostly military men, though it has been a while since we've seen a batch of them. It seems his activities have shifted somewhat, though we remain suspicious."

"Shifted? How?" Holt asked, taking on the role of interrogator.

"We have observed certain comings and goings, the transportation of interesting equipment, meetings with *Official Persons,* and such. Of course, there is the building itself, which is quite an achievement, I must say."

"And you haven't reported anything to the authorities or the Government?" Larissa asked. She had been watching the exchange between Narry and Holt carefully, wondering at Holt's sudden interest in the subject; it was unlike him to show interest in anything.

"We have discussed it amongst a few of us, whether we should act in some way, though it's not really appropriate for us to pry, nor involve ourselves. Besides, we knew it would be a bad idea the day a certain individual paid a personal visit to Orother."

"Who?" Holt asked, almost barking the question at him.

"I will not give you a name, as I fear it would be the end of me if I were to say it aloud. Just be assured it is a man of great power and influence, and if he approves of the Doctor's activities, reporting him to the authorities would be pointless. We felt sure that sometime soon Orother would upset the wrong person, and that that person or persons would do something about it. And here you are."

They turned a corner in the street and paused beside a clock shop. Behind the mildly frosted glass lay a glistening display of elaborate timepieces, each ticking in perfectly timed precision.

Larissa glanced up and spotted the street sign, it read *Clockman Way*. The road led on through twists and turns up the mountainside and in the distance the last house on the street, an imposing mansion, had a huge clock built into the front below the roof apex.

"Clockman Peak?" Larissa asked, though she hardly needed corroboration.

"The very same," Narry confirmed.

"Gods!" Cid exclaimed, and the others turned to see what he'd found. Sailing gracefully across the town, heading towards the mansion, they saw the pirate ship.

"So much for our stealthy approach," Larissa sighed.

Chapter Twenty Six

The pirate ship sailed elegantly around the imposing mansion and descended into the gardens at the back of Clockman Mansion. Doctor Orother stood on a balcony, watching his men aboard the ship guiding it down. Serenia stood by his side, though he had noted she tried to inch away from him whenever she thought he wasn't looking. It became a game in his mind to enhance her discomfort. He started to wonder what he needed her for now that he had the Professor and was about to have the engineer and the girl, too.

Nothing. I don't need her for anything else.

Some tantalising images flashed at the back of his mind of what he could do with her. Perhaps he could kill her first, make the Professor and that girl watch and see what is in store for them. Just as he started to imagine a symphony of screams echoing around his property, the ship touched down and his men headed toward him.

"The ship is secure, Sir," the senior guard said as he climbed the stairs to greet Orother.

"And what of the occupants?" Orother asked.

"We found no one aboard alive."

"No one alive?"

Orother turned back to the ship as he noticed four men struggling to offload a body from the ship. The men had awkwardly balanced the body atop the guard rail and tried to tie ropes around it in an attempt to lower it to the ground. Unfortunately they seemed to have not communicated who was in charge of holding onto the body while the ropes were collected.

Orother took a long, laboured breath as the large cadaver slid gracefully off the side and plopped down onto the ground with a heavy thud. Even at a distance, he could tell from the size of the corpse who it was.

"We found Hans," the guard confirmed. He flinched visibly, expecting a harsh rebuke for the ineptitude of his men.

"Bring him to my lab," Orother instructed.

"But, Sir, he's dead. Very dead. I don't think there's any chance in reviving him."

"I didn't say I wanted to revive him did I, you moron? He is a prime specimen. He will be worth cutting open. I can get a great deal of research out of him, at the least."

"Of course, my apologies."

"There was no one else aboard? You searched the entire ship top to bottom?"

"Yes, Sir, there was no one there."

"Damn. I was looking forward to getting hold of some new toys."

Orother took a few steps towards the mansion when he caught sight of Serenia, and his disappointment faded away in an instant. More of his men returned from the ship, including the four who struggled to carry Hans' large corpse.

"Take the body to the Doctor's lab," the senior guard instructed.

"Very good. And bring the woman down, too," Orother barked.

"Woman? There was no one else on board, Sir."

Orother didn't answer but gave one final glance at Serenia. Her mouth dropped and she reached for her concealed weapons, but it was too late as the guards descended upon her.

"I am sorry, my dear, but you had to realize I don't like to leave loose ends untied."

Serenia kicked and fought the collection of men pinning her arms and legs, and she spat at Orother just as another man tied a gag around her mouth.

"You want her in the workshop to drill holes in her head?" the guard asked.

"No, I have no interest in her sordid little memories. Put her in the lab with the body. I haven't performed a live dissection for a while. It'll give me some entertainment while we wait for our guests to arrive."

"Guests?"

"Yes, we're expecting some form of attack. Double security. Put them on alert and summon the Cleric. Tell him to ready his devices."

"Yes, Sir."

Orother watched as the panicking woman was carried in, followed by Hans' large body. He wondered which he was going to enjoy more.

. . .

Larissa leaned her temple against the cool brick wall of the clock shop and fiddled with the lace of her dress, having abandoned the priest's robe. She stared at the mansion further down the road. The pirate ship had long since disappeared behind the building to land, she presumed, in Orother's back garden.

She let out a loud sigh as she tried not to think of Grubbs and the other man she'd left on board. They were either dead or locked away with the Professor, being subjected to whatever tortures Orother could concoct. It was her plan, her scheme that had failed at even the simplest hurdle, and now doubt riddled her mind.

It had seemed so simple at the outset, rescue the Professor and return to a normal life. Now, as she thought back to her old life, it seemed so distant and ill-suited to the person she had already become. She couldn't decide if she was more terrified of actually succeeding in her plan or of dying in the attempt.

"Friar Narry says he'll be ready soon," Holt interrupted her train of thought.

"Oh." Larissa sighed again "What did he say he was doing, again?"

"He's making some form of spyglass."

"To do what?"

"To detect illusions."

"Magical illusions?" Larissa asked.

Holt raised an eyebrow. "I don't think he would refer to them that way, but yes."

"And you believe in all that, do you?"

"I've seen some interesting things over the years, things that can't be explained in any other way. You've seen it yourself." Holt poked her shoulder, jabbing at the knife wound that took only hours to heal.

"You said that was the Anthonium?" Larissa asked.

"Yes, I believe that is what has aided you, but it is not the only source of mysterious power in the world."

"And why is he so sure we will encounter these illusions?"

"Because," Friar Narry interrupted, joining them, "Orother has a certain person working for him, someone I have had the misfortune of encountering in my travels. A man well-versed in the illusory and mental arts."

"Who?" Larissa and Holt asked in unison.

Narry produced a spyglass from beneath the sleeve of his robe. He lifted it to his eye and scanned the mansion, speaking as he looked.

"He doesn't even have a name, as far as I know. I only ever heard my brothers and sisters refer to him as the Cleric."

Narry lowered the glass and fiddled with the lens. Larissa noticed some form of cog-and-button section attached at the front. Each time Narry pressed a button, a filter clicked into place across the lens, and with each new filter applied he tested the spyglass again.

"Ah," Narry exclaimed, "there it is, or isn't, I should say."

He passed the spyglass to Larissa and she looked through it towards the mansion. The filter cast the view with an odd tint of red. The mansion disappeared out of sight almost completely, leaving a pile of rubble in its place. Frowning, she lowered the spyglass, finding the mansion had popped back up on the landscape, in clear view.

"I...don't understand," she muttered.

"It's an illusion," Narry said, taking the spyglass from her.

"The entire house is an illusion? How?"

"There will be some form of device in place maintaining it."

"Why would someone go to that much trouble?"

"The same reason any illusions exist, to obscure the truth. My brothers and sisters grew suspicious when the mansion was built. Orother got permission immediately, which meant he had connections in Government, as very few new homes gain approval in this town these days. The structure was built far too quickly, and so we suspected it to be an incredibly well-crafted vision."

"And you haven't confirmed it until now?"

"As I said, it's not our place to pry. It's against the rules, in fact. Now, I'm not an engineer myself, but if I had to guess I'd say the actual work was done belowground."

"Wonderful." Larissa's heart sank, the idea of probing around a beautiful mansion house was far more appealing than the thought of slipping into some underground—no, under-mountain lair.

She looked to Holt to try and gauge his thoughts, but Holt was diligently watching the area around them, on sentry duty, his expression unreadable. If he was concerned about the magical illusion, the underground lair, the devices that could create illusions, or anything else that lay ahead, he did a good job of not showing it.

"Where are Cid and Goodson?" Larissa asked Holt, looking around the shop corner to the alleyway where they'd left the other two. They'd found them missing, but she sure she could smell an odd sort of burning.

"Working," Narry answered.

Holt gave her a sideways nod, indicating a place further back behind the shop, and she followed the direction of his nod. Rounding the corner, she found Cid and Goodson huddled together over a small fire which burned with an unnaturally red flame. Each of them appeared to be holding a thin filter clutched between a pair of tweezers over the flame. Larissa opened her mouth to speak but shut it again in silence as she realized they were both in deep concentration and she didn't want to interrupt.

After a while both Cid and Goodson removed their filters from the flame. Cid passed his to Goodson and reached behind to pick up the goggles he'd set down. Larissa watched on in silence as the two men worked quickly and quietly to apply the filters to the lenses of Cid's goggles, the odd material adhering to the glass as soon as it touched.

"You're still intending to go in there alone?" Holt appeared at her shoulder, making her jump.

"I haven't come up with a better plan yet, have you?"

"No. These are for you."

Holt pointed to the goggles and Cid held them up to her. She studied Cid then Goodson. Their expressions were priceless; they looked proud of their work and both appeared to be awaiting some form of praise, though she wasn't entirely sure what it was they had done.

"Thank you. Good work," she said, trying to hide her ignorance.

She pulled the goggles over her head. The strap was far too large and they immediately slipped down around her neck. She spent a moment or two trying to adjust the strap before Holt unceremoniously grabbed hold of them, yanked them back into place over her eyes, and squeezed the strap into place at the back of her head. Next, he proceeded to pull and tug at her hair with rough, anxious hands.

"What are you doing?" Larissa half-yelled as he jerked her head sideways with a handful of her curls. Holt didn't answer. Eventually he let go, and she reached up to rub her sore scalp, finding he had pulled her hair back into a bun.

"You tied my hair up?"

"If you need to run or fight, you will be better off without a face-full of hair. Besides, it will help to keep the goggles in place."

Larissa turned to face him, peering through the oddly tinted goggles at his distorted face.

"If my plan works, I won't need to fight or run."

"Have any of your plans been so simple thus far?"

"No."

"Orother is a maniac. If you somehow manage to sneak in and find him without being detected, he will overpower you. Especially if he has this Cleric in his employment. As far as you have come with your skills, you cannot defeat the entire operation single-handed."

"I don't need to though, do I? I'm the distraction. My task is the procurement of time."

A clock in the shop beside them softly chimed the announcement of five o'clock and the assortment of other time-pieces followed with their mixed bells and peels. Imago rubbed his face across her ankle and let out a soft yowl. An odd chill worked its way down Larissa's spine.

Friar Narry rejoined the group as he tucked the spyglass back into his robe sleeve. He stood for a moment, assessing Larissa, his grey beard shifting back and forth as he ground his teeth together in deep thought.

"It's crude," he began, "but it should suffice. It's the best we can hope for at such short notice. You won't reconsider waiting one more day?"

"No, Friar, I fear we've taken too long as it is."

"Very well. You must not trust your own mind, child. The illusions could be anything, people, objects, doorways, animals. The intention is likely to cause intruders to react to the illusions and draw the guards' attention. When you find one you must find the source, the device that operates it, and shut it off."

"So, these illusions can't hurt me?"

"As far as I'm aware there haven't been any successful devices made that can create tangible illusions to cause actual harm. That level of skill can only be achieved by someone in person."

"The Cleric?"

"He is a dangerous man. If you find him, you'd do well to run."

"It seems I'm entering a yet another den of dangerous men."

"A bad habit," Cid huffed.

"I will follow," Holt said.

"We will follow," Cid corrected him.

Larissa rolled her eyes at the pair of them before she remembered they wouldn't be able to see her eye rolling behind the goggles. Imago rubbed against her ankle once more and a cool breeze blew through the alleyway as the sun started to dip in the sky.

"It's time to go," Larissa said, and silently the men fell into step behind her.

Chapter Twenty Seven

Larissa reached the end of the winding path at the bottom of the flight of steps leading toward the mansion. Friar Narry had directed her to take the Servant's Passage to avoid drawing too much attention to her approach. She had tucked a series of knives in amongst her bodice and skirt ruffles.

She moved the goggles up to her forehead and took a moment to glare up at the structure ahead. It looked like some form of castle from her childhood dreams. The structure was entirely grey, matching the mountain stone much like the other buildings in the town. It had a large balcony at the back and several floors of symmetrical windows. As she pulled the goggles back down over her eyes the main building disappeared, leaving behind a pile of rubble at the front and the balcony at the back with a basic box-like entrance.

She climbed the steps to the top and found the entire structure surrounded by a large wall, too high to scale without the aid of a rope. Luckily, the steps led to a passage, which headed toward a gate. Beyond the gate she could see the pirate ship landed neatly in the back gardens; the large balloon had started to deflate. The sound of voices inside the compound travelled towards her and she ducked behind an alcove in the stone to peek out.

Two men came into view. They ran across the neatly maintained grass, covered head to foot in black soot, leaving black footprints in their wake. As they approached the gate Larissa had to keep herself from screaming at them when she recognized the pair. They were the men she'd left on board, Grubbs and the other man whose name she couldn't remember. Grubbs reached the gate and frantically hacked at the lock with a small axe while the other man watched their backs.

"Shit, there's guards," the second man yelped as Grubbs finally destroyed the lock, flinging the gate open. He ran toward the steps, and Larissa reached out to grab his arm as he sprinted past. Grubbs shrieked and attempted to swing the axe at her. The other man fumbled around at his trouser belt to try to grab at the pistol tucked into it.

"Grubbs, it's me. Calm down." She yanked on his arm and pulled him into the alcove.

"Cap'n?"

"Yes, Grubbs." Larissa removed the goggles again and Grubbs calmed, though the other man still fiddled with his trousers as he looked up at the two of them.

"There's guards coming, Cap'n Rissa. We gotta run," he said, finally pulling the pistol free. She reached out and grabbed hold of him, attempting to squeeze him into the small alcove.

She stepped out onto the path and pulled a pair of knives free, setting her arms behind her back, elbows relaxed, eyes focused. The two guards came sprinting through the gateway and immediately stopped when they saw her, raising their weapons.

"Hello, boys." Larissa smiled sweetly. "I was hoping I'd find some customers up here. Those other two lads were in too much of a hurry, though."

"Just some fucking whore." One man shoved past her and started down the stairs. The other grabbed her arm.

"Get out of here, Miss. This ain't the place for doing business. You'll get yourself killed." He bent over and whispered in her ear, "Though I'd be happy to meet you after my shift is done."

The man caught a glimpse of the two pirates hiding in the alcove for the briefest moment. Before he could react, Larissa slammed a knife into his neck and drew it across his throat. He clutched at the gaping wound, pouring blood onto the stony path as he collapsed. She turned and flung the other knife down the stairs, catching the second guard in the back of his neck. The guard fell forward, sliding down the last few steps, and landed at the bottom with a thud. His arms flailed around as he attempted to grab at the knife. A few moments later both men stilled.

Larissa looked between the two dead guards and the two men, her men, who in turn stared at her with wide eyes. She felt an unpleasant discomfort in the pit of her stomach at having committed such an efficient killing. Yet she knew it was not the time for question or doubt; she had to press on. She'd made the first move and couldn't back out now, as sooner or later someone would come looking for the two guards.

"Nice job, Sir…um, Ma'am…um, Cap'n," Grubbs muttered.

"I'm so glad to see you two. I thought they'd have killed you or captured you."

"We saw 'em coming, Cap'n, knew they'd find us. So we went and hid in the coal pile. Didn't figure they'd dig too deep to look."

"That's brilliant," she gasped.

"It is?" Grubbs beamed a grin, his crooked white teeth a stark contrast to his soot-covered face.

"Yes. It's so good to have such clever men on my crew...you still want to be on my crew, don't you, or are you planning on leaving?"

"Well, we weren't exactly expecting to come across you like this, Cap'n, uhh…"

"It's all right. If you want to leave I won't stop you."

"Really?"

"Of course," she smiled.

"I'll stay on with you, Miss." The other man finally spoke, and Larissa felt like such a fool for not knowing his name.

"Well, now, I can't let Zeb be the braver man than me," Grubbs said. "I'll stay with you too, Cap'n. You got some orders for us?"

"Zeb, Grubbs, I'm very grateful. Listen, we don't have much time. Holt and the others will be coming this way soon. Let them know you're alive and do what you can to get the ship ready to fly again. If we have any form of luck on our side we'll do what we came here to do and escape with our lives. Think you can manage that?"

"Aye, Cap'n," they answered together.

Larissa nodded to the men, reapplied the goggles, and headed through the gate. She quickly stalked her way around the outside wall and climbed the real steps up to the real balcony, virtually the only parts of the structure that actually existed. On either side of the balcony stood two large, orb-like stones, different in color and texture than the structure above. Without the goggles they looked like two sculptures, but with the goggles she could see some form of aura emanating from them, projecting towards the building. She bent down beside one orb and reached out, tempted to touch it. Something made her snap her hand away as she thought better of it.

"If these are the devices that control this *illusion,* the whole town will become rather suspicious if I turn them off and the mansion disappears," she muttered quietly to herself. "I don't fancy our chances at having to fight off the town guards as well as Orother's men."

She stood up, frowning as she realized she'd been talking aloud to herself. Not the best idea when infiltrating a dangerous compound. She left the orbs in place and passed through into the small structure. Inside was a wide staircase leading directly down, apparently without any other guards on watch.

She removed the goggles for a moment, a breathy sigh catching in her throat as the mansion in all its glory reappeared—luscious, dark green drapes hanging down the tall windows, a grand staircase leading up to a second and third floor above, beautiful artwork hanging in golden frames. It looked to be a masterpiece of a building, but all of it nothing more than an illusion. She eyed the row of doors to the left and right, leading to non-existent rooms, and further up the hallway a single open door caught her attention. She wanted desperately to explore but had to remind herself that all she would find in reality would be a pile of rubble.

Pulling the goggles back on, a slight movement caught her eye by the open doorway—a flash of dark red robe disappearing through the gap. She froze, flicking her vision between the filtered goggles and the naked eye, unable to see the movement ahead through either and unsure how to follow. There appeared to be a pile of stone in place of the illusory doorway. A deathly female scream echoed through the building below, and Larissa swayed a little as her legs turned to jelly.

"Narry didn't say anything about illusions that you can hear," she whispered as she attempted to force her legs to regain their strength. Ignoring the nagging voice inside her head that grimly warned against moving on, she began the descent down the stairs.

. . .

Holt stood beside the clock shop, leaning his shoulder against the building corner. He'd watched Larissa walking away, watched her closely as she rounded a bend ahead out of sight. He continued to watch the bend intently for five minutes, counting the time in his head. It seemed more soothing to do so than to simply look at the clocks in the shop.

"How long should we wait?" Goodson's voice cut through the silence between the group of men who stood behind Holt, watching the same bend.

"Not much longer," Cid answered. "Another minute perhaps?"

"Longer," Holt said, his voice even more curt than usual.

"What if she gets caught by the guards?" Goodson asked, unconsciously dancing from foot to foot.

"That is the intention."

"What if she gets into trouble?"

"This is Larissa, trouble is inevitable."

"But what if she—"

"I will decide when it is time to leave," Holt barked. A movement ahead caught his attention. A man flashed into view, falling forwards with a knife sticking out of his neck. The body fell down and disappeared out of sight.

"Was that what I think it was?" Cid asked.

"Shit, she's in trouble. We should go now," Goodson said, panicking.

"She is fine. She has not yet entered the building," Holt responded, chewing on his lip to suppress the grin that threatened his face.

He tried not to wonder if Larissa had been a quick learner or if he was simply a good teacher. A few moments later, after listening to some stifled muttering from the men behind, two figures emerged from the bend. The soot-covered men stepped over the corpse and headed down the street.

"Gods, who are *they*?" Cid yelled.

"The men from the pirate ship," Holt answered.

"You can tell that from here?"

Holt did not reply. Instead, he marched down the street towards the two men, and the others followed.

Chapter Twenty Eight

Orother stood over the basin, watching the crystal clear water gushing out from the copper pipe. He reached up, turned off the faucet, and held his arms out over the water as it settled into a calm pool. He spent some moments admiring the drips of blood that fell from his elbows and fingertips, tainting the water as they hit. His arms were covered in gore up to the elbows, right where his white overcoat sleeves were rolled up.

Over the years he had become incredibly proficient at keeping the overcoat spotlessly clean during his more gruesome sessions, and yet the walls, floor, and instruments in his workshop were as tainted as his forearms. With a sigh he dropped his arms into the icy cool water and watched with mild amusement as the liquid turned a deep shade of blood red. Yet he wasn't finished; in reality, he had barely even begun.

"I really wish you wouldn't wriggle so, my dear," he called out, his voice peppered with a thick Eptoran accent. "I prefer to wait until I'm finished to wash up."

Behind him, splayed out upon a shining metal table, lay Serenia, her wrists and ankles tied down at each corner. Beside her, on a similar table though without the ropes to pin him, lay the lifeless body of Hans. Hans had been sliced open from navel to neck, his innards strewn about haphazardly, the top of his skull removed, brain open to the world.

Serenia had the start of a similar treatment, her body bleeding from the beginning of cuts with a scalpel blade. She twitched and thrashed against the bindings, fighting to break free. Orother returned to the table with clean hands and set to adjusting the ropes that bound her.

"I see you have too much slack. Perhaps one for the neck, too," he suggested to the two young male assistants who stood beside the tables, scribbling notes onto their clipboards.

"Fuck you," she spat.

"Now, now, no need to be crude." As Orother waved an arm at one of his assistants to retrieve more rope from a pile of crates stacked in a corner, a figure appeared in the doorway—the Cleric.

"The female has arrived." The Cleric's voice was soft yet deep, his pale green eyes seeming to glow in contrast to the dark red robes he always wore. His expression was blank.

"Ah, shame, I thought I'd have a little more time. Have the guards bring her down."

"She has killed two guards."

"Oh? Well that is interesting. I thought I told them to double security and put them all on alert?"

"Some of your guards have abandoned their posts. A military contingent would have been preferable. The men you hired are too squeamish," the Cleric said, looking around at the pool of blood and guts on the floor and regarding the assistants with suspicious eyes. The two men averted their stares, apparently terrified that making eye contact with the Cleric would cause them to evaporate into flame or suffer some other mysterious and painful punishment.

"How about the engineer?" Orother asked, returning to tie rope around Serenia's neck. The mercenary had virtually given up the fight and appeared to be resigned to her fate, though she listened intently to the two men talking.

"The female is alone."

"How frustrating. Never mind, I'll discover his hiding place once I have her. Your devices will alert us when she's near."

"She is aware of my devices."

"What? How?"

"She has had help. It is likely there are other men who will follow. I will take some of the remaining guards and stop them."

"Very well."

The Cleric disappeared from the room and Orother turned his attention back to Serenia. He stared at her quizzically for a moment and reached for a scalpel blade from a nearby tray.

"It seems our time is done. You will escape lightly after all." He stepped toward her, knife raised, his eyes flashing wildly. Serenia let out another scream of terror that echoed through the room.

. . .

Holt listened carefully as the two soot-covered men relayed in great detail the story of how they'd hidden in the coal and found Larissa, though his patience wore thin when Goodson began chatting inanely with them.

"You have orders. We have work to do," he stated plainly and the two men begrudgingly headed further down the hillside to search for supplies for the ship.

"So, we're going in there now?" Cid asked.

"Not yet. She needs more time. Perhaps you should go with the other two."

"Not bloody likely," Cid scoffed.

"Goodson, you go." Holt gestured towards the two coal-covered men. Goodson looked as though he were about to argue. The young man thought better of it and did as he was told, leaving Holt, Narry, and Cid.

"I'd have thought it would be better to have more men for this battle plan," Narry said, "especially as I have no intention of fighting anyone."

"I work better alone," Holt said, narrowly eyeing Cid. "Besides, the corridors belowground are likely too tight for a group of men to successfully fight together."

"Perhaps I should stay out of your way?" Narry suggested.

"Agreed."

Narry handed his spyglass to Holt and Holt headed up the staircase. Cid turned to Narry, his face slowly growing pale as the reality of the situation dawned upon him.

"You still look a little lost," Narry said, "though I'm not sure whereabouts you would look at home."

"That makes two of us, Friar," Cid said with a sigh.

"Well, I've no doubt you'll figure it out. At the least, it seems she needs you, more than either of you realize. Perhaps that's somewhere to start. Go well, my son, and Gods be with you."

Cid nodded and followed after Holt, and Imago the cat padded along behind him.

Holt stared up at the mansion for several more minutes, occasionally looking through the spyglass.

"There aren't any more guards?" Cid asked eventually, stepping over the dead body.

"Not outside, it seems." Holt marched through the gate and straight for the airship, heading up to the deck with ease and leaving Cid to stand at the gate, feeling surplus to requirements. Cid leaned against the stony wall, trying to ignore Imago, who wrapped his tail around Cid's ankles.

"Fucking cat," he muttered, but as his gaze shifted back to the mansion entrance he caught sight of a hooded figure in a red robe—the Cleric.

Cid froze, his breath catching. From his position he couldn't be sure, but he thought the man was looking at the ship rather than at him. Slowly, he sunk to his knees and rocked backwards out of view, lifting the cat across his chest and depositing him to the side.

"Fucking hell," he whispered as the Cleric disappeared back inside the mansion, mere seconds before Holt reappeared on the ship deck and jumped down to the ground, heading directly to the mansion entrance.

"Now what the fuck am I supposed to do?" Cid looked down the stairs for Friar Narry, but he was nowhere to be seen. As he turned back, the cat stepped over his feet and headed into the gardens, padding with speed towards the mansion. Cid rolled his eyes and growled under his breath.

"Fucking cat," he said, and he followed.

. . .

Larissa found herself heading down an impossibly long set of stairs on quivering legs. The staircase followed a slight curve in a constant, long spiral, and she spent an inordinate amount of time stopping and listening for footsteps, expecting to meet a guard or some other nefarious character at any moment. Her palms grew sweaty, and every time she adjusted the goggles to check for devices, the leather straps slipped in her hands. At first the way was lit by gas lamps, but after a while the lamps turned to burning torches set in iron brackets. Try as she might, she struggled to erase the vision of ancient torture chambers and dungeons plaguing her mind.

Eventually she reached the bottom, coming into a cylindrical room which opened out into a set of tunnels, like an underground burrow. Still, there was no sign of anyone else, nor any device. She leaned her shoulder against the cool stone wall for a moment, listening for any sign of life or hoping for perhaps some divine inspiration to guide her directly to the Professor.

She felt her body shaking from tip to toe, riddled with nervous energy, all too aware that her plan was incredibly flawed. She felt this way despite the fact that Holt was supposed to be following her down. She started to wonder if it was best just to wait here for him. She leaned her head against the wall and heard a click and a whirring behind the stone. She leapt away from the wall as the ground beneath her feet shook and the entire room broke away from the staircase and twisted around. Larissa dropped to her knees, grabbing for a knife before realizing she wasn't wearing the goggles.

"Shit."

She pulled the goggles down and the filter revealed the wall was filled with switches and levers, though she had no idea which one of them she'd actually pressed.

"Shit, shit, shit!"

The room continued to spin, blocking out the tunnel exits, revealing large cogs and chain mechanisms which controlled the room as the stairwell also disappeared behind a wall. Finally a single tunnel opened up as the spinning room ground to a halt. The room echoed with the sound of a ticking clock, the noise thumping inside her head as she started to panic. The tunnel was as plain and non-descript as the others had been, and still there was no sign of anyone or anything, either in plain sight or with the goggles. She stood dumbstruck, listening to the ticking clock as it gained speed.

"Shit," she whispered, her eyes welling up with tears. "Damnit." She dove forwards into the tunnel just as the ticking ceased and the room swiftly curled back around, blocking her exit.

"Well, I guess that decision was made for me." A laugh spluttered from her lips but was cut short as she spotted a trail of blood trickling along the corridor towards her.

Chapter Twenty Nine

Holt regarded the mansion illusion with minimal appreciation. Though it was no doubt a marvel to fool an entire town into thinking such a grand structure existed, and extra attention had been paid to the illusory inside entrance hall, to him it was really nothing more than an inconvenience. It took enough effort to fight against real enemies; he wasn't so sure his skills would hold up against *magical* foes. He discovered the spherical stones that seemed to power the illusion and checked them carefully with the spyglass, concluding that it would be better to leave them in place. Destroying the mansion illusion may make for a useful distraction during an escape, if they were lucky enough to make it out alive.

He slipped inside, immediately spotting the staircase that led down. An almighty rumbling noise, like the sound of heavy machinery rolling along, echoed up from below, followed by a plume of thick smoke. Holt grabbed a pistol from his belt and raised the spyglass to his eye with the other hand. Immediately the smoke disappeared from view. A wry smile trickled across his lips as he detected the ruse. He slung the spyglass over his shoulder, latching it into a makeshift holster on his back, and proceeded down the stairwell with caution.

. . .

Cid reached the entrance to the mansion and found himself staring up at the great hallway in awe. He'd looked through the spyglass once or twice from a distance and seen the reality of the situation, but now Larissa had the goggles and Holt had gone off with the spyglass. Cid was left with no way of seeing the truth of things. He also had no idea which doorway Holt had taken, or if he'd gone up or down the staircases.

As he stood for a moment, chewing on his lip, Imago padded around in front of him. The cat sniffed at the floor, flicking his tail side to side, stalking along as though he hunted a bug. Cid watched as Imago passed by one door and another, and finally the cat turned around and backtracked toward him.

"Well, bloody hell, animal, if you don't know where we're going then we're stuck, aren't we?"

A plume of smoke came up from the open stairwell leading down, and Cid immediately started to panic, thinking Larissa was in trouble. Imago, on the other hand, paid no attention to the smoke at all. Instead, he had found an interesting piece of floor slab and patted at it with his paw.

"You know something I don't, cat?" Cid asked, joining Imago on his hands and knees to feel around the sunken slab edge. To his surprise it shifted with the slightest pressure, and with one almighty shove the entire slab lifted out of place to reveal a secret ladder leading down.

"Hmm, I wonder if Sir Hot-Shot-Knife-Killer found this?"

Imago sat back on his hind legs and gave Cid an impassive stare.

"Right. Holt doesn't care about secret tunnels, he can just go in and stab everyone to death. I, on the other hand...am talking to a fucking cat. What is wrong with me?" Cid rolled his eyes and slipped down onto the ladder.

"A secret tunnel beats a smoke-filled stairwell in my book." He looked up at Imago, and the cat carefully stretched out his front paws, climbing onto Cid's shoulder. "I'm glad you agree."

With one hand Cid pulled the slab back into place over his head and began the descent down the ladder towards the distant speck of light below.

. . .

Larissa stalked along the rocky corridor, her back to the wall, a knife in each hand, following the trail of blood to its source. She reached a gap in the rock, which seemed the source of the trail, and curled her head around to peek inside. The sight that greeted her was gruesome to say the least, and her first reaction was to turn away and lean back against the wall to stop herself from retching.

After taking a moment to catch her breath and calm her nerves, she turned again to survey the room. There appeared to be no one alive inside. There were, however, two dead bodies laid out on metal tables. She knew instantly who one of them had been; there was no mistaking Hans from the size of his body, though his chest had been opened out like a bull carcass at a butcher's shop. The top half of his skull was missing, brain scooped out and deposited neatly in a jar on a shelf.

Bile jumped up into her throat at the sight of it and she had to cover her mouth with the back of her hand. She stepped into the room, attempting to avoid getting her boots drenched in blood and gore. The second corpse appeared to be female, dark skin, the facial features...removed, though the mop of dark curly hair seemed familiar to Larissa.

She started to wonder if this whole thing was really such a good idea. The body had been tied to the table, presumably because the poor creature had been alive during the recent *dissection*; dead bodies required no such restraint. Larissa couldn't help but imagine herself in that same position; the thought made her toes curl.

"Serenia," she said out loud, finally realizing whom the corpse belonged to, a puzzle piece clicking into place. She remembered their meeting in the bar, how Serenia had warned her that she'd get herself killed.

"You'll be next."

A male voice whispered in her ear and her heart leapt into her throat. She jumped and spun, clutching her knife, knocking into the metal table with her hip. As the table wobbled, the corpse slid to one edge, dragging against the ropes, and the entire thing crashed over onto its side. Blood splatter erupted from a pool on the floor, coating everything in picturesque red dots and splotches. Larissa backed into a wall; she had forgotten to breathe. Her eyes darted around the room but she was the only one alive inside. As her lungs begged to be filled with new air, she consciously forced herself to start breathing again.

"Trick of the mind," she whispered, although not quite managing to convince herself. "Let's get out of the *room of death*..." Larissa headed back out into the corridor and followed the path onwards.

. . .

Holt reached the bottom of the stairs, having encountered no attempted illusions other than the smoke. He studied the surroundings through the spyglass and found the array of switches on the wall. There was no obvious key as to which switch would have what effect. A sound echoed somewhere nearby, a dull thud that seemed to come from somewhere beyond the wall.

As he stood straining to listen, two men appeared in the hallway ahead, one dressed in white overalls and the other in some form of uniform, weapons at his side—a guard. The guard immediately raised his pistol and pointed it at Holt.

"Drop your weapon," the man shouted, "*Now!*"

A thought flicked across Holt's mind, unsure how many other guards were around to have heard the man shouting. The man in overalls had skittered away into a side room. Holt put his free hand in the air, lowering the pistol to the floor, and the guard took the bait to approach him alone.

"Who are you? Where is the woman and the engineer?" the guard asked.

"I believe the woman has taken an alternate route," Holt said calmly, flicking his gaze towards the switches on the walls though he couldn't see them without the spyglass. The guard's stare shifted to the walls for the briefest moment. That moment was all Holt needed; he reached for a knife. The guard saw the movement and pulled on the trigger of his pistol, but Holt launched forwards, knocking the pistol to the side as the shot rang out.

Gunpowder and blood showered the side of Holt's face as he sunk the blade deep into the guard's neck. The bullet from the shot ricocheted off the wall, hitting Holt on the back of his arm. He grimaced at the pain as the guard dropped to the floor. The gunshot echoed down the hallway and Holt growled. He hadn't planned on giving away the game so soon, but as the first move had been made he had no choice now.

Holt flicked a switch on the wall and ducked out into the hallway as the room began to turn, hoping someone would think he headed down whatever passageway it was into which the room opened up. He marched along, stepping into a side room to find the man in white overalls cowering behind a table, some lackey scientist with unwashed hair and ill-fitting spectacles. Holt half-smiled at the man. He'd be unlikely to put up much of a fight.

Cid reached the bottom of the ladder and dropped through a hole into a radiantly opulent bedroom. Elaborate chandeliers hung from the ceiling. The smell of kerosene from the lamps was blocked out by some fruity incense burning in a glass bowl atop a dark wood dresser. In the center of the room beside Cid was a large circular bed, covered in dark green, velvet sheets. Imago jumped off of Cid's shoulder onto the bed and immediately clawed at the fabric.

"Orother's bedroom?" Cid asked Imago, though the cat did not answer. Cid turned around slowly again and again, trying to figure out where the door was.

"Surely he doesn't climb down that ladder every time he wants to have a nap?" As he looked up at the hole in the ceiling, contemplating pushing some bits of furniture underneath it to get back out again, the unmistakeable sound of a single gunshot caught his attention.

"Bloody hell."

Moments later the opening in the ceiling disappeared as a panel slid across it, trapping Cid inside.

"Bloody hell."

Imago dragged his claws along the green velvet, ripping the fabric open with some determination.

"Well, that's just fantastic, cat. That's about as much use as we can be trapped in here. So much for you being sent by the bloody Gods."

Chapter Thirty

Larissa walked through a seemingly endless array of tunnels. Some rooms led off the main corridors, but for the most part they held nothing more interesting than storage rooms filled with boxes. She'd already come across two or three dead-ends and was starting to wonder if she was lost. The hairs on the back of her neck kept tingling and she couldn't escape the nagging feeling of being followed, though no one was visible in the long hallway stretching out behind her.

As she reached yet another dead-end, she groaned aloud and lay her forehead against the jutting rock face. With one long sigh she plopped the goggles down again to check her surroundings in case of any illusions. As she turned back toward the main hallway she froze. In the darkened cavern, blocking her only exit, stood a tall figure in a dark red robe. The hood of the robe was pushed back from his face, revealing short, spiky blond hair, his pale green eyes burning with intensity. He needed no introduction; Larissa knew she'd found the Cleric.

Larissa opened her mouth to speak, hoping upon hope that she could somehow talk her way out of the situation. Instead of words, she spluttered and coughed as a pressure formed across her throat, as though a pair of slimy hands had wrapped around her neck.

Still the Cleric didn't speak nor move; he simply stood at a distance, watching. He was in full control of whatever odd mind technique he used against her. Larissa tried to suck a breath in through her nostrils, finding her throat constricted. As her lungs screamed for air and her eyes bulged out of their sockets, she clutched at her neck and collapsed to her knees. The light in the hallway darkened, black spots dancing on the edges of her vision, and inside her mind a deep voice echoed.

"You will take me to the source." The Cleric smiled as Larissa collapsed to the ground.

. . .

Cid laid his forehead against the dark wood wardrobe door, occasionally allowing his head to rock back and roll forward, knocking against the wood in frustration. The room was a mess; Cid had tossed through every drawer, overturned every ornament, and upended the bed, all to no avail. There was no way out. Cid glared at the ornate casket he'd found in one of the chests.

He wasn't a thief. Really, he had no intention of stealing, even if it was from a loathsome individual, but what harm would it do? It wasn't as if Orother would report him to the authorities, and the casket contents appeared particularly valuable and interesting. Not that it mattered as he still had no way of escaping the room.

"Stop fucking looking at me, cat. It's your fault we're down here." Imago sat atop the wardrobe, looking down at Cid.

As Cid and Imago stared at one another, Cid pondered whether cats could roll their eyes or not. He was sure Imago would be doing so if he could. Imago moved slightly to one side and Cid noticed the small hole in the rock. It wasn't big enough for Cid to get into, but Imago might fit through.

"Well, go on. Come on, animal, go through there," Cid said, trying to coax Imago with a wave of his arms. "Go see if you can find a switch on the other side of the wall or something."

After several minutes of trying Cid threw his arms in the air and sat down on the mattress, muttering a string of expletives to himself. Imago gave one last flick of his tail and disappeared through the small hole.

. . .

Larissa's eyes fluttered open and she found herself bobbing up and down, upside down. As she fought against the nauseous feeling caused by the movement, she tried to focus. The Cleric had slung her over his shoulder and now carried her...where? She didn't like to think, though she still felt groggy from passing out and was hardly able to fight a man seemingly capable of strangling a person without even touching them—and goodness knows what else.

Eventually he stopped and slung her forwards. She landed on her feet and wobbled for balance, coming face to face with the Cleric, who had a perplexed look upon his face. Perhaps he'd expected her to still be unconscious?

"Thank you." A vaguely familiar voice came from across the room.

"She has brought an accomplice. I will stop him next," the Cleric said shortly before leaving.

Larissa turned to find herself in a large room, still within the cave. A pair of guards stood at the entrance, armed to the teeth, and on the opposite wall she caught sight of Orother, who stood beside a body curled into a heap on the floor. Her heart froze as she saw the long, white-blond hair covering the head of the body.

"Doctor Orother?" she asked, her voice cracking.

"Yes, and you are Miss Markus."

"Is he dead?" She pointed to the Professor.

"No, I just rendered him immobile for the moment. I wanted the chance to speak to you directly and privately."

She sucked in a sigh of relief and straightened her skirt ruffles out as she moved further into the room.

"I must say you've done rather well for such an ordinary little girl."

"I have come to negotiate." Larissa ignored his slight, her spine rigid, palms sweating.

"You're hardly in the position to do that, although you are an intriguing creature. I'm listening. Make your proposition."

"I have something you want."

"Yes?" Orother took a step toward her. She felt her toes instinctively curling up inside her boots as though they were trying to dig into the ground, to root her to the spot. She pulled the lockbox from her pocket and balanced it in her palm.

"The *Anthonium*."

"I see. I suppose you'll tell me the code to unlock it in exchange for...?"

"The Professor." She glanced towards the pale and gaunt body bound by a collar to the wall; it looked like a hollow shell of the man who'd been so fixed and strong in her memory. The Professor lay in silence. Orother looked between the two of them and took a few steps backwards to stand beside the Professor.

"You came all this way, through all this effort, to save this man, who barely cares a thing for you?"

"You don't know anything about us," she snapped in defense.

"Oh, but I know far more than you realize."

"I don't care what you think you know. This is my proposition. What is your answer?" Larissa clenched her fist, frustrated at herself, forgetting the plan. She was supposed to be buying time for Holt to pick his way through the guards, but she doubted his uncanny abilities would be much use against the Cleric. The hope in her heart faded rapidly.

"My dear, I will extract the information I require from you, whether you wish to give it willingly or not and without any need for sacrifice on my part. You will tell me the code to your little box, you will tell me where the engineer is hiding, and the location of the *Anthonium* deposit. Once I know everything I need to know, I will use you as a test subject on one of my newest devices. It's quite a daunting thing designed to push the body to the limits of pain and suffering, though I must say its effects are rather gruesome, even for my strong constitution."

Larissa felt the butterflies in her stomach turning somersaults as she tried not to think about Serenia's fate. If a man who enjoyed dissecting people alive found something to be gruesome, it was surely beyond her imagination to comprehend. She looked down at the Professor's listless body, his long hair cascading across the floor, revealing holes in his skull. Her breath caught in her throat as she tried to think clearly, but her thoughts were clouded in a fog of fear.

Orother took another step toward her and she instinctively stepped backwards, finding a jutting piece of rock that stuck between her shoulder blades, blocking her retreat. She imagined Holt would chide her for allowing herself to get backed into a corner. Her mind raced to think of something, anything to try to keep Orother talking.

"What makes you think I know where the *Anthonium* deposit is?" Larissa asked. Her voice sounded small and weak.

"Ah, you must not be aware. Your dear Professor, whom you so gallantly came to save, only wanted you for this." He pointed to the box in her hand. "He traced you through your father. Everyone knows the story of the famed archaeologist, Professor Ronald Markus, who disappeared from the world after he allegedly found the *Anthonium* source."

"You think I know where my father disappeared to? I can assure you, if I had any clue, I would have gone looking for him years ago."

"Really? You care so much for a father who abandoned you as a child?"

"No. I wouldn't have gone for my sake. I would have gone for my mother. I would have tracked him down for her."

She barely registered the fact that their subject had made an unexpected switch to her father. It wasn't something she usually spoke about, even with Mother when she was alive, as every time she tried to ask Mother about him the poor woman had ended up a sobbing wreck.

Now, here she was, standing with the most despicable man she'd ever come across, trying to explain a family connection that had never made sense. It felt more than odd that it would come up now. Would she really have gone looking for her father years ago if the opportunity had come up? No, that part was a lie. Even so, there was nothing in all her memory that suggested she'd know where to start.

"All the same, I feel there is some little piece of information tucked away in your brain, some memory you think is insignificant, that might just hold the key. Not to worry, I'll prize it out of you."

"You are a twisted bastard," she said, grinding her teeth together to suppress the tears threatening to spill out.

"You're afraid? That's good. Perhaps we can still negotiate a bargain. You unlock this little box now, and once I've searched through your memories, I will lock you up beside your Professor instead of torturing you to death. How does that sound?"

Larissa looked down at the Professor. His eyes were still closed, yet she was sure he'd shifted position slightly. There was no reason to believe a single word Orother said. Still, the notion that she might escape from the very worst torment was very appealing, especially as her final hope of Holt saving the day seemed more and more unlikely.

"Fine, have the damn stone, for all the good it's done me." She turned the lockbox over in her hands, trying to hide the tremble in her fingers.

Cat.

She pushed the first dial round and clicked it into place.

Three. Three dates with the Professor. Not sure I can consider this encounter as a fourth date.

The second dial clicked.

Ah, the top-hat.

She glanced to the Professor again, staring at the holes in his head. She was sure she saw him move slightly. The third dial locked.

The dirigible. I imagine Grubbs and the others have run off. So much for my escape plan.

The fourth dial locked. Larissa paused for a moment with the next two dials, rolling them over and over, again and again, trying to remember what symbols she'd chosen. Her finger hovered over a picture of a bird, as her mind tried to think back to the day Cid gave her the box.

Poor Cid. I'll bet he wishes I'd never been born. He was much happier when it was just him and the Professor, just the two of them...Two.

She pushed the dial around one click further and pressed it into place.

"This is taking an inordinate amount of time, my dear," Orother crooned.

Snake.

She pressed down the fifth dial.

"It seems you've gone to an awful lot of a trouble, all for the sake of a machine," she said, locking the final dial down on the letter M.

The box clicked and whirred to life, the pictures whizzing around until the latch unclipped and the box popped open, revealing the familiar silvery-white stone inside. Larissa sighed and pulled the stone from the box, holding it out in her thin and trembling fingertips.

Orother watched her movements closely, his eyes glistening with wild excitement. He inched closer, forcing her to sink back into the wall. He placed one hand against the wall beside her head and leaned in, bringing his lips to her ear.

"The machine is merely the beginning. You are a plucky little thing. I will enjoy penetrating your mind. I look forward to hearing your screams echoing around my home."

His other hand reached up to take the stone from her fingers, though he was interrupted by a guard rushing into the room, panting and flustered.

"Doctor Orother, the assassin is coming."

"What?" the Doctor bellowed. "So why aren't you out there killing him?"

"He's already killed several men. We're not sure where he is. We will stay here and let him come to us."

"Where is the Cleric?" Orother said as several other guards spilled into the room, though none of them seemed to have an answer for him.

Larissa watched on wordlessly, imagining Holt systematically cutting his way through man after man, spilling blood and guts all over the cave corridors. She curled her fingers around the stone, tucking it into her palm. Her heart thumped in her chest and her body tingled with adrenaline. Time, all she needed was a little more time.

Chapter Thirty One

Holt returned to the stairwell, having extracted as much useful information as possible from Orother's assistant. Through the spyglass he found the switches on the wall and pressed the relevant one, as sure as he could be that the cowardly man he'd just interrogated had given him honest information in exchange for mercy.

The machinery controlling the room lurched into life and the walls spun around slowly. Holt stood ready, his rifle following the line of the wall, prepared to fire upon whichever enemy appeared in his path. The room opened out into another hallway, and the ticking timer echoed loudly around him. Holt froze as he saw Larissa, kneeling on the floor ahead, her head full of curls cascading down to the floor as her shoulders shook. She appeared to be distressed, weeping perhaps.

Holt stepped into the hall just as the room turned back blocking the exit.

"Larissa?" he asked softly.

"Please! Help me!" she screamed at him. Holt lurched, acting on instinct to protect her, but something stopped him. She was screaming in hysterics. Though he didn't know her well, she had never done that, not even when she had suffered horrific abuse aboard the pirate ship. The hairs on the back of his neck pricked up and as she screamed at him again, her face contorted unnaturally and her expression turned angry.

"What are you doing?" he asked.

"Help me. Why won't you help me?"

"Say my name," he said, levelling his weapon at her. Her brow wrinkled and her mouth curled into a twisted smile as the illusory Larissa dissipated from view altogether.

"Show your face, you fucking coward," Holt yelled into the shadowy hallway. He received no reply. Gritting his teeth he pressed on, giving no more than a passing glance to the gruesome sight of two dissected bodies in the lab room. The passageway turned a corner and Holt saw a robed figure ahead. He fired his rifle without hesitation and the bullet sailed straight through the man, splintering rock as it lodged into the cave wall behind.

"You wished to see my face?" the man spoke, spreading his palms out. "Come closer, see the truth."

Holt felt a pressure forming across his throat. The tightness intensified as he tried to fight it, keeping his rifle pointed at the figure ahead, though he had no idea how to kill an illusion. Two guards emerged ahead; they raised their weapons at Holt but did not fire.

The rifle fell from Holt's hands and he clutched at his neck, trying to grasp the force that choked him, finding nothing tangible to grip. He watched the Cleric's eyes glisten with sickening pleasure—eyes that, for the briefest moment, focused somewhere behind Holt's head. With a final attempt at salvation, Holt removed a throwing knife from his belt and turned around, flinging the knife down the corridor behind him. The Cleric screamed in pain as Holt's knife hit him in the eye.

The two guards opened fire as the illusion of the Cleric dissipated and Holt recovered, ducking behind an alcove in the rock. Down the corridor, the real Cleric fled, clutching at his wound as he ran toward the room which led to the stairwell.

More shots from the guards sailed past, landing in the rock, splintering shards down the hall as the bullets ricocheted off the walls. Holt tucked his body as flat as possible, waiting for the men to run out of ammo and pause to reload. When they did, he was ready.

. . .

The sound of relentless gunfire echoed throughout the cave; by the time the noise reached the room Larissa was in, it sounded like an entire army of people battling. While Larissa knew that wasn't the case, Orother did not.

"You!" Orother turned to her, his face bright red and burning with rage.

"You fucking bitch, I will make you suffer for this."

She saw the strike coming as Orother raised his arm, his hand balled into a tight fist swinging toward her face. Her legs slipped as she ducked away from the strike and Orother stumbled sideways as his arm missed his target. Larissa sunk to her side on the floor and kicked her legs out catching Orother's ankles.

The shock brought him down, his body crashing heavily on top of her legs and she shrieked as she felt something in her knee pop out of place. The next moment he rolled on top of her, his entire weight crushing her frame, his hands wrapped around her neck, gripping, squeezing with all his might. She tried to stop him, but all she could feel was the pressure inside her skull. The *Anthonium* came free from her fingers and fell to the floor, rolling away.

"Do you enjoy suffering, you stupid girl?" Orother spat through gritted teeth. "You will learn. I will train you."

Larissa's vision blurred around the edges yet again as she struggled in vain to fight for breath. Her lungs burned, her neck stung as he branded her with his fingertips, instantly bruising her skin. She clawed uselessly at his face, fighting to make him stop.

A blur streaked across the corner of her vision, then a fist connected with Orother's face and his grip released as he toppled to the side. The Professor came into view above her, his pale face alive with a flush of red blood, his teeth bared, but his neck still bound by the collar. He placed his body over hers as a barrier.

Across the room the air was filled with shouts and gunfire. Larissa flinched as she expected to feel shots landing in her body. She chanced a brief look towards the sounds and found that the guards focused their attention on the hallway.

"Holt," she gasped just as Orother recovered. His eyes widened with an odd expression at Holt's name, then he scooped up the *Anthonium* and leapt to the wall where the chain that bound the Professor was hooked. Orother grabbed the chain and yanked hard, swiftly pulling the Professor backward. The Professor crashed to the ground as Orother jumped forward and grabbed Larissa, dragging her to her feet and out of the Professor's reach, his arm looped around her neck.

"*Holt!*" Orother bellowed. It sounded like an order, and in confusion the guards ceased firing, though they still raised their weapons and aimed them at the corridor.

"Come in here, Captain Holt," Orother called, "and lower your weapons or I'll snap her fucking neck."

Holt appeared around the corner; he was bleeding from cuts and gashes across his face, his arm dripped blood from a gunshot wound, and his eyes burned intensely. Holt instantly raised his arm, pointing his rifle at Larissa.

"Nice and steady now, Captain," Orother said softly and the room fell quiet, the sound of heavy breaths from all occupants almost echoing inside the cave.

"That was quite an entrance. I'm impressed. Tell me, have you killed the Cleric?"

"Coward," Holt barked, though it wasn't clear if he was talking about the Cleric or just insulting Orother.

Larissa watched as Holt's finger brushed the trigger and she now felt just as afraid of Holt as she was of Orother. Her eyes darted between the Professor, who attempted to stand upright, the guards, who still aimed weapons at Holt and looking to Orother to give an order, and Holt, who seemed to be seriously contemplating putting a bullet through her chest just to kill the Doctor.

She wondered if he were thinking of her incredible capacity for healing, if he were willing to take such a risk, or if he was simply so hell bent on killing Orother that he didn't care if she died in the process. Her mind played through everything that Holt had risked so far to get to this point, and she held her breath, truly not knowing what would happen next.

"I see now that I had the wrong brother. You would have made a much more useful subject." Orother moved Larissa across his chest as he spoke, ensuring her body was as much of a shield as possible. She listened closely to Orother—what did he mean, 'wrong brother'? Her heart tugged at the fact that she had failed to get to the bottom of why Holt was here. She didn't want to learn it this way.

"You will pay for what you did, and when I'm done with you, I will kill the rest of your band of schemers," Holt said.

"You think you've uncovered some plot? You think you have all the puzzle pieces figured out? I'm almost tempted to let you leave here alive just to watch them destroy you."

"One of us will die here," Holt stated, his voice flat, a bead of sweat trickling down his forehead.

"More than one, I suspect." Orother tightened his grip around Larissa's neck with one arm, holding out the *Anthonium* in his other hand.

"Did you know she had this?"

"I did."

"And you didn't simply take it from her?" Orother seemed to be looking between the Professor and Holt, wordlessly calculating.

"She really is an intriguing creature, isn't she?" Orother continued. Larissa watched as Holt's grip on the trigger wavered.

A flash of black and white fur came from the shadows, leaping through the air. Imago. The cat landed directly on Orother's hand, claws extended, mouth open.

Orother yelled as Imago's claws pierced straight through the skin of the Doctor's hand, taking the *Anthonium* and a large chunk of flesh in one bite with his sharp teeth. The guards flinched and faltered, turning their weapons upon the cat as he scampered beneath the heavy machinery, firing a barrage of bullets through the room.

Holt calmly turned his rifle and dispatched the guards as Larissa used the distraction to turn herself around in Orother's grasp. Doctor Orother flung his arm out, trying to catch her again. She rammed her knee up, smashing into his groin, and he pitched forward. Larissa stumbled backward and fell on her backside. Holt fired his rifle and the bullet lodged in Orother's chest. The Professor appeared behind the Doctor and grabbed hold of Orother's head. In one swift move he snapped the man's neck.

The body of Doctor Orother tumbled down into a heap on the floor. The Professor collapsed as well; his shoulders slumped forward as he sat, silently shaking his head.

Minutes passed by in silence. Larissa stared down at the floor, scanning the dips and ridges in the stone, unable to look at either Holt or the Professor and certainly not quite ready to focus on Orother.

They had just achieved the impossible. She should be jumping for joy, and instead she felt lost and a little bit sick. The Professor was silent as well, though he stared directly at Larissa, his eyes locked onto her and his expression unreadable.

"We need to leave," Holt stated flatly from beside the exit. Somewhat reluctantly, Larissa assigned herself the task of searching Orother's body for the key to the collar on the Professor's neck.

Chapter Thirty Two

Holt emerged from the stairwell into reality. The mansion was gone, one of the orb devices that had maintained the illusion appeared to have been destroyed, and the other was missing entirely. Larissa came up beside him, the Professor limping along last with an equally poor-looking cat at his side.

"Did you destroy those?" Larissa asked Holt, pointing to the orbs.

"No. The Cleric escaped."

"Oh." Larissa opened her mouth to say something else, but Holt marched on towards the ship, rapidly bandaging his cuts and bruises with a far more grim expression than usual.

Once they all reassembled aboard the pirate ship, Larissa and the Professor sat in silence on deck for what seemed an eternity, neither comfortable nor awkward, simply silent.

Eventually, Larissa broke the peace, lifting the quiet haze.

"I'm afraid I lost your ship to pirates." She figured it was fairly safe ground on which to begin. A slight grin threatened the corners of the Professor's mouth.

"That's always a risk with so many blasted philistines about. Perhaps I can buy it back from them."

"Unfortunately not. Holt crashed it into a mountain."

"Barbarian. I shall make a note to send him the bill." This time Larissa smiled and something unspoken felt settled between them.

"I am so very sorry, Larissa."

"It's fine."

"No, it is not fine. I could spend the rest of my lifetime apologizing to you and it wouldn't be enough. You saved my life, and after I'd treated you dreadfully. There is nothing I can do to fix the pain I've brought upon you."

"You could start by going back to Sallarium, showing everyone you're still alive, and clearing my name."

The Professor's gaze fell to the deck. "I'm afraid it's not that simple."

"Oh?"

"You see, I didn't have permission to build my machine. In fact, the government specifically forbade me from building it. They were watching me so closely in everything I did. The only place they didn't watch me was at the Hub, so naturally that was the only place I could build it. If I go back now, I expect they'll simply lock me up and throw away the key. They'll most likely peg you as an accomplice and my word on it won't make a blind bit of difference."

"Oh."

"So, once again I must apologize."

"Professor..."

"Please, call me Max."

"Max." She tested the name out loud; somehow it didn't suit him. His formal moniker felt more natural.

"I need to ask something..."

"Ask away. I shan't withhold anything from you now."

"Cap'n 'Rissa." Grubbs stumbled around the corner, his stocky face alight with a proud grin. He was still covered in soot though he had made some attempt to clean his face.

"Grubbs, you came back!"

"Of course, Cap'n, you gave us orders." The Professor raised an eyebrow as he watched the exchange.

"You say you carried out my orders?" Larissa asked.

"Aye, happy to report she's ready, Cap'n."

"What?"

"The ship. You said we was to get her ready and I'm reporting that we done real good."

"I'm not sure I understand," Larissa said, frowning.

"We fixed a few broken bits, topped up the coal, filled the hydrogen tanks and stashed the hull with food and grog."

"What? How the hell did you manage all that? Did you have a stash of gold in the ship somewhere?"

"Uhhh, no. We're pirates, Cap'n. We took it."

"Took it?"

"Yup. These rich folks got tons of great stuff stashed around, filled the hold right up." As he finished speaking, the other crew members rounded the corner, their arms filled with trinkets and jewellery, followed by Friar Narry, who shook his head.

"I must say I do not approve of this," Narry said.

"We heard you the first ten times, Friar," Goodson said.

"Friar Narry, did you not go back to the Citadel?" Larissa looked at him crookedly.

"It was my intention, but when the mansion illusion ended I realized my absence will have been noticed and I would not be able to deny my involvement. I have broken the rules. I cannot go back now. I will stay with you, if you'll have me."

"Of course! The more the merrier."

"Although, I must point out that I disapprove of thievery."

"Yes, well, I'm not sure I approve of it either. I'll have to be more explicit with my instructions to the men." She looked around the deck of the ship, finally noticing that someone was missing.

"Dear Gods! Where's Cid?"

Cid climbed aboard just as she finished her question, carrying a small casket decorated with gold filigree. He stopped in front of Larissa and Max, his eyes flicking between the pair of them; he seemed unsure which one was now his boss.

"I am pleased to see you Cid," Max said.

"Thank the Gods you're alive, Professor."

Larissa pointed to the casket, both her eyebrows raised in a silent question. Cid shrugged and sniffed indignantly.

"Found this stashed under Orother's bed down in that cave. It's got all kinds of interesting stuff inside. I thought it might be useful. I only just managed to get out of there. I assume he's dead?"

"Yes," Larissa said.

"Then it's not like he needs it now."

"We should leave." Holt appeared opposite, his tone clipped and face sullen.

"Why?" Larissa asked.

"The guards in the town have been alerted to our suspicious activities. They are coming."

"Damn, gentlemen, let's get this thing in the air."

"Aye, Cap'n," Grubbs and the three other crewmen acknowledged as they raced to the furnace, the fuel tanks, and to retract the skids. The Professor stood up and then promptly sat back down again when he realized he was completely out of place and more likely to get in the way than to be of use.

"Where are we headed?" Cid asked.

"Just up and away for now, Cid. The guards are going to give a hard chase when they find the mess we're leaving behind, and I think we've all had enough of being locked up for a while."

The furnace cracked with flame, the partially deflated balloon filled with hydrogen, the rotors whirred to life, and as a number of uniformed men spilled into the back garden, the ship slowly rose toward the sky.

Larissa and Holt stood side by side at the edge. Holt raised his reloaded rifle, briefly flicking his gaze to the deck where he'd placed a pair of fully loaded pistols. Larissa took the hint and collected the weapons, matching his stance.

Cracks of gunshot whizzed through the air from below, but Larissa didn't flinch. She took aim, let out a breath, relaxed her elbow, and pulled the trigger. One man dropped to his knees, Holt downed another. Larissa took aim with the second pistol and fired the final shot, bringing another man down until they sailed out of range and out of danger.

Larissa turned to Holt, hoping perhaps to hear some praise or acknowledgement of all they'd achieved. Instead, he turned away, marching across the ship to disappear into the hull. She sighed, catching sight of the Professor; he looked deathly pale. She extended her hand to him and he took it without question as she led him down into the Captain's cabin.

"It's not as well equipped or comfortable as you're used to, but I'm afraid it's all I have to offer," she said with a weak smile.

"Believe me, this is extraordinarily luxurious after my recent travels."

"Good. You should rest. You look like you need it."

"You won't stay with me? You look tired as well, though you're still incredibly beautiful."

He reached up to touch her cheek, and her heart fluttered, knees feeling weak. It seemed, after everything, he could still make her feel like a foolish, needy collection of hormones, and she suddenly didn't mind being so easily overcome. It felt familiar and comfortable to let someone else take control.

As his thumb brushed her lip she opened her eyes. Her vision drifted to the Captain's desk. She recoiled as the memory of her moment with Holt flashed through her mind. She couldn't help but picture Holt brooding, counting the minutes she spent down here with the Professor. The whole thing made her feel terribly dirty and ashamed.

"It seems you have become a very different person from the girl I met merely weeks ago," the Professor said, a warm smile on his lips.

"Growth by necessity, I suppose."

"My greatest loss." The Professor kissed her forehead lightly.

"I'm not saying never. It's just that so much has happened, I think we need to get to know each other—properly, truthfully."

"I understand. We certainly went about things back-to-front, didn't we?"

"I can agree with you there, for sure."

The Professor sunk down into the large chair and yawned. Imago appeared from the shadows and jumped into the Professor's lap, immediately curling into a ball, letting out a similarly lethargic yawn.

"You two look after each other. You've both been to hell and back."

"Indeed," he said, mindlessly stroking Imago. "And what shall you do now?"

"I don't know yet. What about you, Professor?"

"Max," he replied with a wry grin.

"What about you, Max? What would you like to do now?"

"Besides making love to a beautiful female pirate Captain?"

Larissa laughed. "Yes, besides that."

"Well I'd like to build another machine, but it'd be pointless without any more *Anthonium*. Unless, of course, your cat returns the stone to us."

"Well, you're welcome to search through his deposits if you wish."

"Ha, I see. The new recruit gets the best assignments. Even so, if I'm to build a proper-sized machine, I really need a much larger sample."

"And for that you need the location of the deposit?"

"Yes, I need the source." He looked up at her through slightly narrowed eyes, and she let out a long, laboured sigh.

"I have no idea where my father found that stone, Max."

"I know. I'm sorry, once again."

"You should rest now."

"Goodnight, Captain 'Rissa." She watched as he sunk into the chair, his eyes fluttering closed, and she headed towards the door.

With a final sigh she turned and softly whispered, "Goodnight Professor."

Chapter Thirty Three

L arissa looked to the horizon, awaiting the appearance of the sun in the sky. She'd remained awake all night, leaving the Professor to sleep in her cabin; he needed the rest more than any of them. The mountain range had long since disappeared and the tundra below turned to low, rolling hills, the covering of snow thinning away as the temperature warmed. To the east a railway line could be seen stretching out to the distance. Larissa stared at it, thinking about her home, the place she could never return to and pondering where in the world she should go next.

"I'm leaving."

Holt's voice made her jump. She turned to find him behind her, looking towards the rail tracks. His sleeves were rolled up, revealing the bandage on his arm where he'd taken a bullet wound. Aside from that he appeared impeccably well-presented considering everything they had been through. He had even taken the time to shave.

"You have someplace to go?" she asked, her voice cracking mid-sentence. She swallowed, trying to hide the utter panic arising at the prospect of losing him.

"You don't need me anymore," he said, turning to meet her gaze, "and I don't need you."

Larissa's heart froze, her breath caught in her throat. The small voice inside her head screamed, begging him to stay. Yet she knew that if she broke down in front of him, she'd turn to a sobbing wreck, and that kind of breakdown would only make him run off even faster.

"I can't stop you," she said.

"No."

She refrained from pointing out that she had made a statement, rather than asking a question.

"Where will you go?"

"East."

"Descriptive as ever, Holt."

"I don't want you to follow me."

"What makes you think I would do that?"

Holt raised a single eyebrow in response and Larissa blushed.

"Larissa..." Holt began.

"Captain," Larissa blurted.

"My apologies, Captain."

"No, I don't mean that. I mean, that's what Orother called you. He called you Captain Holt." Her sudden change of topic surprised them both.

"Hmm."

"So, you were in the military?"

"I thought you had already established that."

"Oh, for goodness sake, would you stop being so evasive?" Larissa yelled.

"You should try being concise with your questions," Holt said, turning to look at the train track disappearing on the horizon.

"Cid, head east," Larissa called, and Cid obliged, tugging on the wheel to adjust their course. "I can at least save you a bit of a walk," she said to Holt, not mentioning the fact that she was trying to buy time. "Orother knew you, as if he expected you to be there."

Holt sighed and pulled out a piece of paper from his pocket, passing it to Larissa. At the top of the list, the name *Doctor Orother* appeared to be recently crossed out. Her eyes trailed the remaining names on the list. She paused on one name in particular—*Solomon Covelle*. Something about it seemed familiar.

"This is a long list of names, Holt."

"They all need to be held accountable for their actions."

"President Hague is on here." She tapped her finger against the last name on the list.

"Hmm."

"What did they all do?"

Holt sighed and shifted his weight, his jaw flexing back and forth. "Murder, torture, all manner of things."

"I don't doubt it, but what did they all do to *you*?"

"Not me. My brother Daniel."

"I...hadn't imagined you with a brother."

"He's dead," Holt replied, his gaze fixed on a singular spot dead ahead.

"Oh, I'm sorry. What happened?"

"He was just a kid. He always followed me around, wanted to do everything I did. So, as soon as he was old enough he joined the military. When he went for his medical examination he was unlucky enough to be looked at by Doctor Orother."

"Oh." Larissa felt her heart sink, already knowing where the story was headed, yet she felt compelled to let him carry on, to hear the rest. She wondered if perhaps he'd ever told anyone out loud, or if he'd just spent all this time bottling it up inside. She was about to press him to continue, as she usually had to do, but was surprised when Holt spoke voluntarily, offering the rest of his thoughts without prompting.

"Danny was assigned to some specialist division. He was so proud to have been *selected*. It seems the Doctor wanted him for some experiments."

"Experiments?"

"I have no idea what they did to him. The last time I saw him he was like a ghost. Always looking over his shoulder, could barely string a sentence together, and he had these...holes...cut into his head."

"Gods."

"The next thing I knew I had a letter saying he'd died in the line of duty. No one could tell me how or where. Not that it would have mattered what they said. I wouldn't have believed them. I only had one name to go on."

"Orother."

"I researched him. He was a very difficult individual to pin down. When Command found out I'd been poking around for classified information, they stripped me of my rank. When that didn't stop me, they kicked me out. By the time I left I had compiled that list, and that was all I had left on which to focus my time."

"So, you were at the bar in Sherwater..."

"To look for Serenia, same as you."

"It seems we were sadly fated to go through this together."

"No longer."

"Excuse me?"

"I will continue to pursue those who remain on my list. You can go back to your life."

"You know I can't do that. You've overheard enough of my conversations with people when I thought you were well out of earshot. I know you were listening to me speak with the Professor."

"Hmm. Well, whatever you chose to do with your life, I wish you well." He stood up and walked towards the ship's edge.

"Wait!" she yelled.

"You have a ship, a crew, and a hoard of gold. You can go anywhere you like."

"What if I chose to come with you? I can help. You need me."

"I do not need you. I work better alone."

"Oh really? You think you would have managed to come all this way and get into Meridina to kill Orother and escape with your life all by yourself?"

"It is impossible to know the answer to that."

"Gods, you are an irritating man. Why won't you let me help you? Maybe your quest is just the kind of thing I want to do?" She moved to stand in front of him, trying to block his escape.

"You want to travel the world assassinating people?" Holt asked.

"Isn't it more like putting an end to a despicable plot to torture innocent people in the name of *national security*?"

"Giving it a fancy name will not detract from the reality of the task," Holt said, a small glimmer of humor in his tone.

"Either way, it seems like a noble cause, and if you intend to get to the top of your list, you're likely to need help."

A long pause followed. Holt looked at her, his gaze settling deep into her eyes. She held the stare, refusing to feel discomforted by it. She wasn't sure why she acted so desperately to get him to stay. Pursuing his goals would indeed be an adventure; she couldn't swear that she wasn't motivated by selfish needs. A need to keep him close? Did she want to repeat their brief moment of passion? Had she read far more into their joining than there was between them? What of the Professor?

"You have your Professor," Holt said, as if he'd read her mind. He spoke slowly and seemed to choose his words with care.

Larissa visibly hunched over, unable to choose between them. She couldn't abandon the Professor now. He was too weak and she wanted to help build him back up into the man she'd so admired. Yet Holt was so much more, and she wanted more from him, from both of them.

Holt leaned toward her, and cupped her face in his hand. In the distance, the familiar sound of a chugging steam engine floated on the wind.

"Goodbye, Captain Markus," Holt whispered, his lips brushing briefly against hers.

Her eyes fluttered closed and her lungs filled with hot air. After a brief moment, the heat dissipated. As she opened her eyes, she caught a glimpse of Holt's black-clothed body dipping over the side of the ship. She ran to the edge and looked over to see him shimmying off the end of a rope and breaking into a run towards the train line.

"Goodbye, Captain Holt," she whispered as her eyes glistened with tears.

She rested her forehead on the cool wood rail and stared down at her feet, which poked out from the bottom of her dress. Her boots were scuffed and broken, a hole at one side showing the pink flesh of her little toe. She tutted aloud at the sight. It seemed funny to feel so irked by such a small detail, considering everything that she'd just been through. She supposed it was a rather apt metaphor—beautiful, simple things were bound to be destroyed if you treated them harshly.

It wasn't the ending she'd hoped for, though her hopes for the mission at the outset seemed incredibly naive to her now. She mused that luck, rather than judgement, had prevented her from dying on the first day—or any day since.

Yet there she stood, broken, bruised, and changed beyond all recognition. Even if she could go back to her old life in the city, her apartment would feel very small and her job at Greyfort's would be insufferably dull. Larissa Markus, Pirate Captain, seemed a much more exciting—if a little absurd—prospect, though she had no idea where to head next.

"The source." A strange voice echoed inside her mind. It was not her own inner voice and quite unlike a memory. She looked around, wondering if perhaps one of the men had approached, but there was no one nearby save for a flash of dark red material that disappeared behind one of the propeller masts.

She watched the mast carefully, not sure if her exhausted mind was playing tricks. Another movement caught her eye; Imago emerged from belowdeck and padded over to Larissa, flopping down at her feet.

"What's wrong with the cat?" Cid asked as he approached them, setting down the gold casket he'd taken from Orother's room.

"I think he swallowed the *Anthonium*," Larissa muttered.

"Gods. Stupid bloody animal. Why did you do that?" Cid bent down beside Imago.

"He did it to distract Orother. At least, I think that was his intention...it worked." Cid prodded at Imago's belly; the cat did not respond.

"Cid, if I didn't know better I'd say you were concerned about him," Larissa said with a weak smile.

"I don't imagine he'll last another day," Cid said. His prodding turned to a gentle stroke and Imago laid his head on the floor and closed his eyes. Larissa knelt down to join Cid.

"Another sacrifice I had not intended to make." She gently pulled at Imago's ear. Usually he'd respond and rub his face into her hand, but instead he just lay there almost comatose.

"Thought of a heading yet?" Cid muttered. He was trying to be tactful, she knew.

"No idea, Cid. What's in the box?" She pointed to the golden casket.

"Ah, it's bloody interesting." Cid popped the lid open, revealing a spherical, metallic object with a series of holes punched around the surface. At the top of the device was a small receptacle, a sort of dish.

"What does it do?" Larissa asked as Cid lifted the device from the box.

"I have no idea. I've tried to take the thing to pieces but I can't figure out how."

"Why would you want to take it to pieces?"

"To see how it works, of course."

"Ever the engineer. What are those?" Larissa pointed to a crumpled up piece of paper and a pile of fat brass bullets that had been hidden beneath the sphere in the box.

"These are bullets, of course, but they're quite unlike any I've seen before and I don't know of any weapon in which they'd fit. This other thing, I have no idea what this is..."

Cid picked up the paper with care and as it hung from his fingers Larissa noticed that it wasn't paper at all; it was a very thin cloth with symbols printed across it and a red, wriggly line drawn through the middle.

"I'm afraid we may never know, Cid, seeing as the man they belonged to is rather dead."

"True." Cid sighed, visibly disappointed.

"Although it may make sense if you manage to pop that sphere open." Larissa smiled at him.

"Yes, I guess it might. Have you checked on the Professor lately?"

"I didn't want to disturb him, but I it *is* morning. I'll go now."

Larissa descended into the hull, rubbing the exhaustion from her eyelids. As she approached her cabin, an odd fluttering awoke inside her stomach. The air smelled stale and the noise from the propellers seemed to fall flat in the wooden corridor. She instinctively reached for her knife and pushed the cabin door open with the tips of her fingers.

Inside, the cabin was free of shadows and held no hidden danger as she had expected. What she did find was the Professor slumped in the chair, his golden blonde hair hanging like a waterfall, cascading down to the ground. Larissa's knees buckled, their strength failing as she fell, her chest shuddering with shaky breaths. For a long while she knelt there, staring at him with silent tears rolling down her cheeks, until eventually she found her voice.

"Professor?"

It was inane, and some part of her knew it, but they had come so far and suffered so much that she was incapable of giving in to the truth so quickly. She planted her hands on the ground and dragged her body forwards, her fingertips digging into the wooden slats on the floor. She gripped his knee, hauling herself up, tears falling hot and heavy down her face. His head lolled to one side, his body limp and lifeless, and when she touched his face she found the skin cold.

"No...please."

She heard herself muttering, nonsensical words that flowed through her trembling lips as she pulled him onto the ground and into her lap. She cradled his head in her arms and finally let her lungs fill with air for a long, blood-curdling scream, made of the suffering, anguish, and despair of their journey—a journey that had ended in the worst possible way. Her scream was so long it made her head hurt, so powerful it echoed throughout the airship.

Time passed slowly. Eventually, as her sobbing eased, Larissa became aware that Cid and Narry had entered the room.

"Can't you heal him?" Cid whispered to Narry.

"This is beyond my skills to heal. Even if I'd have known he was dying, I could not have helped him. His injuries were too severe."

"Bloody hell." Cid dropped his head into his hands.

As time passed, Larissa's tears dried, her body shuddered with every heavy breath, and her hands shook uncontrollably. It was all she could do to look down at the lifeless body in her arms, her mind a blank.

In the corner of her vision she noticed a crumpled letter sticking out of the Professor's trouser pocket. She reached over and pulled it out, smoothing the paper with her shaking hands, and with a numb, detached interest she read the letter to Doctor Orother, signed by none other than the President himself.

Piece by painful piece, realization dawned upon her. She had lost the Professor, lost herself, and to cap it all off, Holt was gone—all because of some far-reaching scheme by people far worse than Doctor Orother. She stuffed the note into her pocket, rocked back on her heels, and scrambled through the door, racing to reach the deck. Cid and Narry passed confused looks to each other and followed in her wake.

On deck, the other men were surprised when she sprang into view, marching to the bow. The wind caught her matted hair, sending it flying in all directions as she strained to spot the smoke trail from the steam train. Larissa sucked in a deep breath as she saw the smoke dissipating away behind a rolling hill on the horizon.

"You all right, girl?" Cid asked as he approached her with caution.

"Cid?"

"Yes?"

"Fancy going on another *fool's errand*?"

"Not really, though I think I recall refusing to go on the last trip you planned, and here we are. Gods, Larissa, the Professor..."

"Is dead. *We* are not."

"Yes, good point. What crazy scheme are you cooking up now?"

"This is a pirate ship, we are pirates, I am a pirate Captain, and there is something on that train that I want."

"Something or someone?"

Larissa glanced back at Cid and the corner of her mouth curled into a crooked smile.

"Fuck sake," Cid moaned with a sigh. "All right, as you wish, Cap'n."

The men aboard sprang to life, the furnace cracking and whistling as they stoked the fire hard for enough speed to catch the train. The sun burned brightly in the sky above, melting away the winter snow. Larissa calmly buried her grief and despair for the loss of her Professor and his damned Machine.

Epilogue

Colonel Gabriel Kerrigan marched along the cool white corridor of the Presidential Palace. His pace was noticeably quicker than usual. He smoothed his fingers through his short black hair and pulled his dark green dress-tunic straight. He reached the thick metal door at the end, which was flanked by a pair of heavily armed Elite soldiers in black uniforms. They turned to open the door without hesitation. The hinges groaned as the door opened inwards, revealing a large room without windows.

The walls were decorated with ornate paintings of dead Emperors from the days before the Republic existed. The figures in the paintings all wore elaborate clothing and stood in striking, triumphant poses. Beneath the paintings, in the center of the room, sat a large oval table, surrounded by high-ranking military men, all turned-out in their best pressed uniforms. Only the Colonel's seat at the table was empty.

"Ah, Colonel Kerrigan," the only man not wearing a uniform said, who sat at the head of the table. His bald head glistened in the yellow candlelight from the chandelier above, his eyes narrowing slightly as Kerrigan approached.

"It is not like you to be late. I hope you have a very good reason."

"My apologies, Mr. President. I have an urgent matter to discuss with you."

"Is it urgent enough to disrupt the War Council meeting?"

"I have important news from Meridina."

"Ah. Gentlemen, will you please excuse us for a few minutes? General Gott, please stay."

The men around the table, save for General Gott, who was the eldest of the group, stood up in unison, their movements almost precisely timed. One or two let out audible grunts of annoyance before exiting the room. As the heavy metal door slammed shut, the President waved toward an empty seat, beckoning Kerrigan to sit, and the Colonel did so.

"Orother is dead," Kerrigan said.

"Oh?" The President's bushy blonde eyebrows shot up, and the vein on his neck visibly pulsed. General Gott leaned forward in his chair and laced his fingers together on the tabletop.

"There was some form of attack. Professor Watts has not been found."

The President slowly drummed his fingertips on the table and appeared grind his teeth together.

"I must point out, Sir," Kerrigan continued, "that if we'd have given the operation a military team as I originally suggested, we would not be in this situation."

"Orother refused to work under such circumstances, you know that, and he wasn't the sort of man one could convince otherwise. Besides, he assured me there would be no loose ends. Who in all of Daltonia would have managed to infiltrate that town? The Professor had neither family nor close friends who would have risked so much to get him. You're the head of intelligence, Kerrigan, so I presume you know what happened."

"Not exactly. A pirate airship was seen leaving the premises."

"Oh...well, I suppose that makes things a little simpler at the least. Find the pirate ship and secure the occupants by any means necessary."

"You're sure, Sir? It could get messy. It could turn public."

"We'll put a positive spin on it to keep the public happy—*Government cracking down on illegal pirate villains*. No one is going to shed a tear over the spilled blood of such scum. Even if the pirate ship is just some guise. This needs to be wrapped up swiftly. Make sure Orother's property is wiped off Meridina's map. We don't want anyone poking around down in that dungeon."

"I've already issued the order. A team has been sent with instructions to clear everything out and blast the entrances shut," Kerrigan said.

"What of the Cleric?" the other man at the table, General Gott, asked, his voice a deep rumble with calm, dry tone.

"He has not been found, either," Kerrigan answered.

"A betrayal?" The President turned to face the General. "You know the man better than most. Could he have done this to defeat our plans? Might he and the other man have some plans of their own?"

"Unlikely," General Gott stated simply. He gave the President no airs or graces and made no effort to disguise the fact.

"Well, we shall find out once we get that pirate ship, won't we, Colonel? I want you to handle it personally."

Colonel Kerrigan nodded tersely and rose to leave. As he reached the door, he paused to look back.

"Mr. President, is there anything I should know from the War Council?"

"Only that you need to get this business with those pirates and the Professor wrapped up swiftly. The Eptorans are preparing for war and we have very few chances left to stop them."

"Understood." Kerrigan marched out of the room and along the corridor. The Generals returned to their seats behind him. A long sigh escaped through his nostrils. He would much prefer to be in the War Council helping to make preparations for the difficult times to come, instead of chasing halfway across the country after some scummy rogue pirates.

He reached the large foyer where he collected his weapons, then headed out toward his unit of men. If he was going to be forced to babysit the mission, he would make damned sure it would be over quickly and efficiently, and Gods help the bastards on that pirate ship who chose to put up a fight.

Sneak Peek

The Pirate
Book Two
The Blood And Destiny Series

Captain Larissa Markus stood at the bow of the pirate airship, chewing on her lower lip. She watched the distance between her ship and the steam train's smoke plume ahead reduce by degrees. She wasn't sure what the bigger challenge would be—to board the train, or to convince the reticent Captain William Holt that he should come back aboard the airship with her. Either way it was a challenge, and challenge enough to keep her mind from falling into despair over the death of the Professor. His body still lay in her cabin, cold and empty, spirit abandoned.

Larissa blinked away the wetness that formed in her eyes, unable or unwilling to give into grief now that she had a new purpose.

She glared at the dot of the train across the snowy flat landscape miles ahead, as if giving it a deathly stare might somehow bring it to a stop.

"You want me to land the ship up the track a ways to get them to stop, or are you planning on doing some crazy *jump on the train as it's going along at a thousand miles per hour* stunt?" the engineer-turned-pilot, Cid Mendle, called out to her from the wheel of the ship.

"A thousand miles per hour?" Larissa asked, turning to face him with one eyebrow raised. "You seem to have developed a talent for the dramatic, Cid."

"You know what I mean, which is it to be?"

Which indeed.

Larissa poked her chin out, mulling over the options. The train had ten carriages; if she started at one end and worked her way through, it would take a considerable amount of time to find Holt. That was presuming he sat in plain sight and not hidden away. After that, she had no idea how long it would take to talk him into getting off the train. The airship might not be able to keep up with the speed of the steam train, especially if the train driver and fireman spotted the pirate ship following them. They'd likely expect an attack and double their speed. As much as it irked her to admit, getting the train to stop seemed the more practical option, if a little cavalier for her liking.

"Land the ship on the tracks, please, Cid. Can you calculate how fast they're going and how much distance they're likely to cover after they pull the brakes? I'd rather not destroy a second airship and leave us stranded in the snowy wilderness with a train full of angry passengers."

Cid scanned the terrain for a moment, his eyes darting left and right as he appeared mull over complex mathematical calculations.

"There," he said, pointing to a spot far ahead on the landscape where the train track curved around a large copse of snow-covered trees. "They'll slow for the bend. If we land up the track a mile away, when they come out they'll spot us and pull the brake. They should stop before they hit."

"Should?"

"Just remember, you're the one who wants to chase down a bloody train to get to that knife-wielding lunatic. My calculations are sound, provided they pull the brake when I assume they will. I have no control over that portion of the plan."

"Hmm. Think you can drop me off on the train before you go land it over there?"

"What? Why would you want to do that? Have you lost your bloody senses, girl?"

"Captain," she barked at him.

"Apologies. Have you lost your bloody senses, Captain?"

"Not at all. I shall enter the train and make sure they pull the brake. You and the others can look after the train driver while I find Holt. Let's move it, Mr Mendle, before we run out of track."

As the airship closed the distance with speed, the crewmen Goodson, Grubbs, and Zeb shovelled coal in the engine room as fast as they could. Larissa latched a pair of pistols onto her belt and arranged a collection of knives alongside the pistols. The intention was not to fight or kill; she hoped a menacing appearance might be enough to convince the driver to pull the brake, just in case seeing the pirate ship hovering on the track ahead wasn't convincing enough.

The airship approached the last two carriages of the train. Larissa flung a rope over the side of the rail and climbed down, ignoring the nagging voice at the back of her brain that warned against such reckless abandon. As she worked her way along the rope, hand over hand, legs gripping on for dear life, a breeze swung her wide and she clung on desperately.

The smoke from the engine ahead chugged across her face and she quickly slipped a few feet further down to escape the clogging soot. As the roof of the carriages came back into view below, she realized she was not low enough. The airship raced too quickly across the path of the train to make for the simple, neat drop she'd imagined. She scooted a few feet further down the rope, almost dropping off completely when her feet lost the end of it, leaving her dangling by her arms. It was too late, now; her untrained arm muscles screamed out against the strain. There was no way she could pull herself back up.

As another gust of wind swung her wide like a pendulum, she let go and crashed into the roof of the last carriage. The momentum sent her rolling to the side and her arms flailed to find a grip. She finally came to a stop, just as her legs fell off the opposite side of the black carriage roof. Larissa looked up through a head full of curly blond hair that whipped across her face in the wind, and saw the airship moving off ahead, flying over the trees in a straight line to head off the train.

She let out a shaky breath, and with a grunt pulled herself up onto the carriage, crouching down as the speed of the train threatened to send her off balance if she dared to stand any taller. The wind blew the ruffles of her dress around her knees, flicking layers of material up in an immodest fashion.

"You'd better make this worth my while, Holt," she muttered through gritted teeth as she reached the edge of the first carriage. She looked down, wondering if it might be a better idea to go through the passenger cars rather than navigate across the top. A bespectacled elderly gentleman in a top hat glared at her through the rear window of the carriage, brandishing his cane in front of his face as a threat. As far down the carriage as Larissa could see, there appeared to be a combination of angry, scared, and mortally terrified faces, all looking over their seats at her. They'd obviously seen the airship and had probably witnessed her theatrical descent onto their train.

The roof may be the safer route after all.

Larissa straightened slightly, rocked back on her heels, and leapt across the gap onto the next carriage, slipping quite ungracefully onto her backside.

After scrabbling to her feet and battling along the next nine carriages, she'd become adept at making the jump. All that remained between her and the engine was the coal car.

Thick, hot plumes of smoke raced across just above her head. She looked toward where the train approached the bend around the large copse of trees and felt the speed drop off, just as Cid had predicted. She lined up to make the leap across to the coal car, not looking forward to the thought of getting covered head to toe in black muck.

"I hope for both our sakes you have a very good reason for this."

Larissa stumbled as she spun around to see Holt on the roof behind her, crouching to avoid the smoke plume.

"I...uuh...I do."

The train moved through the bend in the tracks as Larissa struggled to find the appropriate words to say in place of *I'm doing this crazy stunt to get your attention and convince you to come back to the airship so we can go off and complete your mission together, because I think I'm falling in love with you.* Instead, she opened and closed her mouth a few times and then resorted to chewing on her tongue.

"Shit."

Holt filled the silence for her as the train completed the bend. Larissa turned to see the pirate airship descending from the sky in the distance ahead. Holt leapt forwards, snaking deftly across the coals on the coal car. Larissa scrambled to her feet and jumped to follow him, smacking face-first into the pile of coals, which left a great smear of black across her face. She clambered along and swung down to the train engine to find that Holt had shoved the terrified train driver and his colleagues into a corner. Holt grabbed the brake handle, and the wheels of the steam train screeched in protest, lurching everyone and everything not tied down forwards.

Larissa braced herself against the doorway. The airship hovered ahead, the point of the curve touching the tracks. She would have doubtlessly commended Cid on his excellent landing if she weren't busy regretting her rash course of action. There was little else anyone could do but wait, and hope, as the train slowed. Holt continued his sharp grip on the brake, the wheels screamed in protest, and the distance to the airship closed at an alarming rate. Larissa gritted her teeth and squeezed her knees together as she struggled to maintain bladder control.

Finally, with one great clunk, the entire train ground to a halt, bumping gently into the hull of the airship.

Holt sunk his head onto his arm as he still gripped the brake.

"Look, we don't want any trouble," the train driver began, his voice trembling. "Just take what you want and then let us get back to work. You don't need to kill anyone, all right?"

Larissa looked at Holt, who eyed her from just above his elbow.

"Well, Miss Markus..." Holt began, his deep voice hoarse from the smoke inhalation. "What is it you want?"

Larissa felt the familiar sensation of blood rushing to the edge of the skin across her shoulders, neck, and face as she blushed, an affliction she still could not hide.

"Just you," she replied sheepishly, wondering if perhaps she needed to take some time to mentally process everything that had led her to this point, lest she cause some complete disaster with her next crazy plan.

"You couldn't have just met me at the station?" Holt asked as he stood upright. Larissa felt the burning blush intensify.

"On reflection, that may have been a wiser course of action."

Holt glanced at the men in the cab who stood dumbstruck by the exchange, and then he marched through the doorway, dropping down into the snow-covered grass. He offered his hand up to Larissa, who accepted his help to get down. Along the train, several people had hopped out of their carriages and stretched their necks to see what was going on.

"If you people are quite finished holding us up, we have a schedule to keep to," the train driver called down, waving his arm at the airship blocking his path.

"My apologies, gentlemen," Larissa called back to them, and she and Holt climbed back aboard the pirate ship.

About The Author

E.C. Jarvis is a British author working mainly in speculative and fantasy fiction genres. For most of her working life, Jarvis has been working her way through the ranks of the accountancy profession in various industries. At the same time she has also been writing.

"It was always a hobby. I'd knock a poem out every now and then, or enter something into a short story competition, with very little success, but that never stopped me. There has always been an underlying need to write. It comes and goes with varying intensity, but it's always there, like an itch that needs to be scratched."

Her first success at publishing was a poem in a collection titled Fear Itself published by Forward Poetry in 2012. Following a three year hiatus where she "couldn't even bring myself to write a shopping list", 2015 saw a turnaround that has seen her complete three full novels, and is on track to complete her first series.

She was born in Surrey, England in 1982. She now resides in Hampshire, England with her daughter and husband.

Find out more at:

www.ecjarvis.com
https://twitter.com/EC_Jarvis
https://www.facebook.com/E.C.JarvisAuthor

Made in the USA
Columbia, SC
25 November 2018